Abandon My Sinking Ship

Gianna Sirrah
and GladysMarie Harris

Abandon My Sinking Ship
Copyright © 2025 by Gianna Sirrah and GladysMarie Harris.

Editing, design, and distribution by Bublish

Printed in the United States of America.
ISBN: 9781647049508 (paperback)
ISBN: 9781647049515 (eBook)

To my husband, who encourages me to explore and live life to its fullest. He is my root to whom I attach my kite so that I may soar high above mediocrity and the limitations of small minds.

♡

When you fully love, you no longer protect your own heart; you give it to someone else to safeguard, treasure, and esteem. You truly believe that they will care for it at all costs, and you will do the same with their heart.

CONTENTS

CHAPTER 1

PEARL

The bar area isn't busy yet, only a few customers. I shift on the barstool once again as the waitress fails to correctly repeat my dinner order. She has attempted to reiterate it twice, and each time she forgets to include or exclude something. At this rate, I won't get my meal until tomorrow. I look toward my beach bag on the barstool to my right, trying to hide the frustration on my face. I'm always concerned about someone messing with my food before I get it if I show disappointment or irritation with the waitstaff's ability. I would really prefer that she stop trying to remember my order and simply write it on a piece of paper.

I've always been a picky eater, according to my parents. My dad never showed his frustration with my special orders as much as my mom did during our meals. But then, she did all the cooking. My brother ate everything that was placed in front of him. As the only girl and the apple of my dad's eye, his comments of disappointment were few. My mom attempted to change my habits after a childhood eating fiasco that stretched to three days, until my grandmother intervened. My mom gave up on the need to change me and began cooking a bland meal for me along with the regular meal for the rest of the family each day.

Sometimes it's easier to tell the waitress what I want on my burger than what I don't want. Burgers have become a work of art. Every chef wants to put their spin on this dish with special sauces or overload it with unnecessary additions. How do you enjoy the burger when you can't taste it? I turn my attention back to the waitress.

The guy sitting to my left is staring at me. I can sense his eyes burning through the side of my face. I wonder if I should just hold up the menu to block his gaze. Or maybe I just think he's staring at me. I slowly turn my head to view him through my peripheral vision. Yep, he's staring. The waitress gets it right this time. Thank goodness. I'll see if she completely understood when my meal arrives.

I scan the other patrons. A few years ago, I began sitting at the bar instead of a table. It doesn't make me feel as lonely because I'm joined by other single people. However, I'm sure some sit at the bar to be closer to the booze and the bartender. Just then, my frozen Bahama Mama is placed in front of me. I take a long exhilarating sip and smile to myself as the drink cools my body.

I turn toward my beach bag to look for my Kindle. My glasses are sitting on the bar. I smooth out my yellow sleeveless dress as I search. I locate my Kindle among the other items and return my towel to the top of the bag to cover everything.

The guy to my left clears his throat. "You're a Michelin chef's nightmare," he states matter-of-factly without any hesitation.

Why does he feel obligated to speak to me? Maybe if I act like I didn't hear him, he'll get the hint that I don't care because I didn't solicit his opinion. I remove my Kindle from its protective sleeve.

"Do you always order your meals so—" he stops and waves his hands in the air—"bland?" he spits out.

I take a deep breath and let it out slowly while counting to ten. This time, I just can't hold my tongue. He is two seats from me, and I am sure he can find another woman to annoy this evening. I turn toward him. "Are you speaking to me?" I calmly ask without any emotion in my voice as I meet his eyes.

"Did you know that you're a Michelin chef's nightmare?" he says again.

"This is not a Michelin star restaurant." I refuse to give him my attention. I place my glasses on my face and turn on my Kindle.

"Have you ever been to a Michelin star restaurant?" he continues, even though he knows I'm trying to ignore him.

This time the obnoxious guy takes a sip from his glass and repositions his knees toward me. I try not to look at his man gap. It's as if men believe they need to spread their legs so far apart to let their balls and cock have a view. I am not inviting any socialization from this guy or his man gap. He's wearing khaki shorts and a designer polo shirt; his ship medallion is on his wrist. I wonder how many drinks he's had between the ship bar and this bar. I can smell the whiskey on his breath as he speaks.

"I wonder if the chef would ask you to leave." The stranger gives a combination laugh and grunt. "I mean if we were at a Michelin star restaurant," he clarifies.

I don't need to deal with this. I don't want to deal with this. Why is this guy annoying me? I'm trying to be nice. What can I say to get him to leave me alone? Yes, I sit at the bar because it makes me feel better than sitting at a table looking at the empty chairs while I eat. I can't help the fact that I'm by myself. I wouldn't be if . . . I had not planned to ever be alone, but my husband—now ex-husband—decided that married life was not what he wanted any longer. Correction, married life with me was not what he wanted. How does true love die? If it dies, was it really true love?

Twelve years I have been in limbo. Twelve years I have worried that I'll never be what a guy wants long term. My breasts are not as perky as they were in my thirties and forties. My curves are just a little more plush.

Unfortunately, I'm going to need to use my tried-and-true statement. The words finally form. "I'm married, sir, and I promised my husband that I wouldn't speak to strangers." Then I flash the wedding band I wear on occasions like this to keep the fools away. "He'll arrive soon." I point to my beach bag. "I'm saving this seat for him."

"Oh, I'm sorry for being disrespectful." He repositions his body toward the bar, once again looking over his shoulder in the opposite direction. At least this whiskey-drinking, obnoxiously rude dude is polite and does not continue to make a pass at a married woman. I should have started with the married story from the beginning.

I always hate to go there with that excuse, but I didn't know what else to do this time. I look at my beautiful diamond wedding band of fifteen years. I would never have thought I would have one this lovely and expensive. We'd eloped and had only plain silver bands for the first four years due to finances. We were in love, and I thought that nothing would ever shake that commitment. Not even when we found out that I could not carry a child to term. He later insisted that my educational pursuits were the reason I couldn't have a baby. We stopped trying and life got busy, or maybe fate decided for us.

The rude guy is paying the bartender. I watch him through my peripheral vision; he's not making eye contact with me. He moves toward a few thin blonde women on the other side of the bar area. He must be attempting to be charming because they giggle. I shift slightly in my seat to get a good look at them. He takes the hand of the taller blonde and heads to the dance floor that is located between the bar and the restaurant's entrance.

The music is why I chose this bar to dine in tonight. I've been in Aruba for the past seven weeks. This was my pick for the year. Each year I select a place to enjoy ten weeks of sun, fun, and beach time. I house swap with someone who wants to visit South Orange, New Jersey. Close to New York City is how I market my home. Enjoy suburban life with a train ride into the Big Apple, local restaurants, and nearby attractions. This year I have a bungalow in Aruba that is walking distance from the beach and restaurants. I chose this place tonight because I wanted to mingle with a few Americans. When the cruise ships enter port, many of the bars will play R&B, smooth jazz, or the oldies to pull in the visitors. I'm being a tourist tonight. The annoying guy happens to be from one of the cruise ships that are docked this evening. I'm sure he probably acts the same way with the women on board as well.

A curl escapes my loose puff bun and falls on the back of my neck. The temperature has been perfect, and my hair is absorbing all the humidity. I pat my pocket to locate a colorful bobby pin to keep my curls from springing to life. It has a little yellow butterfly on it, which matches my beautiful sunshine yellow dress with a flared bottom. I also wore my comfortable strappy sandals that are great for dancing. I might get lucky and find someone who wants to dance. This is always good because I know the cruise ships are here for only one or two days, depending on their itinerary. This means if I meet a guy, the long-term commitment is limited. I sway to the R&B music while sipping my Bahama Mama.

I turn to look at the obnoxious guy dancing with the blonde, who is now rubbing her nonexistent butt against his crotch. I guess someone is going to get laid tonight. I'll spend my night with Spicy. I hope I remembered to charge it. The obnoxious guy has some nice dance moves. Many white guys are stiff, which also means they're clumsy in bed. The blonde might really get a treat from him as long as he's not drunk before she gets lucky. I tap my foot to the music. I love dancing. My ex-husband didn't, but on rare occasions he would slow dance with me.

My food finally arrives. It smells great without any extra sauces or gravies. Although I was given coleslaw in a cup that I didn't want. At least it wasn't placed on my plate to contaminate the rest of my food. I quickly remove the cup and set it about a foot to the right of my plate. Not that it will jump onto any of my food, but never say never. I am not one to waste, but some restaurants feel so obligated to give me sauces, gravies, coleslaw, or condiments, and I don't eat those things. I used to tease my parents about torturing me as a toddler with these types of foods so that I refuse to consume any of those items now. There is a shockingly long list of things I do not eat. I believe that my taste buds did not develop. I also believe that cooks use sauces, gravies, and condiments to hide the actual food. To answer the annoying guy's question, yes, I am a Michelin chef's nightmare.

I remember my first time in Paris. All I wanted was to sit at a restaurant and stare at the Eiffel Tower with the other locals and tourists of Paris while having dinner, which is extremely late in the evening compared to the US. I wanted cheese on my entrée. Of course, I could not get a simple white cheese; it was a mixture of blue cheese and something else. I wanted to know the names of the cheeses, but my French is not the best. After two attempts the waiter returned with my entrée and loudly announced, "*Non fromage pour toi!*" I quickly understood that I had been forbidden to get cheese on my entrée. A few other mumblings occurred, but I would have needed someone to translate for me. I did not return to that restaurant for the rest of my stay in Paris. I ran into a few tourists from that same night who stated they had similar experiences at other restaurants. These have always been my eating habits, and I couldn't change simply because I was in Paris.

The shift in music to a slow Barry White melody brings me back to my current location in Aruba with the food and drink in front of me. The couples on the dance floor move closer, and many more join them. I continue enjoying my dinner and my Bahama Mama. The stress from dealing with the annoying stranger has dissipated. The restaurant is getting crowded, and more people are gathering in the bar area. I move my beach bag and place it on the floor in front of my feet. It would be rude to have it take up a seat during a busy time.

The atmosphere is great this evening with the music selection. A few minutes later, a woman sits next to me and says hello. I greet her with a closed-lip smile and a nod, since my mouth is full. She peruses the menu that sits on the bar countertop. When my mouth is empty, she says, "How is your meal? It looks great."

"It tastes as good as it looks."

The bartender returns with her drink.

"I'll take the same as her." She motions to my plate. The bartender recites the sauces and sides that are also available. This woman welcomes it all.

I wish I could eat everything. I love a good meal presentation. I used to enjoy watching my ex-husband order and eat the most mouthwatering entrées. I just can't do it.

"My name is Seleste," my neighbor says as she extends her hand. "That's Seleste with an *S*."

I wipe my hands. "I'm Pearl. Pleased to meet you."

"Are you on the cruise ship?" Seleste asks.

"No. I'm living on the island for a few more weeks."

"I'm at the Marina Hotel near the beach closer to the Noord area. This is my first time anywhere."

"Really?" I hear the surprise in my voice and hope I didn't embarrass Seleste with my comment. She isn't as old as I am, but she has a few years on her. I have more gray hair than black now, but I refuse to dye it. Seleste has a few grays, but her blunt cut is very becoming. Her smile matches her curves, which are bold and beautiful. And her medium-brown skin is a combination of sun and a gorgeous blessing from God. I've always been horrible at identifying people's ethnic backgrounds, but I'm not ignorant like most misinformed white Americans who believe that Black and white are ethnicities.

"I always wanted to travel, but my husband thought it was a waste of money."

"So he finally changed his mind, and you decided to take him on a trip?" I look across her in an effort to locate her husband. But there are two younger guys sitting next to her. Seleste follows my eyes.

"Oh no, not exactly. He died, and I decided to do something I always wanted to do."

"My condolences," I say sincerely.

"No, don't be sad." She pats my hand. "I found out he didn't take me traveling because he took his girlfriend instead."

"Oh." I couldn't think of anything else to say. Now I'm sure I have a stupid expression on my face. "You didn't help him in the dying process, did you?" I quietly whisper.

Seleste chuckles. "I did not, but I should have." She sips her drink. "I didn't know anything until I got an STD."

"Really! My goodness."

"He got it from his girlfriend, mistress, or whatever they call them nowadays."

"I'm sorry. Being cheated on is never a good feeling, but I'm glad you've decided to travel and see the world."

Seleste raises her drink. I mirror her, and we clink glasses.

"So what have you seen so far in Aruba?" I ask Seleste.

"I've seen the bars, restaurants, and beaches. I've even spent time with a very loving guy."

"You can't take a vacation and not have a holiday romance," I state boldly, as if I would ever consider doing the same. Or maybe that's just what I need. I know my dildos would probably like to have a rest.

"He was really good, but I only have my dead husband to compare him to."

We both smile. I'm thinking about the last time I enjoyed a man and did not rely on Spicy for an orgasm. I take a breath and come back to reality. "You can't leave Aruba without seeing the murals in the San Nicolas area. There's also a beautiful beach there," I say as I place my fork on my plate. "You can take the bus to the San Nicolas region, but to get to Baby Beach, you'll need to take a taxi if you're not driving yourself."

Seleste's food arrives. It looks great with the gravy and the different sauces on the side. The restaurant is busy now, with many more tourists dancing to the R&B music. I've lost sight of the obnoxious guy, but Seleste's company has been a pleasant surprise, since I spend so much time alone. I very much like my own company, but it's nice to encounter another soul who has survived the bullshit of life and come out on top.

"Do you have children?" I'm always curious about other women my age. In my mother's generation, it seemed like they all had children unless they were barren like me. But in my generation, a lot opted out of raising families. Many women have lived extraordinary lives and have had fulfilling careers.

"Yes, I have one son from whom I am estranged. I think that's what they call it when your child gets angry with you and decides you're the scum of the earth because you choose not to give him money to waste."

"Yeah, unfortunately, that is what it's called. Many women have fraught relationships with their children."

"Do you have any children or estranged children?" Seleste asks.

"No. I wasn't blessed with children. Just an ex-husband."

"I loved being a mother and expected so much more when he became an adult, but it didn't happen." Seleste repositions herself on the barstool, showing that she might be uncomfortable talking about her inconsiderate son. "I expected calls to check on me and maybe enjoy grown-up family vacations and possibly grandchildren."

"Yeah, I wanted that mother experience and possibly grandchildren, but it was short lived." I take a sip of my drink and smile. I don't like to talk about my losses because I feel shame, but why keep it a secret? "I tried but couldn't carry a child full-term."

"Many of my friends had a similar experience."

"Society doesn't realize how common it is and wants to ostracize women. My mother-in-law was the president of that club and reminded me at every opportunity."

"I have stretchmarks and a sagging stomach to remind me of my ungrateful son and it makes me angry." She pokes at her stomach.

"You can always get a tummy tuck."

Seleste thinks for a few seconds. "You're right. I'll take his inheritance and get a tummy tuck. That will show him."

We both laugh. I continue my conversation with Seleste, and we exchange telephone numbers before I leave the bar for the evening. There are too many people here now. I had finished my dinner, and no one had asked me to dance. Seleste and I plan to connect tomorrow at the beach and have dinner together that evening.

Seleste catches the eye of a guy who wants to dance. She's excited to cut a rug. I wonder if my interaction with the obnoxious guy prevented anyone from asking me to dance. When I get to the door of the restaurant, I turn to see Seleste being twirled on the dance floor. Both she and the guy are laughing. *Seleste might get lucky again tonight*, I think to myself.

CHAPTER 2

KELTON

I watch the bikini-clad women near the pool from the upper deck as the sun reflects off the water and a warm ocean breeze moves across the deck. It seems like each year the bikinis get smaller and smaller, not that I'm complaining. I'd like to think my daughter doesn't wear anything that skimpy. However, I know the women at the pool are attempting to reel in a guy to take them shopping. Trading shopping for a night of extracurricular bedroom activities isn't always worth the hassle. As I've gotten older, I prefer a woman with curves instead of one who is extremely thin and bony. There is nothing wrong with a little extra weight, as long as the woman is happy with it. I've seen curvy women in bikinis, and they look so good. I guess I've always liked a little something to hold on to. It's hard when their thighs are so thin and their buttocks is lacking—or should I say missing.

Wow, like that one over there. I don't remember seeing her around here. A new group of cruisers joined the ship in Fort Lauderdale a few days ago. We're here in Aruba for two days and then one day in Curaçao before we return to Fort Lauderdale.

"You see anyone worthy of your time?" Richard asks as he approaches, an orange juice bottle in hand. He's dressed in his traditional workout attire. He faithfully exercises every day.

"Good morning, Richard," I say with a slight British accent. I point toward the voluptuous woman dressed in orange with the perfect coloring of brown sugar and waves of curls tumbling down her back. "She's new on the ship."

"Kelton, you have a good eye. Yes, she is definitely new. We should probably introduce ourselves. I'll find out if she has a friend for you."

"I'll let you handle the inquiry, then you can get back to me regarding her story." I slap Richard on the back.

"Game on." Richard smiles, then downs the rest of his juice.

I turn to see the beautiful horizon. "I'll never get tired of this view." I shake my head as I think about the horrible view in prison. The dingy walls in my cell that needed to be painted and the limited sunlight. Three years locked in a dreadful tomb because my COO was either greedy or totally ignorant. Matt could never have gotten away with his embezzlement scheme. He triggered so much heartache, which caused my world to come crashing down around me. I lost everything the day my mother died when I was still a child. It was years into my adulthood before I could love again and not fear losing someone to something tragic.

"I'll never get tired of all the women." Richard waves toward the lower deck, where the female sunbathers are positioned around the pool wearing very little in the way of swimming attire. They return his wave with one of their own. "I was concerned about leasing this suite for twenty-four months and traveling the Caribbean." Richard's smile grows larger. "But I believe it's well worth the money." He winks at a woman who is staring at him from the pool area.

"If you decide you want something permanent after the twenty-four months, tell me. I might be willing to sell you my one-bedroom unit." I walk toward the stairwell leading down to the pool deck from the owner suites. "I need to get breakfast. I'm meeting Lyndsey later. We're going shopping—or shall I say she's going shopping with my money."

"Is she worth it?" Richard asks as he lifts his eyebrows.

"I'm getting old. I think I'd prefer more than just sex."

"Shut your mouth. Sex is all I want. Sex in every position is all I need. I avoid those women who require a commitment, and since my vasectomy, I don't worry about asking about protection."

"Yeah. I know that some don't even discuss protection. Sometimes I can't get it out fast enough or even get my clothes off." I retreat from the stairs and return within earshot of Richard. "You got a vasectomy?" I whisper.

"I did it a few years ago when a young woman attempted to get pregnant by piercing all of my condoms with a needle while they were still in the foil."

"Really?" I'm surprised and shocked. "How did you find out?"

"You don't want to know. But I decided not to take another chance that someone could make me a father."

"Do you tell the women about your vasectomy?"

"No. Of course not."

"Did it hurt?" I point to my crotch.

"Just a little pinch from the needle to numb everything." Richard taps the empty orange juice bottle against the railing. "A few weeks later, I returned to the urologist to confirm that none of my swimmers were in fact swimming."

"I never thought about permanent birth control."

Richard clears his throat. "It doesn't stop you from getting an STD. I've had a few of them."

"Thanks. I might consider it, since I have no need for another child, and paying child support again is not how I want to spend my golden years."

"Yeah, I didn't get to sixty years old to raise another child."

"Agreed. I didn't get to sixty-two to raise another child either. I've got to go." I jog down the stairs holding the handrail.

Lyndsey had a great time shopping for everything designer. The dresses look wonderful on her, and she insisted on a pair of shoes for every outfit. I don't mind letting the women shop with my money because it makes them feel good to look nice, and I want them to appear beautiful when they're with me.

Lyndsey's arm is around mine as we stroll down the sidewalk while I carry the shopping bags. We hear R&B music playing from a nearby restaurant and decide to have dinner there. It's crowded, and we wait in the bar area until we can be seated. I place the shopping bags on the floor in front of me while Lyndsey excuses herself to locate the restroom.

I notice a woman in yellow at the bar. She's trying to avoid speaking with the guy next to her. I can't determine whether they're together and she's upset or whether he's a stranger and she's attempting to ignore him. I observe their interaction. A curl bounces from the top of her head and falls on the back of her neck. She brushes the hair back in place. I notice a wedding ring on her hand, but I don't see a husband. He's a lucky man.

As I get a better view of the woman, I realize she's the same one I met at the soccer field earlier today. She's now wearing a sunshine yellow dress, and she looks great. It complements her skin beautifully. If I wasn't with Lyndsey, I'd probably approach and get rid of the guy for her. I didn't get her name when I spoke with her earlier. Why didn't I ask her for it? I was so astonished that this woman decided to buy ice cream for all the members of the youth soccer team. She didn't even have a child playing on the field, nor was she a grandmother to one of the young players. She just wanted to buy ice cream for them all. It simply surprised me. She also knew the name of the ice cream vendor. Maybe she hangs out at the soccer field every game or just makes a point to be nice to the vendor. I asked if I could get one of the ice creams, and she said she would pay for mine as well. I declined. I just wanted to know if her generosity would also extend to me.

"I think it's too crowded. The waiter is going to rush us through our meal," Lyndsey says when she returns and sits next to me at the bar.

"We won't let him do that," I reply, attempting to reassure her.

"They always rush the diners when the restaurants are crowded."

"Hey, folks," Richard calls as he approaches. "Any good shopping?"

"Oh yes. The shopping was great," Lyndsey says with a smile.

Richard winks at Lyndsey and stands next to me.

"Can we go?" Lyndsey asks me in a demanding tone. "We can get dinner on the ship at the steak house restaurant."

"I'll join you," Richard says.

I look at him with a smirk. "That sounds like a good idea as long as Richard accompanies you."

"Really?" Lyndsey says. "You don't mind?"

"Of course not. Richard wanted to talk to you about your organic sunscreen." This gives Richard a reason to hang out with Lyndsey. "I want to stay and possibly dance."

"In this crowd?" Richard looks at me.

"Yeah. I'll get some dinner and find someone to dance with me."

Lyndsey begins collecting her shopping bags from the floor. "Thanks for all the gifts." She leans in to kiss me on the cheek.

Richard reaches for some of the bags and then Lyndsey's hand to guide her through the crowd and out the door.

I order a drink and ask for a menu, then look down the bar at the woman in yellow. When I spoke with her earlier, I noted a hint of magnolia. I don't know if it was her hair or her perfume. Her curls are pulled up and clamped at the back of her head. A few are trying to escape and move every time she sways to the music. I could spend the rest of the evening watching her. Maybe I'll ask her to dance. I hope she won't think I'm being annoying like the other guy and dismiss me. I wish I could have heard their conversation. I always thought I should learn to read lips.

I order my meal and stare at the woman in yellow in an effort to devise a plan to ask for her name. As I watch her, I see another woman sit next to her and begin a conversation. I enjoy my dinner and the music in the hope of telepathically conveying a message to the woman to look my way. What if I send a drink to her and her friend? Is that too bold? I have only one more day on the island before the ship departs. It's been a while since a woman has been intriguing enough to get my attention.

Why would she buy ice cream for a bunch of youth soccer players when she didn't know them? Is that her character, or did someone dare her to do it? Is she on holiday, or does she live in Aruba? Why would she be here in a tourist restaurant with this crowd? She's not on the cruise ship because I would have seen her. She keeps watching the dance floor while rocking to the music. She has a beautiful smile, and I could just swim in her large hazel eyes. It would be nice to meet a woman and have something else to discuss other than fashion. I can't remember the last time I showed any interest in a woman other than for sex. After my divorce, I swore I would keep women at a distance, or, like my former COO used to tell me, I like keeping them in a box and opening it only when I need them.

Why am I thinking about Matt? He's still serving his remaining sentence for embezzling from our firm. It might not have been so bad, but because we were a publicly traded company, the shareholders needed someone to take responsibility and serve time. I ended up in prison even though I did not embezzle a penny, but in the end, the shareholders held me responsible for not monitoring the COO and the CFO. Not in a million years would I have ever believed I would be jailed for something I did not do. Now I live under the radar, and most of the women I meet have never heard my name or anything about the case.

If I could go back in time and make the decision to embezzle money, I would have taken enough to disappear and never be found again. But Matt embezzled just enough to trigger an investigation. He cried at the sentencing, as did his family. He never told me why he did it. I would have helped him solve his financial problem. That's if it was a financial problem. It could have been a greed problem. There's never enough money to address greed. My family was in shock, as was I. But they didn't cry. Not a single tear. My wife told me that she never knew anyone who'd gone to jail. She also said that the children were embarrassed and never wanted to see me again. *I felt like crying.* She filed for divorce a few days later, and my children have not spoken with me since the night before my sentencing. I gave her the house and all the furniture, then packed my personal items into a storage unit. After the attorneys were paid, my wife realized her lifestyle was going to decline considerably with me in prison. Her friends ghosted her, along with some of her family members. No one should ever make a decision in a few days that will prepare them for three to five years in prison. After my mom died from cancer, I worked so hard to make her proud of me. I promised on her deathbed that I would be a good boy. I held to that promise except for a few occasions. But a good man? That might be questionable, since I ended up in prison.

I don't have any true friends. The few people who know me aren't aware of the real story. I'd like to spend time with someone who won't judge me, and I worry every day that someone might recognize me. If that happens, I'll need to hide in my stateroom. I wonder if the cruise line would ask me to leave the ship. Everything is so volatile and secretive in my life.

I pay for my meal and drink, then walk toward the woman in yellow. Another curl has fallen from the ball on the back of her head. That single curl floats across the nape of her neck as she moves. She's picking up her beach bag. I might be too late to ask for a dance. She pulls out her cell phone and shares something with the woman next to her. I slide closer, hoping to hear their conversation. They're talking about yoga on the beach tomorrow around 10:00 a.m. I don't catch the name of the beach. I lean in closer while trying not to look obvious. The woman in yellow is leaving, and I still don't know the name of the beach. Her friend heads to the dance floor. Would it be weird if I followed her to where she's staying? Yeah, that might look bad, and I could end up in jail or get clobbered over the head. Neither sounds like a good option. I guess I'll go back to the ship, determine how many beaches are in Aruba, and design a game plan for tomorrow.

C H A P T E R   3

KELTON

This morning's goal is to find the woman in yellow, whom I didn't get an opportunity to introduce myself to or dance with at the restaurant last night. The ship will leave for the next port this evening at eleven. I spoke with the concierge after breakfast and obtained a map of the beaches. I'm up and off the ship early. The plan is to visit the beaches closest to the ship, then expand out from there. If those two women are going to hang at a beach today, I guarantee I'm going to find them. I'm dressed in comfortable clothing and have brought along my beach bag with a few additional items. I don't want it to appear creepy if I just show up as if I had no intention of visiting a beach. I don't want to give the appearance that I'm stalking them if they remember me from the restaurant. I make my way off the gangplank and toward the first beach.

I can't believe I didn't hear the name of the beach when I attempted to eavesdrop on their conversation yesterday. I must be losing my touch. I used to be so good at listening in on my children's conversations with their friends. It would have been so much better if I had asked the woman in yellow to dance. She was swaying to the music throughout the evening, which gave me the impression she wanted to dance. I had approached them once and then went down on one knee as if my shoe was untied. I was wearing deck shoes with no laces. She stared at me as if I was attempting to steal her bag or look under her dress. I could feel her eyes piercing through my skull, an expression of confusion on her face. I eventually stood up with a grunt and gripped the bar top. My knees don't work as well as they did when I was younger. She gave me a side-eye glance as if she was concerned or maybe just totally confused as to why I knelt in the first place. Regaining my composure, I continued past them and headed to the men's room.

Now I'm walking across another beach, shoes in hand. "Ouch!" I don't see that shell because I'm watching a yoga group not far from me. I hope it's the one I'm searching for. As I get closer, I see several in the group suddenly start to fall like dominoes. Either this is a new style of yoga or someone is having a problem. One woman takes down two more people, and the one on the end is quick to move. I hope no one is hurt because I have a smirk on my face that I can't remove. I try deep breathing and walk in a circle to readjust my thinking so that I don't laugh. When I turn around again, it appears someone did get hurt. Now it's not funny. Maybe later when the person is feeling better, I'll laugh with them about the arms and legs that were flying all over the place when they all went down. A few from the group help a hopping person to her towel, and I realize it's the other woman from the bar last night. The instructor suggests spreading out so that they don't play the domino game again as they stand in warrior pose.

Everyone moves back to their mats. I scan them to find the woman in yellow, my ray of sunshine. She is adorable in her yoga pants and sleeveless top. Today she's wearing pink. The woman in pink. I haven't had this type of pull to someone in a very long time. In fact, I can't remember the last time I've wanted to get to know someone of the opposite sex. She sets my heart on fire just watching her. I don't even know her name. I walk directly to the woman in pink's companion, who is now recovering from her injury. My plan is to spend time with her and get invited to hang out with them both on the beach.

Before I left the ship, I got a nice little snack spread for the beach and a board game. I thought the women would enjoy something after yoga class. No one ever turns down fruit, cheese, crackers, and drinks. I haven't attempted to woo a woman in a while because most aren't looking for something long term. They know I'm here because of the cruise ship and that when it leaves, I'm gone to the next port.

"Hello," I say as I approach the woman on the towel.

"Hello yourself." She smiles and removes her sunglasses.

"May I sit here?" I motion to the spot next to her.

"Sure." She readjusts her sunglasses to shield her eyes. "My name is Seleste," she says as she extends her hand.

"I'm Kelton." We shake. I drop my backpack on the sand and spread out my towel, then open my beach chair and sit.

"The chair is a great idea," Seleste says.

"My back needs support, or I'll be in agony tomorrow." My sunshine, the woman in yellow who is now pretty in pink, looks at me, then continues to follow the yoga instructor's directions. I make small talk with Seleste and ask about her ankle. She's icing it, but it's not bruised or swollen. When the group finishes, my sunshine joins us. Asking Seleste if she's doing better before spreading her towel on the other side of Seleste. Introductions are conducted by Seleste. I offer my hand and Pearl reciprocates.

"I brought fruit and cheese for a snack, since I had plans to sit on the beach this morning. I'd like for you both to join me. I have enough for the three of us." Pearl looks at Seleste as if to find an excuse not to include me. I wonder if she thinks I might drug them and take their belongings.

"I'm going to soak up the sun under that umbrella over there." Seleste points to an area farther along the beach. "Since you brought snacks and our granola bars don't look as appealing, you're invited as long as Pearl agrees." Seleste begins the process of standing on one leg. She looks like a pelican until she begins to lean to one side. I stand and reach for her elbow. Pearl still has not said anything.

"Okay," she finally replies, a note of reluctance in her voice.

Pearl helps Seleste move toward the beach umbrella as I grab the remaining items on the sand and follow in silence. I wonder if the woman in yellow who captivated me at the bar last night will give me an unforgettable memory before I ship out this evening. I open my beach chair and let Seleste sit. "I'll be back." I head to the beach stand near the hotel. They place umbrellas on the beach for everyone and hope the tourists will rent chairs. I look back and see Pearl sitting on her towel talking to Seleste; it looks like they're having an argument. I hope the conversation is not about me, since Pearl is being very animated with her gestures. I wonder if a few strawberries will console her.

I return with two chairs, and Pearl gives a half smile and thanks me. I quickly place her chair next to Seleste and mine next to hers. I don't want Pearl to sit on the other side of Seleste, as it would be impossible to have a discussion with her. Seleste looks sleepy, or maybe she's just really enjoying the ocean breeze.

I get situated and then pull out the snacks, placing them on the towel in front of us along with the travel size version of Scrabble. I pass the container of strawberries to Pearl. "They're sweet; you'll enjoy them." She accepts it and taps Seleste, motioning for her to partake in the fruit. She's going to be a tough nut to crack. Pearl eventually eats one after placing the container on the towel. She's surprised by the sweetness. I pass her a bottle of water, then assemble the cheese platter. Seleste eats a strawberry.

"Do you play Scrabble?" I ask both while giving my undivided attention to Pearl as I hold the small platter. She takes a few slices of cheese and some crackers. Seleste shakes her head no to Scrabble while taking another strawberry. "What about you Pearl?"

"Yes, I play but I'm not very competitive."

She still doesn't trust me. She crosses her legs under her. I can't read her expression.

"I'm not very competitive either. I just like to play and don't find many people who enjoy word games or board games." I watch her face as I pull the game out of my backpack. I was lucky to find a travel version of Scrabble at the gift shop this morning. I remember seeing Pearl playing some type of word game on her cell when I passed her at the soccer field. This would give us something to break the ice.

She asks Seleste if she needs anything. She says no and closes her eyes. She mentioned taking Pearl with her to dance all night long. We all laughed about all-nighters after I invited myself to join them. I asked about her wedding band. Pearl didn't get a chance to answer before Seleste mumbled Pearl was not married.

After a few minutes, I get a laugh out of Pearl. It's angelic and is followed by a beautiful smile. I don't believe I've ever had such a good time playing a board game. I even laugh a few times, which surprises me. I've been hanging out with women who are focused only on what they can spend with my money. I even tell her about owning a stateroom on the cruise ship. I was hesitant to do so because many don't believe you can purchase a stateroom and live on the ship, but she surprises me. She had considered doing the same but changed her mind. I believe I would really delight in spending time with her every day. Our conversation was lighthearted and flirty. The wedding band I noticed earlier had disappeared from Pearl's finger.

Seleste's cell alarm goes off, and she wakes. We've enjoyed these two hours on the beach and agree to meet in the Marina Hotel lobby this evening for music and dancing with Seleste's friend. I'm glad Seleste didn't think I was imposing on their dance night. I'm getting closer to my goal. We can dance and go to her place for a little evening activity before I return to the cruise ship.

I get to the hotel early. I'm surprised I managed to, since I changed my clothes three times before leaving the cruise ship. I don't know if it's nerves or if I just want to make sure Pearl likes my outfit. I'm people watching. The bikini-clad women walk by me without cover-ups and smile or wink at me. Every time the automatic doors open, I turn to see if Pearl has arrived. Why am I so nervous? I check my wallet for my condoms. As I get older, sometimes I think of doing something and then forget to complete the task. The horrible downside of aging. I'm glad my body parts don't detach because I'd probably misplace them and never find them again. Sometimes I'll put things in a safe place and then can't remember where the safe place is located.

The automatic doors open again. I turn to see Pearl step through them and into the lobby. She waves and walks toward me. She looks lovely. Her hair is up, and a few strands frame her face. Her dress is a beautiful navy blue. I'm glad she wore a dress, as it gives easy access. Pants are so difficult when trying to get a quicky. I can do wonders with a woman pushed against the back of a door. She has just enough padding in the back that it draws attention when she walks. I return her wave. She joins me on the sofa bench and tells me that Seleste is on the way. The delay has something to do with Seleste's hair or makeup. I'm not really listening. I'm daydreaming about Pearl's taste. I nod a few times, but I'm really watching her lips. I make eye contact every once in a while. She finally pulls me out of my trance by asking about the next cruise port. I tell her the ship is headed to Curaçao and that I'll be in Fort Lauderdale in three days.

Seleste finally arrives, and we grab a taxi to the bar where her friend and the band that he manages is playing.

We hear music rolling out of the building as the taxi pulls up. People are dancing in the street and on the sidewalk. Seleste says our names are on a list at the door. I reach for Pearl's hand to guide her through the crowd. Her hand is soft and warm. It feels like silk. When we stop so that Seleste can find the guy who invited us, I interlace my fingers in hers. She doesn't attempt to pull away while we wait. I watch as she sways her hips to the music. I wish I could read her mind. Seleste returns with a guy who introduces himself as Weston. He kisses Pearl on the cheek and gives me a bro hug.

We follow Weston to the side of the bar. The place is packed. I'm sure the fire marshal would shut it down if we were in the States. The dance floor is full, so people are dancing near their tables. I secure one for us when I see a couple leaving. Weston has to check on something and will return soon. I make my way to the bar to place our order after Pearl and Seleste decide on tropical drinks.

We sit for a while and dance in our chairs until I decide I don't want to keep leaning in to talk to Pearl. I want her in my arms. I slide my hand into hers and point to the dance floor. I don't think she understands, so I rise from my stool and pull her to her feet. I love having her in my arms. Because the dance floor is still crowded, it's easy to pull her closer. I feel her hips rub against mine. I thought I forgot many of the dances, but she challenges me every time the music changes. I love it. As we slow dance, her signature scent of magnolias wafts around us. I move my hand up her back as I kiss her jaw. I tilt my head and let my lips brush against her. Her lips brush against mine more firmly and then part as my tongue explores her mouth. I hear her moan, which causes my manhood to twitch, and I moan too. Her arms wrap around my neck and pull me closer. When my cell alarm vibrates, I realize we've spent the entire night laughing, dancing, and rubbing against each other. Tonight's objective was to get laid before my cell alerted me to return to the ship. The goal was not met.

I whisper to Pearl that I need to leave and that I can walk her home if she's ready to go. We hug Seleste and Weston, then hold hands all the way to her door. I kiss her and thank her for a wonderful evening, then reluctantly walk away. I'll be in a new port tomorrow and will find someone else to share my time with. I still have Pearl's cell phone number. Seleste was nice enough to give me hers and Pearl's while we sat on the beach. I'll call her the next time I'm bound for Aruba, and we can continue what we started.

CHAPTER 4

PEARL

The air is laced with salt and warm against my skin as the waves dance along the beach. I stretch through my fingertips before touching my yoga mat. I'm glad I found this morning yoga class. I'm dressed in my soft pink yoga pants and pink striped T-shirt. Even my sports bra is a light pink. My hair is pulled back into a curly ponytail. I feel great even though I'm not a fan of anything early morning. But a 10:00 a.m. yoga class is doable for me, especially in these perfect surroundings.

"Downward dog," the instructor says. A total of twelve people are attending the class this morning. I glance at Seleste, who is holding the form perfectly. I'm struggling. Pointing my buttocks toward the sky might be healthy for my body, but my upper arm strength needs some work. I keep reminding myself to breathe. Why do I think my poses will be better without breathing? It would be so embarrassing to pass out.

"Simply challenge yourself. You're not competing against the person next to you or behind you," the instructor reiterates as she walks through the students, correcting and repositioning poses. We move into warrior 3 pose, which is one of my favorites. The woman next to Seleste grunts. I try to block out everything other than the instructor and my breathing, but today I hear others gasping and grunting. A couple in the second row keeps whispering, which is becoming very distracting. I hear another grunt and a shriek before I see flying sand. I quickly close my eyes while trying to keep my pose. Suddenly, I feel someone tumble against me and knock me to the ground like a falling tree. What in the world is happening? I wipe my eyes with my hand and open them. Seleste's body is splayed across my hip, and the grunting woman is lying on Seleste's leg. I've been pushed into the sand. The woman is apologizing and attempting to get up. I'm a little dazed. The instructor and a few of the students help get everyone back on their feet. Seleste is hopping on her left leg in an attempt to keep from putting pressure on her right ankle. The thought that I'm too old to fall, even in sand, keeps repeating in my mind.

"I think I twisted my leg when I went down." Seleste grimaces and speaks through gritted teeth. The previously grunting woman continues to apologize. The instructor asks everyone to return to warrior pose. I try not to laugh as I compose myself. Someone has a small cooler and gives Seleste some ice for her ankle. I help get Seleste situated on her beach towel and assure her that I'll get her back to her hotel to rest after the class. I also move two additional steps to my right, which is falling distance away from the grunting woman. She's embarrassed about taking Seleste and me down like dominoes. But if she falls again, I'll be far enough away to not be impacted. Seleste mumbles something under her breath as she holds the ice on her ankle. The yoga instructor continues with the class.

As we finish and namaste, I look over at Seleste and see that she has male company. Maybe he can help me get her back to her hotel. The gentleman has set up his chair next to Seleste's towel. I wonder if he migrated to Seleste because she's holding ice against her leg, or could this be the guy she told me about? I walk toward them.

"Good morning," I say to the man before turning to Seleste. "Is it feeling better?"

Seleste removes the ice and attempts to rotate her ankle. "A little." She returns the ice to her injury. "I'll keep it there until the ice completely melts, then I'll do a test walk."

"Okay. Sounds like a plan." I spread out my towel on the other side of Seleste.

"Oh, this is Kelton." Seleste motions to the man. "And this is my friend Pearl."

Kelton stands and offers his hand. "Pleased to meet you."

I extend my own and we shake. "Nice to meet you."

"Is that Pearl like the jewel of the ocean?" Kelton asks.

"Yes."

"I believe we met the other day at the soccer field. You bought ice cream for all the players."

"I don't remember you."

"I was the guy who asked if you would buy me ice cream."

"Oh yes. I recall that now." But I really don't remember.

Seleste repositions herself to allow Kelton and me to see each other without her between us. She rotates her ankle again.

"I'm thinking we should move over there under one of the umbrellas and chill for the rest of the morning," I suggest to Seleste.

Kelton nods as if in agreement. I'm still not sure whether Seleste has invited him to spend time with us or whether he's a serial killer or a scammer looking for desperate women. I help Seleste to her feet.

"My ankle feels much better. I had no idea I could get hurt doing yoga on the beach. I was just taken down, and it came out of nowhere. I heard her grunt a few times, and then the sand went flying." Seleste frowns in disgust.

"Getting hurt doing yoga is a new one for me." I grab our beach bags, and Kelton picks up our towels. He follows us to the umbrella.

"Were you just passing by and decided to sit with Seleste?" I need to know his intentions.

"Yes. I was simply walking by and decided to watch the yoga class. Maybe tomorrow I'll join in."

"You do yoga?"

"Don't sound so surprised. Yes, I like the benefits of yoga. And I promise not to fall on anyone."

Seleste and I chuckle.

Kelton places our towels on the sand. "Seleste, you can sit here in my chair." Once she's settled, Kelton says, "I'll be right back." He runs off toward the rental hut. A few minutes later, he returns with two chairs and places them next to each other.

We're all situated on the beach under the large umbrella. I'm between Seleste and Kelton. I also notice that Kelton has a beach bag. He pulls out a travel size version of Scrabble and a Tupperware platter of snacks.

"Do you play?" he asks us as he motions to the game.

Seleste shakes her head but takes a strawberry from the platter.

"What about you, Pearl?" Kelton asks.

"I play, but I'm not the best." I'm wondering why this guy has latched on to us. What is he up to? He brings a board game, specifically Scrabble, which is one of my favorites, and snacks. Fresh healthy snacks.

"Nor am I. Would you like to play?"

I look at Seleste first. "Do you need anything?"

"Oh no. Go ahead and play while I lay back and close my eyes. I'm resting for an evening of dancing. Weston's band is playing. Did I tell you that you're going dancing with me tonight?"

"No, you didn't tell me." Maybe tonight I'll find someone to dance with me.

"I'd like to join you both if I'm not imposing," Kelton states with confidence.

Seleste is excited. "That would be great. You're invited, and we'll dance until sunrise." She grabs a strawberry from the platter.

"You do know that we're too old to do all-nighters anymore," I say with a laugh.

"Speak for yourself!" Kelton and Seleste reply in unison.

"That was a long, long time ago when we had the ability to stay up all night," I answer.

Kelton smiles and continues to set up the Scrabble game. A few minutes later, the competitive nature has taken us over while Seleste quietly snores next to us. I had planned to read while sitting on the beach, but it's nice to play a board game and have someone to talk with. Since I've been in Aruba, I've had limited interaction with others. What a perfect day to enjoy the beach and a game.

"Are you staying at one of the hotels in the Noord area?"

"No. I'm on the cruise ship."

"You decided to sit on the beach instead of taking an excursion?"

"It's not my first time in Aruba." He looks at me. "I live on the ship."

"Oh, you work on the ship," I clarify.

"No. I live on the ship. I purchased a stateroom a few years ago and decided to visit all the Caribbean islands," Kelton says, then watches my reaction.

"Wow. I considered purchasing a stateroom." I smile at Kelton. "You're the first person I've ever met who has actually done so."

"I have a one bedroom. It was one of my better purchases. You and your husband could visit all the Caribbean Islands or all of Europe or Asia."

"My husband and I?"

"I see your wedding band."

I look down at the ring that is still on my hand.

"She's not married," Seleste mumbles.

"I'm . . . I'm divorced," I stammer. I'm so embarrassed to be flirting with Kelton while wearing my wedding band. Or am I embarrassed because I failed to keep my marriage together?

"I'm divorced too. It's not something that I planned or even wanted," Kelton confesses.

"Let's change the subject." I did not want to admit my husband divorced me because I gained weight. The divorce papers actually state, along with a bunch of legal mumbo jumbo, that I failed to complete my wifely duties due to being overweight. I quickly pull the gold band off my finger and drop it in the outside pocket of my beach bag.

"No problem. If you decide you're interested in living on a cruise ship, I know there are a few more lease options available."

"Thanks. I had considered it because I love visiting ports, but I decided that I would visit places I liked and stay ten weeks out of the year. Each year I select a different place."

"Now that sounds interesting. Where have you visited?"

"First was Grand Caymans, and last year I spent time in London."

"Sounds nice. I'm from the Southwick area of London."

"I'm horrible at determining accents. I pegged you as Australian. It's not always present, but I hear a hint of an accent."

"I was born and bred in London. I moved to the States for college."

"What do you do?" I want to see if he's trying to scam Seleste or me out of our money.

"I don't work anymore. I studied finance at Rutgers University in New Jersey. And you?"

"I studied business at Case Western Reserve University in Ohio, and I win again." I clap my hands symbolically so as not to wake Seleste from her nap.

"Do you think I might be letting you win?" Kelton grins.

"Are you letting me win, Kelton?" Our eyes connect, and I let out a long breath to calm myself. This guy is extremely charming. Ted Bundy was also charming. Should I worry about him being a Nigerian prince attempting to scam me out of everything I have? Okay, he might not be Nigerian, but maybe he knows a Nigerian prince. I wonder why scammers use the Nigerian prince character when most scammers are European.

Seleste's cell alarm wakes her, and she stretches. "Did you two enjoy your game of Scrabble?"

"Yes, we did," I answer with a smile.

"Well, it's past lunchtime, and I need to shower and get ready for this evening." Seleste stands, being careful not to put too much pressure on her right ankle. I move next to her and take her elbow.

"Okay, stand on your ankle. I'll grab you if you start to fall."

Seleste slowly puts her body weight on her ankle. "It feels good. The pain is gone."

Kelton packs the Scrabble game and towel into his bag. "Where are we meeting, and what time?" He stands, then lightly brushes sand from my arm and moves a loose curl behind my ear. I feel a tingle. I haven't been touched intimately in a while. I can't remember the last time, since I've been celibate for the past twelve years.

"Meet me in the Marina Hotel lobby at five, and we'll go from there. I'll need to call Weston to confirm the location."

"Would you like me to help you back to your hotel?"

"We're good. I'll find a taxi for Seleste so that she doesn't overdo it before tonight, and I'm walking distance from here. Thanks for asking."

I pack my towel into my beach bag. "So Weston plays in a band?"

"No, he manages the band. They play R&B and pop music," she clarifies.

We begin walking toward town, and I flag a taxi for Seleste. I'm still curious about Kelton. I'm sure there are more than enough women on the cruise ship to keep him busy. Why did he invite himself to spend time with us today and then go dancing this evening? What is his motivation?

When I arrive at the Marina Hotel, Kelton is already sitting in the lobby. He's wearing dark-blue khakis and a sky blue polo. His deck shoes make him look as if he just stepped out of a catalog. His peppered curly hair is combed back, not like the wind-tossed look he sported at the beach. His beard and mustache are trimmed perfectly. I hesitate and think again about the Nigerian prince scam. My navy blue wraparound dress gives the impression that we planned our attire. I'd swept my hair up into a lose puffball and let a few strands fall to the sides of my face.

Kelton stands and waves to get my attention when I enter the hotel. Am I getting into something that I don't want? Or do I simply enjoy this man mentally and physically because he's leaving on the cruise ship tonight at eleven? We'll have a few hours of dancing and rubbing against each other before he turns into a pumpkin and disappears.

"You look gorgeous," Kelton says with a more pronounced British accent than earlier. He kisses me on the cheek.

"Thanks. You look good too."

He motions for me to sit, then joins me on the bench. "How much longer are you here in Aruba?"

"Only ten more days." I fold my hands in my lap. My small purse hangs across my chest. I brought only the necessary items and locked everything else in the safe at the house. My necessary items consist of a door key, lipstick, a debit card, a credit card, fifty dollars, and my cell. I didn't bring my eyeglasses, so I hope I won't need to read anything.

"Where is your ship going next?"

"The next stop is Curaçao for one day, then we'll be at sea for the two days it takes to return to Fort Lauderdale."

"So in three days you'll be back in the States." I'm not sure why I'm counting the number of days, but I feel a little nervous. I watch as bikini-clad women walk through the lobby. I know he also sees them because some attempt to make eye contact with him. I clear my throat. "You don't have to go with us. This is your last evening in Aruba. I'm sure you could find other entertainment tonight." I don't want to look at him, so I focus instead on the women strolling around. It's only right to give him an out for the evening.

I feel his finger on my chin, which he turns so that I'm facing him. I glance up to meet his beautiful mocha-colored eyes. "I'm going dancing with you tonight. That's what I want to do on my last evening in Aruba."

My heart begins beating like the steel drums in the Caribbean. A few seconds later, Seleste arrives and pulls us back to reality. She's wearing a pastel summer dress that bares her arms and back. She spins, and the skirt billows through the air. Her white sandals are strappy with a low heel. "Are you two ready?"

"You look beautiful," I say. Kelton nods.

"I feel magical." She touches her upswept hair that is held in a clam-shaped clamp. "Let's go!"

We arrive at a restaurant and bar combo. The band is already playing. The place is beyond packed, and everyone is moving to the beat. Weston is waiting for us at the front door. Seleste is excited to see him again. He has locs that give him a cool vibe, and he's impeccably dressed. I like when men wear suits with a T-shirt underneath instead of a dress shirt. Weston kisses Seleste on the lips. He pecks me on the cheek and gives Kelton a bro hug. He's reserved a table for us. He takes Seleste's hand, and Kelton places a hand on the small of my back to guide me as I follow her. I'm sure my awareness of him is due to the fact that I've had only battery-powered intimacy for so long.

Kelton had previously set his cell alarm for ten o'clock. I don't want him to miss boarding his ship. The night is enchanting. We freestyle, dance the mambo, electric slide, and cupid shuffle, and slow dance. The cherry on top is slow dancing to Barry White. Our first slow dance is close but not as close as the next. I can feel his erection, and it's glorious to rub against it. On the last slow dance of the evening, his lips travel down my jawline. I close my eyes and pray not to faint before he reaches my lips. His are soft and plump with just the right amount of firmness. He continues to sway as we kiss. I'm lost to everything around me until his phone vibrates, startling me. I'm breathless and don't want the night to end. But Kelton has to go. He insists on walking me to my rented cottage, and then, with a quick kiss, he's gone.

CHAPTER 5

I wake to the smell of the ocean breeze. I prefer the natural air instead of the air-conditioning. The windows are slated to prevent anyone from climbing into the house. I usually don't feel safe in the gun-toting United States, but here in Aruba, I'm always completely relaxed. Ever since the police broke into Breonna Taylor's home in the middle of night and she died by their bullet because her boyfriend was trying to protect them after being awakened from a deep sleep, I haven't felt safe. We don't expect judges and law enforcement to commit unsavory acts in the United States, especially against its citizens. It's very unfortunate that neither the judge nor the officers nor anyone else involved accepted responsibility for killing someone so innocent.

What a great night dancing with Kelton. I had a much better time than I'd expected to. He turned out to be interesting, charming, gracious, and alluring. I guess he's not a serial killer or running a scam. He definitely knew how to pull me close and be a sensual gentleman. I'm not sure I needed him to be as much of a gentleman last night. If he'd asked to return to my place before his ten o'clock alarm, I probably would have led the way. I'm glad I had charged my dildo yesterday because I needed it last night. I have two, depending on my needs—Spicy and the Magician. Last night I used the Magician. He does wonderful magic tricks.

I plan to start the day with a walk along the beach, then have brunch. There's no scheduled yoga today, so I'll connect with the group tomorrow morning. The book I wanted to read this week is still sitting on my nightstand. It's the first published novel by a friend of mine. I'll come back and hang out on the patio after I call Seleste. I'm sure she didn't return to her hotel until late, unless she decided to stay at Weston's place after dancing. Weston is handsome and charming. After his band finished playing, he was at Seleste's side for the rest of the evening. They danced and rubbed up against each other like two teenagers. It's so nice to be footloose and fancy-free.

I lock the door behind me and place the key in my shorts pocket along with my cell, credit card, ID, and a few dollars. As I turn toward the sidewalk, I see a guy sitting on the rock at the end of the driveway. He has on sunglasses and a baseball cap, so I can't determine whether I know him. He's wearing a white T-shirt and khaki shorts. I'm not expecting anyone, so I think maybe he's lost. I look down at his shoes, then back up to his sunglasses. He sees me and stands. My mouth flies open like a trap door. I'm surprised and horrified at the same time. It can't be. Concerned and worried, I say, "Kelton?"

"Good morning." He approaches me with a smile and a wink.

"Oh my. You missed the cruise ship?" It comes out as a question, but I meant it as a comment. This isn't my first crisis on vacation, and because I've been to the neighboring islands, Bonaire and Curaçao, I know we only need to get there by boat. Kelton begins to talk, but I'm not listening. "I'll call Seleste. I'm sure Weston knows someone who can take you to Curaçao. I'm sorry you missed your ship." I haven't allowed Kelton to say anything as I ramble. Still, there is no concern or worry showing on his face. I unlock my cell phone and go into my contacts. He doesn't seem upset. I wonder how he missed the ship. I purposely didn't keep him long after he walked me home, even though I wanted to give him a reason to stay with me last night.

Kelton's hand wraps around my mine. He takes my cell phone, then places it in his front pocket. He sets his hands firmly around my waist and moves me toward him like a gravitational pull. I look at his eyes; they're solid and securely fastened on me like his hands. His lips slowly brush against mine, and I stop trying to solve his problem. I feel his lips touch mine again, and I part them slowly to give him access. It's nothing like the kiss he gave me last night. I lean against him as my hands grip his biceps and pull him closer. When we break apart, my head is whirling. I know there's a problem that needs to be solved, but I need a moment to remember what it is.

"Good morning, lovey."

I don't have words. I don't know what to say or do. I simply nod.

"There is no problem. I decided to stay on the island a little longer and fly into Fort Lauderdale in three days. So we have two whole days together before I leave for good." I think he realizes that I'm not processing his words, but he continues anyway. "I'm at the hotel down the road so that I can be close to you. I got lucky, and they had a vacancy for the next two days."

My brain is starting to work again, and I repeat everything he said in my mind. "So you didn't miss your ship?"

He shakes his head, then leans in to place a kiss on my neck. "You smell so good."

My breath catches from his kiss. "You're going to spend a little more time with me?" Oh, I'm going to get in trouble with him. I've kept men at a distance, and with Kelton leaving yesterday, it helped me with boundaries. Now, in the blink of an eye, he's decided to crush my little boundaries and step into a land I've forbidden men to enter.

He smiles and nods this time. His eyes are looking into my soul as I try to regain my composure. "I hope you don't have plans with anyone else for the next few days."

This time I shake my head. "No, I don't have plans with anyone else." Only me, myself, and I.

"I'm glad, because it would be awkward, since I'm about to kiss you again in front of all of your neighbors." He pulls me against him and lowers his lips. My knees turn to Jell-O, and I lean into him for support.

A half hour later, we're walking on the beach and holding hands as if we've known each other for years. It feels so right, and he changed his plans for me. Am I reading too much into this grand gesture? To cancel leaving yesterday evening is a grand gesture. I'm sure it is. Though I didn't need him to do that. Now that my wall is crumbling and the boundaries I've created are blurring, what am I expecting for the next two days? What is he expecting for the next two days? Suddenly, my cell phone rings, bringing me out of my thoughts. It's one of my clients in the States. Murphy Home Care Services is one of my very lucrative contracts that has allowed me to purchase my two-family home and pay for this year's ten-week vacation. I look at Kelton. "I need to take this. Give me a few minutes."

He nods and sits in the sand. "I'll be right here waiting for you."

I walk a few steps away and answer the call. Jonathan is upset and needs someone to talk through his concerns regarding the government contract he acquired for his home care agency. I listen and give some practical advice, even though I'm not looking at the papers that are causing him such worry. I turn to look at Kelton, who is watching the waves break against the beach. What am I going to do with this man who loves to dance and hold me close? Oh, and his kisses are just perfect. I finish the call and return to Kelton. If the world stopped right now, I would be happy for the rest of my life. He intertwines his fingers with mine, and I snuggle closer to him.

We spend a few hours listening to the lapping of the waves on the beach and people watching. Seeing the children running on the sand, splashing in the waves, and laughing just warms my heart. My mind begins to wander. I always wanted to relive vacations through the eyes of my children. There is such an innocence to their questions and the look in their eyes. All of the why questions that continue throughout the day. Families arrive with tons of items in tow in wagons, their children so excited they can't stand still while their parents assemble beach accessories. Many just run with unbridled abandon. I remember babysitting my niece and nephew before the fire that took my brother and his family from this world. A tear forms in the corner of my eye, but I don't want to explain anything to Kelton if I start to cry, so I suggest that we have brunch. I believe he's thinking the same thing because he promptly stands and reaches for my hand to assist me to my feet. We walk toward the main street where the restaurants and hotels are located.

We decide to eat at the hotel where he is staying. I'm hoping he doesn't have other plans that include removing our clothes and having orgasms. The wall that I've been hiding behind and that no one has cared enough to attempt to scale is slowly dissolving. He does have a plan after brunch, but it's more intimate than sexual. He's reserved a hammock for us to nap in. It's been a while since I shared a hammock with anyone. The problem is not the sharing once we're situated; it's the process of two people getting into the hammock without flipping one to the ground. I vividly remember falling out of a hammock when I was much younger. I am definitely too old to fall on the ground, and so is Kelton.

Kelton sees my hesitation when we arrive at the hammock. I try to smile, but I'm sure it seems more like fear. "What's that look for?" Kelton asks.

"Do you think we both can get into this hammock without falling? I think we should take our nap on the lounge chairs."

Kelton steps closer and kisses my forehead. "You're always safe with me. I got you." He smiles like a Cheshire cat.

"We're too old to fall. We might break something."

Kelton steps between me and the hammock.

I look up at him and let out a slow breath. "I trust you." He wraps his arms around my waist, and his lips touch mine. The next thing I know, we're falling. I already had my eyes closed during the kiss, but now I squeeze them tighter. A scream comes out of my mouth as he lands in the hammock and I fall on top of him.

"You're safe, lovey," Kelton whispers in my ear. I open my eyes and look up at him. He's right.

"We're in the hammock," I say, then smile and kiss him.

"Ye of little faith." He pulls me closer—as if I could get any closer, since I'm lying partly on him and partly on the hammock.

"You're good. I will never doubt you again." I place my hand on his chest.

"I have skills you've not learned about yet."

I moan. "Really?" I'm intrigued as I slowly close my eyes and drift off to sleep.

I stand in front of the steak house waiting for Kelton to arrive. I feel beautiful and wanton. I turn around to watch my dress twirl. It's silk with a drop bodice and bell-shaped sleeves. The fuchsia color against my brown-sugar skin makes me glow. My hair is down in full bouncing curls. I feel free and want my hair to be the same and to do as the curls please tonight. I didn't expect to have an audience. I look up to see Kelton and a few other guys watching me. I tuck a curl behind my ear and grin. Kelton and another man approach me from the bar. They stop to talk before they reach me. Kelton pats him on the shoulder, then continues toward me alone.

"You look absolutely beautiful." He leans in and kisses me on the lips gently so as not to mess up my lipstick.

"Thanks. You look good too."

"I thought I was going to need to fight those guys to take you to dinner tonight."

I look toward the bar. One man waves at me. I return my gaze to Kelton. "I only have eyes for you tonight, Mr. Anderson."

Kelton winks at me.

We walk to the hostess station. Kelton's hand is on the small of my back to guide me but also to make sure everyone knows I'm with him. Dinner is great. The conversation and the food are more than I expected. I love Kelton's attention when I'm talking, and his smile lights up my world. Afterward, he walks me to my rented home and gives me the best good night kiss I've ever had. He also asks if I'd consider letting him stay overnight tomorrow. I think for a moment as my heart beats wildly.

"I don't do one-night stands." I watch his mocha-colored eyes for a reaction.

"No one-night stand." He leans in to kiss me.

I don't know if that's a question or a comment.

"I'm here for two more nights. You set the rules, and I'll follow them."

I can hear my mother in my head. All the no-no's. If I set the rules, who's going to enforce them? Do I need to do both? When I get weak in the knees and wet between my legs, who is going to remember the rules? Why would I use my dildo when I have a perfectly good cock available?

"Can I stay with you tomorrow night?" Kelton asks again.

"Yes." I think he might want to stay tonight.

He kisses me one last time before saying good night and turning toward his hotel.

The following morning, we agree to meet for yoga on the beach. Seleste is also joining us. We all think it best to space ourselves so that if one of us topples, we won't all be taken out. We follow up with lunch after sitting on the beach. That evening we dance until 2:00 a.m., and I let Kelton stay over. I didn't want it to feel awkward, but I was excited to tuck my butt against him while sleeping. I haven't had a hot-blooded man in my bed in a very long time. I agree that he can sleep in my bed with me, but there will be no intercourse. I let out a long sigh of nervousness. I turn to watch as Kelton connects his cell phone to charge. I hope I didn't make a mistake by telling him he can stay the night but that there'll be no sex. We're still completely dressed other than our shoes. Kelton places his cell on the nightstand, and I hear jazz fill the room. I strategically left a night-light on in the bedroom; it and the moonlight cast shadows on the walls and across the bedroom.

"Come here to me, lovey." He reaches his hand toward me. I take it, and he pulls me close to him. We dance to a few jazz numbers and to a few Barry White tunes. I know I should embrace this, but I wonder if this is what he does with all the women. Or did he simply have a playlist for us tonight? After a few dances, he whispers, "I didn't bring any pajamas, but I would like to get you into yours tonight."

I nod. I try to leave his embrace and collect my pajamas, but Kelton doesn't release me.

"I have our pajamas." I smile, and Kelton kisses me, solid and sure. He pulls his shirt out of his pants and unbuttons it. I see his undershirt beneath it. "I'll sleep in my underclothes tonight."

I don't say anything. I simply watch. I want to touch him but fear that if I brush my fingertips along his chest, I might not stop. He steps closer to me.

"Can I take off your dress?" I turn around so that he can reach the zipper and pull my hair up. He kisses my neck and begins to undo my dress. As he unzips it, he kisses my skin all the way down my back. He pulls the dress off my shoulders and lets it drop to the floor. I step out and pick it up. He takes the dress from me and places it on the chair. I'm now wearing only my lace bra and matching panties. "You're beautiful," he says with a growl while his eyes caress me from my toes to my head.

"My pajamas are under the pillow." I point to the bed.

He shakes his head and begins to remove his dress shirt. He sets it around me and places my arms into the sleeves. The shirt carries the smell of his cologne. I'm totally overwhelmed with excitement, and wetness pools between my legs. I tell myself that he's only here to sleep. I'm not doing anything else tonight. But in this moment, my defenses are crumbling fast. He leans in and kisses me before securing three buttons on his dress shirt. When he finishes, he pulls me back against him again to continue dancing. My head rests against his chest and shoulder.

"Do you want to do more than sleep?" I ask, then look up at him.

"Yes." He lets out a breath. "But I promised to be a gentleman and to follow your rules."

I smile. "I'm happy you remembered because I might forget." He twirls me and pulls me back to him.

"I'm glad you wanted me to stay overnight."

"I have a second toothbrush, and you're welcome to use anything in my toiletry bag." We brush, and I wash my face and pull my hair up in a silk scarf. He watches me. "You can't sleep in your pants; you can wear your underwear."

He smiles devilishly.

"You do have on underwear, don't you?"

"Yes, but you have me excited."

"I can handle excited. I would be disappointed if you weren't." I'm excited too.

"Do you sleep in underwear?" he questions as he unzips his pants.

"I usually don't, but I can tonight since I'm wearing your dress shirt." I attempt to slide into bed, but Kelton's hand stops me.

"Can I remove your panties and bra?"

"I'll remove my bra, and you can remove my panties." I quickly unhook my bra and pull it through his sleeve. He kneels in front of me and reaches under his shirt. I feel his hands at my waistband. He slowly pulls my wet panties down my legs. I step out of them, and Kelton picks them up and smells them. His lips kiss my mound where his dress shirt is open. I close my eyes and suck in a breath. I quickly move toward the bed, and he follows with a large, firm bulge in the front of his underwear. He lies on his back, and I cuddle next to him.

"Good night."

"Good night, lovey."

In the morning, I wake to find that we're spooning. I feel his bulge pressing against my butt, with only his underwear separating us. His dress shirt has ridden up, and his arm is firmly around my waist. The tapping of his bulge woke me. It's a pleasant way to welcome the morning. It's a feeling I miss from a lover. It triggers a long overdue, hidden sensation, and I can feel the wetness between my legs.

"Good morning, lovey. I didn't want to move and wake you."

"Good morning."

"I want to make breakfast for us this morning."

"Oh, you cook?"

"Of course I cook. What do you like?"

Something that I haven't had since I became celibate and a dildo became my lover. "I don't eat anything fancy."

"I don't need to do fancy to satisfy your appetite. I just need to provide what you want."

Kelton gets out of bed and heads into the bathroom to turn on the shower. A few minutes later, as I'm standing at the window looking at the flowers in the backyard, Kelton comes to stand behind me and slides his hand into mine. I lean back against him, and he kisses me on the temple.

"Our shower is ready."

I turn to look at him. "Our shower?"

"Yes, and I remember, no intercourse." He leads me to the bathroom.

My walls and rules continue to crumble as I discreetly look at his erection pushing against his boxer briefs, then into his eyes.

"You shouldn't look at me that way, lovey."

"I know." I slowly unbutton his dress shirt and let it fall to the bathroom floor. I turn to glance at him and then back myself into the shower. Kelton crosses his arms and moves against the counter to watch me through the glass doors.

"I would join you, but I might violate your request." He rakes his palm over his face.

I lather and slowly run it over my arms and neck, then across my chest, circling each breast. I run the soap over my stomach and hips before moving it across my butt cheeks and down one thigh, then the other. As I pick up my feet, I raise my eyes to meet Kelton's. I finish soaping myself, then step into the shower flow before washing my hair. When I reach for my conditioner with my eyes closed, I touch Kelton's hand. I open my eyes, and my breath catches as I see the full Kelton in all of his naked glory. He has the conditioner in his hand and steps toward me. It's only when he whispers in my ear do I realize I'm holding my breath.

"Breathe, my sunshine. I'm just here to condition your hair." I turn around to give him access.

"May I soap you while I leave the conditioner in for a minute or two?" I turn around to meet his eyes.

"You may do anything you want, lovey."

I swallow. He smirks as I watch the soap move across his body. I lather his erection and thighs before he turns so that I can get his back and butt.

"I hope you don't mind, but I'll definitely be hard while making breakfast."

"I don't mind as long as you don't mind me watching it."

We finish showering, then dry my hair and body, leaving my private parts for me. I can smell my essence, and I'm sure he can as well. I throw on a swimsuit cover-up with a built-in bra and pull on a lacy pair of panties. I dry Kelton, and he pulls on a pair of shorts and a T-shirt.

I slice fruit, and Kelton prepares omelets. I also make coffee and set the table after selecting a little smooth jazz for us. Afterward, Kelton challenges me to a game of Scrabble while we sit in the sunroom. The ocean breeze is perfect, and we curl up in the hammock together and nap.

Over the course of the remaining days, we repeat coupling, laughing, and preparing meals in between sleeping. In the afternoon we either read to each other from the same book, play a game of Scrabble or Gin Rummy, or watch a movie. We venture out only one evening for jerk chicken, then walk along the beach before returning to the house. The following morning is the end of our holiday romance, and he takes a taxi to the airport so that he can leave for Fort Lauderdale. He assures me that we'll do this long distance, but I tell him we'll play it by ear.

CHAPTER 6

KELTON

J hope I'm not doing anything that will reveal my past. I've been in a lot of ports and have spent time with many women, but the woman in yellow called Pearl has captured a piece of my heart and won't let it go. From the first time I saw her, I began to fall for her quirky idiosyncrasies that many may find annoying. I find them cute and endearing. I could grow old living day by day on the moments and memories with her.

The question that keeps coming to mind is my true history. My secretive past. Will she still give me the time of day if I tell her the truth? Will she still let me pull her close if she knows I'm a convicted felon who has spent time in prison? Prison is a third world country inside of America. The rules of humanity do not apply. Darwinism is alive and well within the prison walls. How can such an environment exist that is designed to reform people? The average person in society might not know what life in prison is like, even though many television series have tried to depict it, but those in the justice system must know, along with the lawyers. They probably realize that many of the guards are also the problem because they're paid to conduct illegal activities inside prison.

I sit on the rock in front of the house Pearl is renting in Aruba. I had originally planned to leave with the cruise ship last night to continue to the next port of call. Instead, I gathered a few clothes and checked into a hotel down the street. I hope she'll be excited to see me, but only time will tell. I'll have two days of fun in the sun with the woman in yellow before returning to my bachelorhood.

I hear the side door open, and Pearl steps out. She's wearing shorts today instead of her yoga attire. She doesn't see me yet. When she does, she freezes as if I'm a vagabond camped outside of her house. She slowly approaches until she recognizes me. Her expression is one of utter horror, for me, I guess. She asks if I missed the ship, then wonders how could I have if I returned in time last night. She insists on solving my missing-the-ship problem by calling someone. I think she mumbles Seleste's name, then Weston's. I'm confused and need to stop the madness, so I kiss her. Oh, the kiss is sweet, and she welcomes my tongue while leaning into my warmth. This action, of course, stops her from talking, and her expression of horror has dissolved. Breathless, we pull apart. I can start explaining now, but the kiss is so sweet. I decide to simply enjoy kissing her for now, so I do it again, this time longer and with more intensity. When we finally part, I explain that I've decided to fly to Fort Lauderdale in two days to reconnect with the ship.

I have truly enjoyed the entire adventure on the cruise ship, moving from one exotic location to another in the Caribbean. I've returned to enough of the islands to have favorite restaurants and sometimes a regular woman. These opportunities are to replace the unplanned hideous experience of going to prison. A woman in every port is every man's dream. I hope no one ever plans to go to prison, because if that is their mission in life, they should get another one.

After Pearl welcomes the idea of spending time with me for the next few days, we head toward the beach, where she'd planned to walk this morning instead of participating in yoga. I hold her hand. She tells me that when she's with a man, it's important that he holds her hand to indicate that he wants to be with her. Apparently, her husband said it was only necessary to hold her hand while they were dating. Her telephone rings, and she looks disappointed. She tells me it will take only a few minutes and steps away to answer the call. I walk closer to where the ocean is washing across the beach, take off my shoes, and sit on the sand. I watch as the waves run up the shore, as if touching an invisible line. The ocean is mesmerizing. I feel the spray against my face and taste the salt on my lips.

The sense of freedom overwhelms my senses. I close my eyes to push away the tears that are welling because of the unexpected situation that caused me to lose my freedom.

The day I was sentenced, the judge informed me that I would start my jail time immediately, and that frightened me most. My attorney had said the judge would give me a few days before I reported to prison, but that didn't happen. I had packed all of my personal items and rented a storage unit a few weeks prior to my sentencing. My wife, Chanel, was in denial, and there were important family photos and antiques that I wanted to hold on to. My personal keepsakes. I didn't want anything to happen to those items. Chanel thought the judge would allow her to keep the house because she didn't have anything to do with the embezzlement. I also didn't have any direct ties to taking the money, but there I was sitting in court with a very expensive attorney who was trying to keep me out of prison for the next sixty months.

I remember the cuffs being attached to my wrists after the sentencing. It was so surreal. Everything happened in slow motion. I could see and hear all the commotion and noise, but I couldn't process what was taking place. My wife was crying and screaming, but I heard only the judge sentencing me to sixty months. I didn't hear anything after that statement. My children did not attend. I thought it would be best to spare them the heartache, and I didn't want the media taking pictures of them. It was hard enough when my name and picture were plastered on the front page of the newspaper. I did nothing wrong. I never took one penny of the money, but there I was on the front of the paper with a startled expression on my face. Not my best photograph. The headline read "Stolen Money and Stolen Investors' Dreams." My daughter was embarrassed and asked what I did with all the money. My son wanted to know why I didn't buy him a car. I explained that I didn't take the money, but because I was the CEO, I was responsible for anything that happened at the corporation.

The deputy sheriffs led me to a holding area, where I waited in my suit for two hours before taking a transport with three other men to the Hudson Correctional Facility. I never in a million years thought I would follow this path. I've always attempted to do what's right. I started with a small tool company that was going bankrupt and turned it into a large competitive business that obtained its IPO eight years after I purchased it. That move provided enough money to give my family, grandchildren, and great-grandchildren a very comfortable life. I was so proud of myself, and I prayed that my mother in heaven was pleased with what I had created and the status I had gained.

The entire prison experience is something that I never want to talk about. The intake process to the first night were overwhelming. Everyone had single cells, but the room was only large enough for a single bed, toilet bowl, and sink. I remembered similar images from television, but to see it in person and to experience it was another thing. I was targeted by larger inmates and by anyone who thought I could be bullied. To think the correctional officers and the warden know this takes place, but the fact that no one does anything is concerning. Because you're in prison, you have no right to be human or to expect to be treated in a humane way. I'm sure the judges and the deputy sheriffs know, but nothing changes. It's survival of the fittest.

I open my eyes to see if Pearl is still on her cell or watching and realizing I'm hiding something important and wearing a mask to spend time with her. She's animated as she tries to explain something to the caller. I turn to stare at the ocean once again and touch my right wrist, as if I'm still wearing handcuffs.

I was targeted to be raped by someone in the same section I was assigned. Apparently, this guy liked to break the newbies, then decide who he wanted to keep around or pass to someone else. How do you live knowing you have no control over what could happen to you at any time of the day or night? The fear of being raped and controlled was unbearable. I tried to get moved after telling my attorney, but it was no longer his concern when my wife decided not to pay the balance of his fee. Then Chanel showed up at the prison that first weekend to inform me that she had filed for divorce and all our assets had been frozen. She wanted to tell me in person that she'd never met a man who'd failed to provide for his family, even though I had promised her father that she would always be taken care of. This was after she told me my children never wanted to see me again because of the choices I made. That was the day I realized I was all alone in the world and no one would care if I were raped or abused or if I died. No one would miss me if I was gone.

Pearl startles me when she sits next to me on the beach and hooks her arm in mine. I want to spend the next two days with her under the lie that I'm a nice guy and only want to give her a good time in the sun. I smile down at her and kiss the top of her curls. She raises her head and looks at me. I kiss her on the lips this time.

"I'm glad you decided to stay," she whispers.

"Me too. Let's get some lunch." I stand and pull her to her feet.

The day moves along quickly, from lunch to a nap in a hammock. I know Pearl naps every day to recharge after lunch. Her siesta. I had reserved a hammock at my hotel, and even though she looks concerned about us both getting into it safely, I assure her we'll be fine. Later, we have dinner at the restaurant in the hotel across from mine. Afterward, I walk her back to her rented home and return to my hotel. I remember that I originally wanted to get laid and that my mission was not accomplished yet. I ask her to think about having me stay overnight with her tomorrow. She agrees to consider it.

Day two consists of yoga on the beach with her friend Seleste and then dancing after our nap. Weston joins us again. I believe he knows all the good hangouts on the island. The next time I visit Aruba, I'll need to contact him so that he can hook me up with the nighttime activities and maybe someone to keep me company. Pearl says I can stay over, but there's a catch. No sexual intercourse. I might have wasted my time by staying and not heading to the next port on the cruise ship. I enjoy the dancing and putting my shirt on her for bedtime. I hope maybe she'll change her mind if she gets horny enough. I do everything to get her in the mood.

When I finally ask to remove her panties for bed, they're soaked. But she holds to her rule. I could smell her desire, and I was harder than I've ever been. I get up in the middle of the night to relieve a little pressure because nothing I thought about got the blood to leave my cock, especially when Pearl rubbed her naked butt against the front of my underwear while we slept spooning.

The following morning, I cook breakfast with no gravies, sauces, or condiments. I decide to make the best of this situation and enjoy it to the fullest without sexual intercourse. But I do get to taste her and hear her moans as I send her to ecstasy land. That gentleman act occurs during a shower one morning.

I take a taxi to the airport after a very long and endearing kiss. I've accomplished my mission with the woman in yellow, my sunshine called Pearl. I remind myself that next time I encounter a woman who makes my blood boil with desire, I'll pass if she tells me that sex isn't readily available and will look for someone else who will embrace it. I mention the long-distance thing to Pearl, but it's only to pacify her.

CHAPTER 7

PEARL

I feel the sun on my face and the spray from the ocean as it laps the beach. The water runs across my feet, then retreats. I twirl, then walk into the ocean and float on my back. The water is perfect. The seagulls fly above. I feel a tug as the water becomes rough. The waves get bigger, and I bob beneath the water. Each time the waves rise, they take me under for a few seconds. I flip over and begin swimming for the shore. I tell myself not to panic. I kick my feet and claw at the water, but I can't make any progress toward the shore. I slowly drift farther into the ocean.

The alarm goes off, and I awake in a cold sweat. It was only a dream. I've returned home to South Orange from a beautiful vacation in Aruba. My existing clients are my first priority, then I'm meeting with two new ones. My schedule is packed, and I'm ready to solve problems and help grow businesses. I'm recharged, refreshed, and a force to be reckoned with. I begin my morning routine, then head to the office.

Jaynea is making coffee when I arrive. She's been my assistant and right hand for the past four years. She was not my first choice from the temporary agency. Her hair was neon green the day she started. Over the course of these four years, her hair color has changed from yellow, to blue, to blonde, to red. As I said, she was not my first choice. I tried two other temps who could not manage their own time let alone run an office. Because Jaynea doesn't interact with clients on a face-to-face basis, I no longer worry about the color of her hair. She's a beautiful mahogany woman who is confident in everything she does. A fancy dresser. Much more so than I'll ever be in this lifetime. Her nails and shoes always match. Because I'm not as into fashion, I don't know if she wears expensive designer clothes and shoes or if it just looks like it.

"Coffee is almost ready, and I brought scones to welcome you back," Jaynea calls as I wave and walk by the kitchen nook.

"I'll be back after I drop my stuff in my office." I pick up the pace, then return to the kitchen. I give Jaynea a hug and a gift from Aruba. "I hope you like it."

Jaynea rips the bag open to reveal a multicolored silk scarf. She yells as she jumps toward me for a big embrace. "It's beautiful." She wraps it around her shoulders. "I feel like a Nubian queen ready to address my people." A smile spreads across her face and brightens her eyes even more than usual. "It's nice to have you back. I've updated your schedule for the week. You have another new client. He's worried that his profit isn't being reflected in his sales numbers." She twirls the scarf, then wraps it around her waist and ties it in the front. "I can't see how you can have good sales but no profit."

I fill my coffee mug and then Jaynea's. "It can happen if your expenses are higher than expected and no one is monitoring the fixed and variable expenses." I grab the flavored creamer from the refrigerator, then add a little and pass it to Jaynea. She likes a lot more flavor in her coffee. I take a scone from the box on the counter. "You read my mind this morning. I was just too lazy to plan for scones. I'll treat on Friday." I leave the nook and head to my office. I'm still shaken from the nightmare. I never go that far from the shore. I've always been concerned about undertow, and I've never been a strong swimmer. I wave the nightmare away as I bite into the scone, then sip my coffee.

My first appointment is with Hazel Hanson-Brown. She owns four arts and craft stores in the area and caters to community centers and schools with active parent groups. The main office is located in a historic building in downtown Cranford, New Jersey. I've always loved the Cranford community and the small intimate shops. The town council has been very successful in keeping franchise establishments and large box stores out of the downtown area. I've always believed this is best for the small business community. They could never compete with box stores that order large quantities and lower the price to eliminate competitors. I park in a community lot and place the parking pass that Hazel had given me on the dashboard. I gather my things and go inside, where I'm greeted by the receptionist.

"Good morning. You must be Pearl Jermaine. Welcome."

"Good morning. You are absolutely correct. I'm here to see Hazel Hanson-Brown."

"Have a seat. I'll tell her you're here."

"Thanks." I sit a few chairs away from the receptionist but position myself to see Hazel when she comes through the glass doors separating the waiting area from the other offices. It's a beautiful day, and I'm wearing a sky blue dress and a bolero jacket with an abstract pattern. My hair is up and held in a clamp; curly strands frame both sides of my face. During the summer, I try to keep my hair off my neck because it might trigger a hot flash. This time of year also allows me to wear only a little lipstick because my skin has been blessed with a golden glow. I can also forgo a foundation to even my completion. I always wear comfortable professional sandals, since many times I'm standing or walking to understand the situation of a company in large warehouses and office buildings.

"Good morning," says a voice from the doorway. Hazel looks like Queen Amanirenas. All she needs is an entourage to announce her presence. She smiles and waves for me to join her.

"Good morning." We hug, and I follow her to her office at the end of the hallway.

"I'm going to apologize now. I can't give you as much time as I had planned because we had an order that wasn't complete due to missing inventory." We sit, and I pull a legal pad from my bag to take notes.

"Is this part of the reason you hired me?"

"Yes. I don't understand how to stop the bleeding of inventory."

"Give me a few examples."

Hazel explains some of the situations that have occurred in many of the stores.

"So this is happening in all four locations?"

She lets out a long sigh and explains the ordering process, the inventory monitoring, and the excessive loss that is now affecting her bottom line.

"When did you first notice the losses?"

Hazel opens a folder and recites the dates and the amount of financial and inventory loss.

I ask a few more questions and get a timeline for her situation before she is forced to inform her investors. I ask permission to visit each of the stores and speak with the managers and employees. She closes the folder and passes it to me.

"I've given you the managers' names and numbers along with all the employees at each store. I've also included the shrinkage reports." She places both hands on her desk and rises. "I know you've already signed confidentiality agreements along with our business agreement, but I ask that you keep everything close to the vest. Some of the managers don't know the amount we're losing. I hope you can get to the bottom of this before I'm forced to file for bankruptcy and my investors take out a contract for my head." She chuckles briefly. "Unfortunately, I'm serious."

"I know you are. This is your baby, and you don't want anyone to hurt it." I place everything in my bag and stand. We embrace again, and I return to my office to analyze the numbers and review everything before devising a plan of action.

When I arrive, I find Jaynea in therapist mode. She's speaking with someone on the telephone and occasionally asking probing questions. I shrug and mouth, *Who?* She flips over her legal pad and writes on it: Fred Armstrong.

I started working with Fred before I left for my vacation in Aruba. We addressed a few of the concerns he had for his gym, Trim and Fit. Now that I've returned, I'm meeting with him at 3:00 p.m. We had first tackled his employees' flexible schedules that were nonexistent. Fred thought they had flex hours because they'd show up two to three hours late for work. If the gym opens at 5:00 a.m. and no one arrives to prewipe all the equipment, replenish the towels, and do the laundry, there's a problem. To solve it, everyone has a schedule that is set two weeks in advance. Time off for any reason must be planned and approved accordingly. The only flex is for emergencies, as none of his workers have children. That might need to change in the future if someone has a baby, but we'll revisit that if and when it's necessary.

Fred's next issue consisted of terminating the repair contract with a good friend who could not fix the machines in a timely fashion, which began to impact membership and profit margins. Unfortunately, they're no longer friends, but the new repair company has a twenty-four-hour timetable that's been wonderful.

I motion to Jaynea that I'm headed to my office. I need to take a few minutes for myself as I eat my chicken burrito and prepare to meet with Fred this afternoon.

A knock on my door startles me.

Jaynea pokes her head into my office. "Are you ready for Fred?" She enters and places a legal pad on my desk.

"I'm not sure. Why did he need to call since we're meeting today?"

"He asked to reschedule for tomorrow at seven a.m." Jaynea looks at me before frowning.

I shake my head and roll my eyes to the ceiling. "Are you serious?"

"Yep. He said today at three is going to conflict with something at the gym."

"Okay. Call him back and confirm seven a.m. tomorrow at Fit and Trim. I don't like early mornings!" Now I frown and form an ugly face.

Jaynea backs out of my office. "I know. I tried." She closes the door.

Since Fred canceled and I have some free time, I decide to investigate Wash Me Laundromat. Roger Reid is the absentee owner. He likes to travel and thought a laundromat would be the perfect business. He's seen a decline in profits since his nephew, Ryan, started managing the day-to-day operations. Ryan is thirty-seven years old and has never held a position longer than six months. I look at his résumé and shake my head. He's had twenty different jobs within a five-year period.

The largest part of the Wash Me Laundromat profits comes from their daily laundry service. The laundromat advertises the washing, folding, and pressing of clothes that are dropped off by 10:00 a.m., and they'll be ready for pickup any time after 4:00 p.m. I decide to take my clothes over for a little laundry service and identify the problem. When I arrive at Wash Me Laundromat, I don't see Ryan anywhere. I ring the bell, then stand and wait. Ten minutes later Ryan comes through the front door with a bag from the fast-food restaurant across the street. There was no sign indicating that he was out to lunch or when he would return.

"Hey," Ryan says when he sees me at the counter.

"I'd like to get laundry service on my bag of clothes." I lift the bag for Ryan to see. I didn't give him much, just a few exercise outfits, a couple pairs of jeans, and some T-shirts.

"It's too late to get your items by four o'clock today," Ryan says between bites of his hamburger.

"No problem. I'll pick them up tomorrow." I place the bag on the counter.

"Well, because you can't pick them up today, why don't you drop them off tomorrow in the morning since I'm at lunch now." Ryan pulls up a stool, then grabs a few fries out the bag and places them into his mouth.

I understand why Roger is losing loyal customers. I've learned when I go undercover to carry my purse, which has a place for my cell to record video with audio. I try to smile; Ryan is ignoring me.

"No. I'm going to leave my clothes now, and I'll pick them up at four tomorrow."

"Whatever." Ryan licks the salt off his fingers, then wipes them on his jeans before writing out a ticket and handing it to me.

"Thanks." I know I'll need to use hand sanitizer when I return to my car.

A few hours later, I return with a load of underclothes to be washed. I'm using the washer and dryer in the laundromat because I want to observe Ryan at work. I don't see him when I step inside. A few customers are there, and a man is sitting close to the counter. A concerning smirk on his face makes him look suspicious. I load the washer and pour a cap of detergent into the designated compartment. I start it and take a seat near the counter where I spoke to Ryan. The suspicious man is now leaning forward as if he's listening for something. I don't remember seeing a television behind the counter. Maybe there is one, and I just didn't notice. I collect my purse and set my cell to video record, then move toward the counter. I'll see if Ryan is behind it and ask a question. As I get closer, I hear a few low moans; it sounds as if someone might be hurt. I glance at the man, and he looks at me. I ring the bell. A few minutes later, Ryan comes from behind a curtain that divides the storage area from the counter area. He's not wearing a shirt, his pants are unbuttoned, and he's breathing hard. I'm perplexed until I hear a female voice say, "Hurry up, baby. You don't want me to get cold."

Now I'm sorry I left my clothes. I like my exercise outfits, but I'll never get them back. I clear my throat. "I'm sorry. I dropped my clothes off earlier around one—"

He cuts me off. "I told you they won't be ready until tomorrow at four."

"I know, but I changed my mind. You were right; I should drop them off tomorrow."

He stares at me for a few seconds that feel like minutes. I wonder if he's thinking about the ticket, the clothes, or letting the female get cold. "Do you have the ticket?"

I fumble it out of my purse and hand it to him, making sure he doesn't touch my hand. I have no idea where his may have been or what may be on it right now.

He looks at the bags on the floor and locates mine. "Next time wait until the morning to drop it off."

I take the bag and return to where my underclothes are washing. As soon as they're finished, I'll take them home and dry them there. If only I would have been more curious of the suspicious-looking man before I put my clothes in the washer. I sit in a chair along the wall. The place is clean, which surprises me, until I see a cleaning woman enter with supplies. Ryan has hired someone to make sure the place is spotless because he's too busy with someone behind the counter. I smile and nod to the woman. She returns the greeting before beginning her work.

I'm not sure what Roger is going to do when I speak with him after sending my report regarding the problem, along with the two videos. I guess he'll stop traveling long enough to address the issue before this place becomes a money pit. Sometimes nepotism can be a good thing to teach the next generation how to operate a business. But in many cases, if your family member is an idiot, nepotism is a poison pill that is as lethal as fentanyl. Since I started consulting, I've never suggested that someone must be fired. I recommend additional training or mentorship. But in this case, Ryan needs to be fired. I just won't tell Roger that so directly.

As soon as the chime rings on the washer, I remove the wet clothes, place them in my laundry basket, and head to my car.

CHAPTER 8

KELTON

I stretch and open my eyes. But I'm not in my bed or in my stateroom. I try not to invite women to my stateroom because then they get very clingy and want some type of commitment. I don't see the woman I stayed with last night. As I get out of bed and pull on my boxer briefs, I spy a note on the nightstand. I walk to the balcony door and pull back the curtains, then read the note.

K,

I'm at the gym and didn't want to wake you. You were great last night. Maybe we can do this again in a few weeks. I'll see you around the ship.

xoxo,
Ginger

I place the note back on the nightstand and begin to dress.

I wonder what Pearl is doing right now. I miss the smell of my woman in yellow. I miss having her tucked close to me. She had to go back to work in New Jersey while I move on to the next port.

When I arrive at my stateroom, Richard is standing in the hallway knocking on my door. "Good morning, Richard."

"Hey, how are you? You've been bed bouncing since hanging out with the woman in Aruba. Didn't you get any from her?" Richard leans against the wall while I open my door.

"I got everything I wanted from Pearl." I smile as I put my breakfast on the table with my cup of coffee and sit. "I didn't bring any extra food or coffee from the buffet, but I might have some juice or water in the refrigerator."

Richard reaches into the refrigerator, then sits at the table with a small bottle of orange juice. "Did you hear about the guy who was removed from the ship yesterday? He was wanted by Interpol."

"What?" I move my food around my plate, then shovel a forkful into my mouth.

"Something about selling guns and money laundering." Richard takes a swig of the juice. "I played poker with him." He snaps his fingers a few times. "I can't remember his name."

"It's Ian." I continue to eat.

"Yep, that's it. I can't believe he's a criminal." Richard takes another sip of his juice.

I wait for additional comments from Richard. This is why I refuse to tell anyone about my past regardless of how close I become with them here on the ship. They will judge me. There were plenty of news articles and interviews about how I was irresponsible and had possibly participated in embezzling from my beloved business. I was so proud of my company, Tool Depot. And I wanted to make my mother proud. I didn't have the same opportunities as others to have a sturdy family foundation. Sometimes life deals horrible hands to young children, and many don't get the opportunity to overcome them.

I remember when I was nineteen, and I lost my job at the burger place in Newark on Main Street. I didn't like my boss very much. He reminded me of my social worker when I was in foster care. Always giving the presence of being better than me and telling me that I can do more. Don't be a problem for my foster parents or they'll have me removed. Don't eat too much. I was a growing boy, and I felt like I was always hungry. I took the burger-flipping job because I could eat any leftover food at closing, though I had to share with the other employees. The day my boss asked what I would do to get my check earlier than 4:00 p.m., I didn't answer.

He stood behind his desk. He hired only young kids who had aged out of the foster care system. The ones who didn't have anyone to advocate for, support, or believe them if they told. That should tell you everything you need to know. He was a predator, and we were his prey.

Richard snaps his fingers in front of my face, bringing me back to the present.

"Sorry. I was thinking about something. What did you say?" I redirect my focus to him.

"I was saying that he could have robbed us all here on the ship. That's why I only trust you, Kelton."

"I hear you."

"Can you imagine a person so low in society that he would need to go to prison? I've never known a convict before." He's silent for a moment. "I thought convicts couldn't own a weapon."

"I don't think they're supposed to." I finish my breakfast and take another sip of my coffee. I didn't own a gun before I went to prison. I definitely don't want a gun now. Why is Richard concerned about someone owning a weapon?

"I heard the men have sex with one another in prison. Or do they find a weaker male and use him as their sex partner?" Richard shakes himself, as if a blast of cool air hit him. "I can't imagine. I like pussy too much to ever decide on an alternative from a man. But I guess a butt is a butt. Butt—is that a pun?" Richard laughs as if it were really funny. "I'm not a fan of anal sex, and I tell my female friends that."

I stare intently at Richard as he reacts to Ian being a criminal. Why do I hang out with this guy?

"Do you like anal sex with the women?" Richard asks, a curious expression on his face.

"No. I tried it one time but found it wasn't for me," I reply.

"Yeah, I know what you mean. I think it's our generation. I hear the younger guys find it appealing, depending on their mood. Oh, and of course the mood of the woman they're with that evening."

I clear the table, then discard my napkin after scraping the contents of my plate into the trash can under the sink and setting my dishes on the counter for housekeeping. "I need to shower and hit the gym. I'll see you later." I hope Richard gets the message that it's time for him to leave.

Richard throws his empty juice bottle in the trash and heads toward the door. "I'll see you later. I'll go check on the beauties around the swimming pool."

I walk to the door, flip the security lock, and begin stripping off my clothes as I walk to the bathroom for a much-needed shower.

I awake in a cold sweat. I had another nightmare about being back in prison. I've done everything possible to remain out of jail. I refuse to consult, be a bookkeeper, or even audit business accounts. But I get so bored, and I miss working with numbers immensely. I wonder if my dreams are a reminder that I shouldn't even consider it.

I started as a bookkeeper when I was studying for my CPA exam. I was so proud that I had graduated from Rutgers. I definitely wasn't the best student before I became a bookkeeper, since I had to work full-time and take evening classes. The latter were always an afterthought, as many of the full-time or daytime teachers didn't want to bother with working after 6:00 p.m. I would nap in my car after my job ended in the career services department. My role was to assist students with résumé development, and I answered the telephone and scheduled appointments for students to meet with career counselors.

I was so grateful to have a job. I had been sleeping and eating at a local homeless shelter for weeks. I spent my days at the library on the computer applying for jobs. When I finally landed the position at Rutgers University in Newark, I was so relieved. My goal was to not let anyone know I was homeless. I was given two pairs of dress slacks by the shelter social worker and five long-sleeve polo shirts. After work, I would change into my jeans and T-shirt so as to not accidently soil the items. That opportunity happened after two years of living on the streets. Those years weren't good. I thought I could just do what the others my age were doing until I realized that they weren't going anywhere fast. And I was going nowhere fast with them.

After receiving my first two paychecks, the first thing I bought was a hooptie. It was all mine for $1,100.

I tried to buy a car when I was working at the burger place. There was a dealer who didn't mind if you had no credit or bad credit. I picked out a beautiful blue Camaro with a racing stripe. I had to pay $210 for the car plus $75 for insurance each month. They actually offered car insurance at the dealership. I was so happy that I could buy the car. I needed only $285 each month. My burger job paid $7.25 per hour for my twenty-hour weekly shift. I thought I had made it. Until I had engine problems. I couldn't get it fixed and make the monthly payment. It was repossessed while I was at work. It was so embarrassing. I felt the same way I did when I realized my mother had died. I was ashamed when the social worker told me that I couldn't stay in the apartment by myself. She gathered a few clothes, and I packed my favorite toys and a few trinkets of my mother's. I asked the social worker when I would be back to get the rest, and she told me the landlord would clear out everything. When I got to the first foster family, my toys were taken from me. I hid my mother's bracelet that spelled out her name and a tarnished heart necklace that had my picture inside. Mom called it a locket. I remember telling myself that it locked my picture inside the heart, and that's why it was called a locket.

I found a good spot in the employee lot at Rutgers to park my hooptie. I didn't want to drive and have it break down and need to be towed. Or even worse, have it towed by the police if it broke down in the middle of the street. The impound lot charges the owner the price of towing and a daily fee to keep the car. I only needed my hooptie for shelter and storage. I reclined the passenger side seat and put a few blankets inside that the shelter gave me because they were a little raggedy. (They were a lot raggedy.) I took the six blankets, washed them at the shelter, and arranged them on my seat like a mattress. I bought a thicker blanket from the Salvation Army, and my bed was perfect. I also bought a pillowcase and stuffed it with rags. I now could lock my duffel bag of clothes in the trunk while at work and in class. One day, a construction worker who was part of a crew renovating a section of the college decided his lunch box cooler with a broken handle was useless. He tossed it in the trash, and I retrieved it when no one was looking. I could now store food items like bologna and drinks and keep them cold on those hot nights with a little ice.

My cell phone buzzes and scoots across the nightstand, bringing me out of my reverie. I reach for it and see my ex-wife's name on the screen. "Hello."

"Hello, Kelton," she squeaks out.

"How are you doing?" I longed for a family during my foster care days. I know my mom was in pain, and it was good that she wasn't suffering anymore. But I swore I would have a family when I got older. A happy family with a wife and children. I accomplished that task—at least I thought I had.

"This is not a social call. I'm phoning on behalf of your children to tell you to stop leaving messages on their cell phones."

"I want a relationship with my children. They never visited while I was in prison, and I understood that." As the words leave my mouth, I realize my balcony door is open. I don't want anyone to hear my conversation. I stride to the door and close it. "I'm no longer in prison, and I want to speak with them at least once a month. Why is that a problem?"

"You embarrassed them by going to jail," Chanel states in a flustered breath.

"I was also embarrassed by going to jail. Especially because I didn't do anything wrong and I didn't take a penny of that money. Matt embezzled the money, not me." I spit out the words like venom.

"I've heard all of this before, Kelton. I don't want to rehash any of it. I'm simply calling to tell you not to contact your children."

"But they're my children. I participated in making each of them, and they need to respect their father." I'm pacing. I want to hit something. Why can't I get Chanel to understand how important my family is to me?

"If you call them again, they'll change their numbers."

"Can I at least call them on their birthdays?" I close my eyes and pray that she'll agree.

"I think they should reach out to you when they're ready. You know we had to move out of our house and the neighborhood after you got indicted and went to jail."

"I know."

"They froze the bank accounts." Chanel is getting choked up. "I didn't know how I was going to pay the bills and take care of our children."

"I know."

"I had to marry William McKensie to provide shelter and food for my children. He doesn't trust me and thinks I'm still in love with you."

"Are you?" I ask with hope.

"How could I love a criminal? A convict? A man who let me down? I'm no more than a prostitute. I'll be that for the rest of my life to William McKensie, all because of you. It's simply disguised as the word *wife*."

I let out a long sigh. I was hoping she'd say that she's still in love with me. I could put my family back together. I knew she had divorced me and remarried before I started losing weight from the inedible prison food. My family, who I was so proud of, who I created and loved, didn't love me back. Maybe I don't have the right to have a family. Maybe all I'm worthy of is a few women friends who use me to purchase their seasonal wardrobes in exchange for sex. "Goodbye, Chanel. I won't call them again." As soon as I hang up, my cell buzzes again. I'm hoping she's changed her mind until I see the name. Matt Marek. I'm not speaking to him. I decline the call and place my phone on the nightstand.

Maybe I'll get dinner and hide in my stateroom this evening. I'm not up for witty discussions and flirting tonight.

PEARL

*I*t's 6:30 a.m., which is way too early for me to start my day. I'm not one of those chipper morning people. I'm sitting in my car outside of Trim and Fit, drinking my coffee and whining to myself. I'm observing the many cars in the parking lot, and I occasionally see Fred through the large floor-to-ceiling glass windows that allow the gym fanatics to look outside. *Why would anyone want others to watch them sweat while exercising?* I wonder. Fred works out of this location in Elizabeth; however, he has ten locations in two states. He's originally from Allentown, Pennsylvania, where he opened his first gym. He's grown a lot faster than he'd planned, but the need is prevalent. Old age and obesity are taking over. Many learned bad habits in their youth and are now dealing with the aftermath. His gyms also include personal trainers, self-defense classes, tai chi, weight training classes, boxing, and nutrition classes. Some even provide a personal chef who teaches how to minimize carbs, fat, and sugar. His YouTube channel doubles in clicks every forty-five days. I'm looking forward to visiting all ten locations and exposing myself to some of the classes offered. It's a perk of being a consultant to experience firsthand the services of my clients. I take another sip of my coffee before stepping out of the car. I'm dressed to work out today. I want to blend in with the members as I observe. I'm not visiting the other locations at this rooster hour unless it's extremely necessary.

I step into the building and approach the front desk. Fred sees me as I enter. "Good morning!" he says excitedly to me and two others who followed me in. They swipe their badges and proceed through the gate.

"Good morning." I return the greeting, trying to sound enthusiastic this early in the morning. Fred informs the smiling front desk person that I'll be visiting this week and hands me a one-week free gym badge.

I thank him and slide the pass into the front pocket of my messenger bag after swiping to enter the gym gates.

"I figured I'd show you around, then we can sit down and talk." Fred nods and greets people as we start at the left side of the gym near the machines. After spending an hour walking through the facility and taking notes, I'm very impressed. Fred discusses his concerns about rapid growth, staffing, and investors. The quick expansion of his gyms hasn't allowed him to gain full control of all the moving parts. The investors are requesting a return on their investments that Fred is unsure is possible. And as each gym expands, so does the staff.

I explain that every company experiences growing pains. I'm not as familiar with investors and guaranteeing a return on their investments. I assure Fred that each of his concerns will be addressed. I'll need to visit the other locations and continue to evaluate the services and programs. Fred will contact the other gyms and set up a schedule for me to visit them.

I return to the office to address two 611s Jaynea texted that morning. It's our code that means I have to handle a growing problem that hasn't reached 911 yet. I try to deal with the 611s before they become a 911 situation. I feel like a firewoman constantly putting out fires.

I'm floating in the ocean wearing my beautiful yellow swimsuit. The day is gorgeous. The sun warms my face and body as I drift on my back. I see Seleste and Kelton on the beach waving at me. I motion for them to join me. Kelton attempts to get into the water but keeps ending up on the shore. I realize I'm moving farther and farther from where Kelton is standing. Seleste is telling me to come in. I flip over and begin swimming for the shore. I urge myself not to panic. *Swim harder!* I continue to kick my feet and claw at the water. I cannot get back to the shore, and I slowly begin to drift farther into the ocean.

I wake in a cold sweat and am breathing heavily. I begin my day and try to ignore the nightmares I've been having over the past few weeks.

I arrive at the first of four Country Crafts stores. The manager, Amber, is expecting me. I want to see the inventory tracking and then the stocking process. It appears that someone is simply walking out of the store with items. Could it be the customers? I'd like to think that parents aren't the ones doing the pillaging knowing that this is the only arts and crafts store within a forty-five-minute drive. What I always keep in the back of my mind are the dirty things competitors will do to make you look bad or even put you out of business. Could one of the employees be working for the competition?

"Good morning," Amber says with a warm smile. Hazel had sent my picture to Amber to ensure I'm the correct person with whom she's sharing company information.

"Good morning." I extend my hand, and we shake. I didn't think Amber would understand the sister hug, since she is not a sister. She directs me to the back of the store and into her office. For the next two hours, I ask all the questions that were on my legal pad, along with quite a few more that were not. We review the numbers and the processes. I ask her opinion of the inventory loss. She gives me a practical answer but nothing that is going to stop the problem. I ask for permission to walk around the store. She agrees and also indicates that cameras had recently been installed to view the cash register area. The employees weren't happy but understand that it's for everyone's benefit. I spend another hour observing and taking notes on the inventory and its storage. My watch vibrates, indicating I've reached ten thousand steps already. I know it's going to be long day because it's only a little after one o'clock.

I proceed to the second Country Crafts store and conduct the same analysis with that manager. This store is much bigger than the first. Drew has been managing it for more than seven years and occasionally floats to the other stores when needed. I learn that many of the employees also work in different stores during inventory stocking, special promotions, or vacation coverage. This is the largest of the four stores, and it's also had the greatest inventory loss. Drew immediately mentions the new cameras and how they've lowered morale. He's lost two employees because they refuse to work somewhere that might accuse them of stealing. Because the loss has continued, we know that the two employees who resigned were not stealing from the company.

I also ask Drew's opinion of the inventory loss. He simply shrugs. I'm not sure whether his lack of response is because he doesn't want to say or because he's much older, and sometimes things aren't always the way they should be in life. I call Jaynea from the car to get any messages, then tell her I'm heading home and will see her in the morning.

I'm on the road today visiting three Trim and Fit gyms. I still have six more to observe. I've created an evaluation form and obtained permission to speak with a few of the members at each location to gauge their experiences.

Each location is in a trendy community, which means the rents are probably expensive. The members love the facilities, but a few state they would like more classes. On my way to the final gym, I learn that one of the investors will meet me there to discuss his concerns. That's all I need—someone questioning my skills and ability while mansplaining something I already know.

When I arrive and swipe my badge, a fit middle-aged man is waiting in the lounge area dressed in sweats and a T-shirt. He approaches and extends his hand while introducing himself as Sebastian Tallen. He's not overly handsome and isn't someone you would recognize if you met him on the street. But he's extremely charming and witty. We talk for a while about the gym and why he invested. Apparently, he owns a few other businesses in the area. His cell vibrates a few times during our conversation. Each time he looks at it, then ignores the call. Afterward, he asks if I have a meeting with Fred to address services, and I confirm that it's tomorrow afternoon.

He opens an envelope and shows me a few of the member evaluations regarding the classes. I'm pleased that evaluations are being administered and collected. He wants me to give them to Fred the following day. I scan a few before returning them to the envelope. I excuse myself and assure Sebastian that I'll reach out to him with any other questions. He shakes my hand and leaves the gym.

I return to my original evaluation process of assessing the gym and speaking with a few of the members. I like the evaluation concept and wonder how many times they've been conducted. Back in my car, I place the envelope on my front seat to remind myself to give it to Fred. I'm heading home for the evening. I'll complete my summaries over dinner while in my pajamas and bonnet after a shower.

The following morning I'm scheduled to meet with Samyl Kumari. He's been a client off and on over the past two years. He operates a home care agency with his wife, Tamie. Samyl has been having staff problems, but I'm not sure what that means. His wife has never been warm toward me, so I always ask Samyl to include her in our meetings. I'm not sure if the reason is a cultural aspect or a woman aspect. I look in my rearview mirror and eye the box of towels that I was asked to deliver to Fred at the Elizabeth gym. I'm not sure why he couldn't send an employee to do it instead of asking the consultant. I'll need to address that issue with Fred. I know he's able to pay my consultant fee, especially because the gyms are doing remarkably well with the new path of sponsorships, so he can also afford to hire someone to deliver towels and evaluations.

I park in front of Happy Home Care and collect my briefcase before removing my driving clogs and sliding into my sandals. I've scuffed more sandals than desired while driving, so now I keep my clogs under the front seat. I've always wondered why it's illegal to drive barefoot. I have a better chance of getting into an accident if my clog slips from my foot than if my bare foot slips off the end of my leg. I leave that thought in the car as I enter the offices.

"Good morning," Tamie says as she smiles at me. That's a first, and I wonder why. I feel she might be leading me to slaughter given her friendly demeanor. "We've been expecting you. Would you like some coffee or water?"

I wave my hand slightly. "No, thank you. Are we meeting in your office?"

"Yes." She walks in front of me, and I follow, even though I know the way. We usually meet in her office, which is much more tranquil than Samyl's. I take a seat, and she heads for the chair behind her desk. The melon color of the room and the smell of incense relax me.

"Is Samyl joining us?" I ask.

"Samyl is rotating aides this morning. I wanted to meet with you regarding a concern that I've heard from the aides." She doesn't make eye contact with me; instead, she looks past me at the wall behind my head.

I take out a notepad and pen. "What's the problem?" I watch her actions and again note the lack of eye contact.

"I believe a few of the aides, particularly the female aides, are being blackmailed." Tamie finally turns her gaze to me.

"I'm . . ." I let my words trail off. I feel uncomfortable. I'm not equipped for blackmail. "I'm not an investigator," I finally say.

"I know, but you're always discreet." Tamie taps her index finger on the desk.

"Do you have any idea who is blackmailing them? Or what they're using as blackmail?"

"I know that my husband is keeping something from me and that the women don't feel comfortable coming to the office anymore." She lets out a long, deep sigh.

"What do you think I can do?"

"I want you to talk to them. I'm thinking if you—" A knock interrupts her. "Come in." A man opens the door and speaks something in a foreign language. Tamie answers him, and he leaves. She looks at me again. "I would appreciate it if you can come in as an aide and mix with the current employees to find out what is going on."

I'm really starting to feel uncomfortable now. I've gone undercover before. I've even sent Jaynea undercover, but do I want to try to address a blackmailing scheme? I think about it for a few minutes. "Does your husband know you're meeting with me?" I'm curious. Why didn't we schedule a time when both would be available to speak with me?

Tamie folds her hands on the desk. "No. He doesn't know. I'd like to put you with the laundry crew at the Hampton Nursing Facility. There are three women there already, so you'll be the fourth."

"Why there?" I slip my notepad back into my bag.

"I overheard two of them saying something about paying two hundred dollars to keep the pictures off the internet." Now Tamie teepees her fingers and folds them back onto the top of the desk.

I think about it for a moment. I'll be at a single facility and will interact with only three other female aides. I can do this investigation. "Okay. Tell me when."

"Is tomorrow too soon?" She opens a folder and hands me an employee ID badge with my name and picture.

"Tomorrow it is. I'll clear my schedule. What time?" I hope she doesn't say 6:00 a.m.

"The shift starts at seven a.m. and ends at two p.m."

"My fee will be double, and I'll have a report to you within twenty-four hours of completing my shift tomorrow at two." I stand and place the ID in my purse. "Do I wear scrubs, or is there another uniform needed?"

"No, scrubs will be fine. I'll call Cassie and tell her to expect you as a floater tomorrow. You'll need a lunch. Report to the laundry room when you arrive."

"Not a problem." I feel as if I'm making a clandestine deal. Other than the unknown man, no one else saw me enter and leave the Happy Home Care facility that apparently is not very happy.

I sit in my car and look at the sign with the smiling character next to the business name. I wonder if Samyl is blackmailing the women. And who is the unknown male? I should have asked.

Fewer than twenty-four hours later, I'm typing the report as I sit on my bed with the laptop. After a day at the laundry center at the Hampton Nursing Facility, I'm exhausted. The women were as sweet as pie. Many are working because they're not eligible for social security because they're refugees and don't have forty quarters to be eligible. But, according to them, it's better to work here in America at eighty years of age than to die of starvation in their home country. None of them wanted to leave their country, but they had no other choice. They had to leave family possessions and all they had worked for to move to America. Climate change is real, and until people understand, we will continue to have a much older workforce of refugees.

The women didn't automatically divulge their blackmailer. After talking, sharing, and getting to know them over break and lunch, one told me not go to the office unless Tamie was available. I, of course, wanted to know why. Another said to never change my clothes in the back room of the office. I learned that a hidden camera takes pictures of them as they dress there. The blackmailer told them that if they did not put $200 in mailbox 219 in the break area every week, the pictures will be sold on the internet.

The women are worldly and wise but also very humble and private. Each five-day workweek, the aides sacrifice two days' wages to pay the blackmailer. None know who is behind it. I don't think it's Tamie, because why would she ask me to find out what's going on? One woman told me that the unknown male I saw in Tamie's office tried to kiss her when Tamie wasn't there. She stopped by to collect her paycheck, but he wouldn't give it to her. She sat outside until Tamie arrived and got it then. She never told Tamie. "Don't go there by yourself," the woman said before she hugged me at the end of the shift. I assured her I would not.

I'm not sure how Tamie is going to welcome my report. She'll need to monitor mailbox 219. I'll pick up a little spy camera that connects to her cell phone to watch the mailbox. It's either Samyl, the unknown male, or both. All I know is that I would not want to endure the wrath of Tamie. She might be small, but I think she carries a very big stick.

CHAPTER 10

KELTON

I'm having breakfast in the dining room this morning. I wanted a change of scenery. I'm reading yesterday's newspaper from Newark, New Jersey. A new passenger left it on the table after breakfast. I wonder if it's simply a coincidence that it's from New Jersey, where the woman in yellow resides. I've thought about reaching out to her just to talk. I've also thought about deleting her number from my cell. What if I drop my guard, and she realizes who I am? I was prosecuted in Connecticut, but the news probably made it to New Jersey.

I straighten the pages and reassemble the paper by page number before starting with the front-page news. A teenager killed his mother after confronting her about his true ethnicity. She had been lying to him about his father and where his father's family lived. She had been perpetrating a lie or passing for white. His father's family is part Ghanian. That's America, because white doesn't exist anywhere else. Maybe in South Africa when the European whites stole the land from the South Africans. Their day is coming to kill the Boer.

The teenager decided to test his DNA as a silly joke with his friends about the percentage of English each of them possessed. When the results were available, he was blindsided and demanded another test. The company obliged, and the same results were posted.

He and his friends had ridiculed and harassed the minorities in his school. Hazing minorities and posting inhumane pics were the norm. One friend's dad, who is an attorney, encouraged the teens to bully minorities, saying that all comments were covered under the First Amendment. Telling minorities to go back to their country. Now he finds out that he is an ADOS, American descendant of slavery. There is nowhere for them to return to. There are currently fifty-four countries in Africa. America's government officials stripped the ADOS of their country, their family name, their language, their culture, and their humanity. Which country do you return to? Which family do you belong to?

I can understand this teen's shock and horror when he found that he's been ridiculing himself all this time. Participating in ignorance because some want to put a percentage on your level of humanity. It doesn't feel good when you learn that you've been a buffoon and that the people, including the attorney, are justifying ignorance. Everyone's day is coming. If you fail to see everyone as human, one day you too will be seen as less than human, and no one will save you because of your conduct and actions.

I think about my two children, Elisabeth and Kelton Jr. Chanel did not want the children to know that my mother, their grandmother, was Jewish. Because I was orphaned at twelve years of age, I was never taught the customs and practices of the Jewish religion. I was sorry that my mom had gotten sick and couldn't pass down her customs to me. I've never subscribed to any type of religion. How can I believe in something bigger than myself that is supposed to guide and protect me after watching my mother slowly die before my eyes and never knowing my father? All I learned about my father was that he worked at the same company as my mother and that he had another family. My mother assured me that she hadn't known this and made me promise to never break up a happy home. I couldn't believe that my father was happy in his home if he was spending time with my mother. I don't acknowledge that I'm an atheist, but I don't believe in a greater being.

I told Pearl that I was an atheist. She didn't flinch. She said everyone must believe what is best for them. Pearl is a Christian, and it's important for her to believe there is a God, all-powerful and all-knowing, that will avenge the weak and the innocent. She said that if there wasn't a God, then she would be forced to seek revenge on those who prey on the weak and innocent herself. I laughed and hugged her close. I could just imagine Pearl dressed in leather with guns tucked everywhere, looking for predators. She would be a sexy female version of Charles Bronson in *Death Wish*.

One day, my children will also learn that they are Spanish in addition to being English. Chanel thought that teaching them about their culture would single them out to be bullied in school and in the community. Speaking Spanish or any other language doesn't allow for full assimilation into the American white world. You must erase your culture and learn to hate minorities.

"Hey! There you are." Richard slides into the seat across from me.

"Good morning, Richard."

"Did you forget that we have an excursion with the twins this afternoon?"

"No. What time is it?"

"It's almost eleven, and the bus leaves in thirty minutes."

"I must have lost track of time." I get up and fold the newspaper before tucking it under my arm. "I need to change shoes, then I'll meet you at the gangplank."

"I'll be waiting with the twins."

Richard heads to the elevator bank while I go upstairs to my stateroom. I'm not sure if I should continue to contact my children or if I should do as Chanel requested and let them reach out to me when they're ready. They're fifteen and seventeen years old. I hope they don't decide to do a DNA test and kill their mother after learning the results of their ethnicity. It would be best for Chanel and her attitude about my Jewish and Spanish heritage to have the children learn their ethnic DNA. If Chanel dies, I'm sure her new husband will not be heartbroken.

The excursion results in riding throughout Saint Thomas in a jeep visiting the different beaches. Richard assures me that I'll be impressed with the women. At fifty-five, they no longer look like twins. They dress alike, but that's the end of being identical. Neither has been married or has children, but the one who continues to rub against me like she's a cat and I'm a couch is named Tandy. She would rival a bean pole, and when I mention dinner, I didn't know they would share an appetizer-size salad. I did expect them to eat a little more than what a ten-pound rabbit would.

I watch Tandy's antics as she places her fork into the cup of salad dressing that was requested on the side by her sister, Candy. Candy is Richard's date. Then she'd spear the vegetables in the small plate of lettuce and put it in her mouth. When they split the salad, Tandy counted the cherry tomatoes, and Candy counted the cucumbers. It was an even divide. They passed on the crotons because a moment on the lips means a lifetime on the hips.

When we return to the ship, Candy says they'll meet us poolside after they go to the gym to burn off their dinner. I look at Richard, who shrugs. When they leave us at the elevators, I tell Richard to enjoy the twins. I return to my stateroom to make an important call.

"Pearl Consulting. How may I assist you?"

"Hello, lovey. Did I dial the wrong number?"

"Hello. No, you didn't. I just forgot that I was answering my personal cell instead of the office phone."

"How are you doing?"

"I'm doing well. However, I'm sure you're probably doing much better enjoying the fun, sun, and everything else."

"I wish you were here to enjoy the fun, sun, and everything else with me."

"How did you get my number? I didn't give it to you, and you didn't ask me for it."

"I got it the day Seleste hurt her ankle on the beach."

"So you've had it awhile?" Pearl says slowly.

"I didn't know if you would be upset if I called you."

"But today you decided to try?"

I can't determine whether she's happy I called or pissed that I took so long to do so.

"Yeah. I went on an excursion today and thought you would have loved it." Of course, I'm not going to tell her that I was joined by another woman who was unbearable and who was definitely not her.

"What type of excursion?"

"I'm sorry. Is this a good time? I forgot to ask."

"Yes, this is a good time. I needed a break from writing a report."

"Is it okay that I called you?"

"Yes, it's okay."

"Is it okay if I call you more than just this one time?"

"Yes, you may call me in the future. Now can I hear about the excursion?"

"We're in Saint Thomas for the next few days. The excursion was a jeep tour of the island and a few of the beautiful beaches."

"It sounds great. Did you soak up a little sun for me?"

"Can I ask what report you're working on?"

"I'm limited as to what I can say, but the situation involved me going undercover to investigate an employee claim. I worked harder today than I have in quite a long time. But I met some really great women."

"I'm sure you were fantastic. Did you wear yellow? I like you in yellow."

"No. I wore blue."

"Did you wear that lacy bra and panty set?"

"Oh, you just called to be nosy and nasty."

"What did you have for dinner?"

"I had a vegetable stir-fry this evening with a glass of red wine. I found a vineyard in Pennsylvania that might be my new favorite place. What are you doing tonight?"

"It's poker night with the guys."

"Well, I'm going to wish you good luck and say good night. I need to get up early in the morning."

"Okay." I hesitate before speaking again. "I miss you, Pearl. Good night."

I end the call. I don't even let her say good night. I wasn't quite sure what to say or not to say about my life on the ship. She knows I'm probably with a new woman every night. I'm surprised that I spent three days and two nights—or was it four days and three nights?—with her. It's unlike me to even consider such a long-term commitment. I never thought to ask for her cell number because I already had it. However, I assumed she was just a notch on my bedpost. She might be a little more, since my heart is still racing and my libido twitched when hearing her voice.

An hour later, I'm ready to leave my stateroom. I touch my shirt pocket to confirm I have my cigar, then place my wallet with the $1,000 buy-in into my back pocket. I head to the selected poker stateroom for this evening. I hope I don't accidentally run into Tandy or Candy. I also wonder if the discussion will lean toward Ian and how Interpol saved us from interacting with a known felon with multiple criminal enterprises. If they only knew that I was also a felon.

CHAPTER 11

PEARL

My dreams have gotten so vivid recently. I usually don't dream, but since I've returned from my Aruba trip, something has changed. I'm sure I'm probably overworking myself.

Kelton called a week ago. It was a little awkward, since I believed I was simply a blip in his cruise ship life. Over the past week, I've received some inspirational texts from him. Then, out of the blue, he scheduled a date with me remotely. I didn't know what to expect, but he FaceTimed me that evening. At the beginning of the date, my doorbell rang. Kelton told me it was my dinner, since he wanted to eat with me and play Scrabble via the computer. He'd ordered my favorite curry chicken from a local restaurant with a bottle of red wine that he wanted me to try. Everything was delivered to my door. He ordered Thai for himself and a bottle of pinot noir. We ate, talked, and played a few games of Scrabble. It was a great evening and a fantastic date.

He was in Fort Lauderdale and wanted to know if I could spend the week with him in Savannah. I was surprised by the invite but was willing to coordinate my schedule and move a few clients to free up a week. He asked if I wanted him to reserve two rooms, but I said that one would be more than enough. He laughed; he hadn't wanted to assume anything. I'm definitely not one to waste money, and reserving two hotel rooms would be a waste. I left all the reservations to him. I'll meet him next Wednesday at the Savannah airport. We coordinated our arrival times, then I said good night and blew him a kiss. He did the same, and we ended the call.

I clear my food containers and plate from the dining room table while reminiscing about the first night he stayed with me in Aruba. I was so hot after Kelton slowly and methodically stripped me down to my lacy bra and panties. His hands caressed my butt all the way up my back while kissing me first on the lips and then on the jaw, neck, and shoulder. He moaned every time he kissed me. My skin was on fire from his touch, and his kisses were the fuel. He placed his shirt around me and secured a few buttons to prevent it from falling off my body. He picked me up as I wrapped my legs around his waist. He backed me up against the wall to leverage the grinding of his erection. I thought I was going to explode. He ground just enough for my body to hit the peak of orgasm. I wailed a breathy scream of his name as my body reacted. He didn't stop until I finished convulsing. He whispered in a raspy voice, "Thank you for sharing your pleasure with me."

He slowly lowered me to the floor, and I held him to get my balance on shaky legs. After asking to remove my panties, he planted kisses on my thighs as his fingers caressed my skin on their way to my waistband. He pulled them down, revealing my swollen pussy. He planted a single kiss there before he held my hand to help me step out of my panties.

He pulled back the covers, and I climbed in, then watched as he removed his pants, his erection straining the front of his boxer briefs. He laid on his back and reached for me. I curled against him and pulled my right leg across his body. Our breathing finally leveled out, and we fell asleep.

To prepare for seven days in Savannah, I ask Jaynea the following morning to clear my schedule. She rearranges my appointments while I review my client timetables and confirm that I can squeeze in seven days with Kelton and not upset anyone.

I have only one client with whom I need to meet before leaving. It's regarding Stephen Santorini's marketing issue. He's operated his tax office for the past three years alone, following the death of his sister. Another consultant recommended he change the business name to emphasize a definitive brand. He refused to rename the company after his sister passed away unexpectedly one evening after work. He terminated the contract with that consultant and reached out to me. Mari Hall was Stephen's younger sister, and she had pushed him to open the tax office after his youngest child started college. They wanted to leave a legacy for their children. His two kids and her daughter were interested in following in the family footsteps as bookkeepers and accountants, ultimately reaching the coveted position of certified public accountants. CPAs are the monitors and protectors of other people's money or, in this case, company money.

When I enter the office, no one is in the lobby waiting to get their taxes filed. I'm surprised. In the past, the office was always jam-packed with people. The chime above the door signals that I've entered. A few seconds later, Stephen appears from his office in the back.

"Hello, Stephen." I extend my hand.

"Hello, Pearl. How are you?" We shake, and he directs me to the conference table in front of the cubicle area. I take a seat and pull out a notepad and pen.

"I'm doing well. I was surprised to hear from you until I drove around the community."

"Yeah, the community has changed. They knocked down many of the older homes and built affordable housing units on three of the four corners and in between." He shakes his head.

"Does that 'affordable housing,'" I reply as I make air quotes with my fingers, "mean the tenants can actually afford the rents?" I watch Stephen's reaction. He's gotten older and grayer. He's always been distinguished. It looks like the loss of his sister has taken some of the fire out of him. His wife never wanted to be involved in his business. She wanted him to take care of the money while she took care of the house. The problem with that thinking in this day and age is that men die and leave women to fend for themselves for ten to fifteen years. If they never learned how to budget, negotiate, and survive on a fixed income, they'll be overwhelmed. Old age for them will be hell.

"I don't know what affordable housing means," he admits. "That's the buzzword. Everyone uses it, but no one has a definition for it. The units were built to accommodate the lower wage earners, but they can't afford the rent. The city has reclassified two of the buildings from affordable housing to regular housing. The people moving into the community don't need someone to complete their taxes. Technology and AI permits them to accomplish that task without me or my office." Stephen taps two of his fingers on the conference table before he takes a long deep breath and then lets it out slowly.

I nod in agreement. "Technology has changed many things."

"That's the problem. Those in affordable housing are transient, and people not living in affordable housing don't need my services. I can't get a handle on the change."

"Have you thought about relocating to a less transient community that may need your services?" I believe he knows what needs to be done. He's simply hesitating.

"I have, but . . ." He looks at me, then down at the floor. I want to reach over the table and hold his hand. I know what he's thinking. If I show him compassion, will he assume I'm flirting with him? There's a fine line between compassion and unprofessional conduct. I decide not to reach for his hand.

"Her spirit will go wherever you go. She'll always be with you." I didn't know I needed to bring my therapist hat today. I thought Stephen wanted to talk about marketing or managing his employees. At the present time, I'm not sure he has any employees.

"I know." He's still looking at the floor.

"She would want you to do what's necessary to keep the office active and vibrant." I can just imagine her spirit sitting with us at the conference table.

"I feel her presence here in the afternoon." He looks up at me. "I miss her."

"I know."

"I have something to show you." Stephen disappears in the back and returns with a picture of the three grown children.

"How are they doing? They all should be graduating soon from college." I decide to motivate him by addressing why he and Mari started the tax office to begin with. They wanted to leave a legacy for their children.

I also believe he knows that there will be no legacy if he decides to stay in this new affordable housing community.

"My oldest has graduated and so has Mari's child. They have good-paying jobs at firms in Newark." He looks at me. "They didn't want to join me here."

"They're still young. They don't know any better than what their friends have or are doing." I cross my legs at the ankle under the table as I think about what else I need to say to convince him to move or to close.

"I know I have two options. The first is to close my doors, which will also close the door on the legacy Mari and I wanted to leave our children. The next generation." He stops and takes a deep breath. "Or I move and pick up a few business clients and permanent tax filers."

I smile at him. "It sounds like you just wanted someone to talk to today."

Stephen smiles in return, and the light appears in his eyes. The light I always saw when he worked with his sister. I developed a marketing plan for them when they first opened their doors. Mari's skill set complemented what Stephen was lacking. They worked perfectly together. She had a heart attack one evening after work and died before the EMTs got to her house.

"I guess I did."

"Well, that's simply my personal opinion. You also didn't need a consultant, just a friend."

He repositions himself in his chair. "Next time I'll have coffee and muffins." He laughs.

"I have a fantastic commercial realtor. She can find you the perfect small office."

"It sounds like a plan." The smile stays on his face this time.

"I'm also going to refer you to BNI, which is a networking group that meets once a week early in the morning. You'd be perfect for it." I stand and put my messenger bag on my shoulder.

He steps forward to give me a hug. Before I leave, I remind him that Mari would be proud of him. I tell him to call me when he's ready to move. I'll probably end up packing Mari's office. I remember how hard it was to box up my grandmother's belongings after she passed away. I cried throughout the entire process. Every single item reminded me of her, as I recalled the stories she'd told about many of the pieces—why she bought it or who gave it to her. Many tears were shed that day.

The following morning, I learn my flight out of Newark is delayed. I text Kelton and tell him I'll be late getting to Savannah, arriving at 4:35 p.m. instead of 1:20 p.m.

I turn on my cell when I land. Kelton replied to my earlier text and followed my advice about not waiting for me in the airport. Instead, he's texted me the address of our hotel. I schedule an Uber, and it brings me to a warehouse. A warehouse? I'm hesitant, thinking the driver mixed up the street name, until he shows me that it's the correct address. On second glance, I realize the entrance is located on the other side of the building. The owners converted this old abandoned warehouse to loft-style condos.

The lobby displays exposed brick, which creates an endearing charm. As I read the welcome sign and the process for checking into the building, someone whispers in my ear. "You look lovely." A smile spreads across my face as I turn to see Kelton holding a few bottles of wine and two wineglasses. "I've already checked us in." He leans in and kisses me ever so tenderly. He hands me the wineglasses and bottles as he takes the bag off my shoulder and grabs my suitcase. "Follow me, lovey." On the way to the airport, I stopped and purchased condoms because I'm still a responsible person, even though I cannot get pregnant. I'm sure Kelton has been with other women, and I don't want to receive another's germs, diseases, or what have you. Have fun and be responsible.

We're on the second floor. The condo is beautiful. It's a one-bedroom, one-and-half-bath unit decorated in a classic contemporary theme all in shades of mauve. I place the wine and the glasses on the kitchen island. It's an open concept design, so we can cook and see the television in the living room. The furniture looks comfortable and plush. Kelton has stowed my luggage and is watching me from the bedroom door.

"Do you like?"

"Yes. It's beautiful."

I cross the room and slide my arms around his waist. He envelops me in his embrace. I take in his smell and place my head on his chest. I wasn't sure what I was getting into this week, but everything feels good. It feels right. He kisses my forehead. Then his finger tilts my head up, and his lips capture mine. The connection that we had in Aruba is still present and strong.

"I'm glad you accepted my invitation."

I smile like I'm ready to burst. "I'm glad you offered."

He rubs my back and pulls me even closer.

"I had the refrigerator stocked with food, and I have a surprise for you." He takes my hand and leads me into the bedroom.

"Is it the king-size bed?"

"No. I have one better." He leads me into the bathroom. I'm blown away by the size of the tub. "I remember you had a fantasy that involved you, a special someone, and a bathtub." His deep voice repeats exactly what I was thinking. He steps a little closer to me from behind, and his arms circle my waist and pull me back against his chest. "I'm your special someone this week."

I always wanted to take a long hot bath with a special someone wrapped around me. I place my hands on his and smile. "Thank you."

He whispers in my ear. "You set the pace this week. I'm all yours."

I don't realize I'm holding my breath until he kisses me on the cheek. "Okay."

I'd been a desert before the day of passion in Aruba. A sexual apartheid had happened in my life. I turn in his arms to gaze at him. I don't know what I'm looking for, nor can I determine his level of health. But I'm going to feel very badly if I end up killing him in the middle of an enthusiastic fuck. He reaches for my hand and pulls me out of the bathroom.

"I made reservations at a restaurant off Bay Street. It's walking distance from here." He stops at the living room sofa and sits, then pulls me onto his lap. "I've missed you. We need to speak more often and possibly see each other more."

"I agree." His lips slowly caress mine. The kiss becomes more intense as he sweeps his tongue into my mouth for a taste, then gently bites my bottom lip. He pulls me closer to his chest. I feel so protected. I smell his scent and lay my head against his. His lips nuzzle my neck. I feel cocooned in his embrace. I want to stay here forever. It's perfect.

A few hours later, we have a magnificent dinner. The steak and garlic potatoes are fantastic. We finish the bottle of wine, and Kelton buys another for the week. I'm buzzed just enough to let my inhibitions down but not drunk. I want to be present if I'm going to enjoy Kelton.

I open my eyes to find that I'm lying on my stomach. I blink a few times to adjust my vision. I look under the sheet that's covering me and see my peach-colored sexy silk nightgown. I also feel an arm on my waist and someone pressed against my side. I hope I didn't embarrass myself, because I can't remember doing anything with Kelton. I don't believe anything happened last night because I'm still wearing my nightgown. Nightgowns are for foreplay. I love sleeping naked. I touch my head and feel my bonnet.

"You feeling better?" Kelton whispers.

"Was I sick?" I feel flushed now. I don't want to scare him away. I turn to look at him.

"You thought you might get sick last night." He brushes his fingers across my cheek. "You wanted to show me your nightgown."

"Did you get me into my nightgown?"

"No. You found it in your suitcase and insisted last night was the night."

"I was nervous."

"I did place your matching bonnet over your hair after you collapsed on the bed."

I touch my bonnet again before pulling it off. "Thanks very much."

"I would never have insisted on anything last night. I want us to both be in the moment, and I think you're a lightweight with alcohol." Kelton smiles, then leans in and kisses my lips. "You look great in your nightgown and matching bonnet." His hand slides up the back of my thigh, which pushes the gown up toward my waist. He moves to my butt and squeezes. My heart is beating wildly, and the space between my legs is getting wet and starting to ache. His other hand brushes my lips, then his lips touch mine. He pulls me closer. I can feel his manhood against my belly. He kisses me passionately.

"I need to get you two aspirin and some water." He slides out of bed and disappears into the bathroom. He's wearing only his pajama bottoms. When he returns, I look at his chest and the dusting of gray and black hair there. "Take these, then I'll prepare breakfast. What would you like?"

"I'm not fancy. Toast, bacon, and eggs. Scrambled eggs with only pepper."

"I can do that." He leans over and kisses me on the forehead. "Are you up for joining me?"

"Yes. As long as I'm not forced to do anything too fast."

Kelton takes my hand and leads me to the kitchen island. I sit while he preps and cooks breakfast. He's proficient in the kitchen. I never had that ability. I can cook enough for myself and my bland, simple taste buds, but I've never felt comfortable cooking for others. I feel better after breakfast and clear the dishes since he cooked. I return to the bathroom to brush my teeth and shower. I pin up my hair because I don't want to wash it and take the next sixteen hours to let it dry naturally. When I come out of the shower stall, Kelton is leaning against the sink.

"I probably shouldn't have suggested we finish both bottles of wine yesterday," Kelton says.

I hold the towel tightly around myself. "I was nervous. I usually drink only a glass or two of red wine or share one bottle at the most."

"Are you feeling better? I had plans for us today."

"Yes. I don't want to mess up your plans. Were we going to walk along River Street?" I reach for my lotion from the toiletry bag.

Kelton takes the bottle out of my hand and places it back on the counter. He leans in and kisses my lips. I shiver as if I'm cold. He takes my hand and leads me to the bathtub. I see bubbles. "I know I told you that I'll follow your lead, but if you're willing to give me a little leeway, I'd appreciate it." He kisses the inside of my palm.

"Okay." I smile. "What do you have in mind?"

"I want to place you into this warm tub and ask for an invitation to join you." Kelton watches me until I look at him. "Would you like me to join you?"

"Yes," I say enthusiastically.

His finger traces my lips, then he kisses me gently. "Afterward, would you let me kiss every spot on your body while I explore?"

"Yes," I whisper breathlessly.

He untucks my towel and lets it drop to the floor. He smiles. "You're beautiful," he says as he admires my body. I haven't had this type of attention in quite some time. He takes my hand for balance as I step into the bathtub. I slide into the bubbles while watching him. My eyes rake over his body, paying attention to old scars and tan lines. I linger at his crotch a little longer than I should, and he looks down at himself. He smiles and slowly slides his pajama bottoms over his erection. I am going to delight in riding him.

"Do you want me to sit behind you or across from you?" His erection bounces as he walks toward me.

"May I touch you?"

"I'm all yours. Touch wherever you want to touch."

I firmly grip the base of his erection and slide my hand up to the top of his cock. Brushing my fingertips across the head, I say, "You're beautiful." I release him and slide forward in the tub. "You're sitting behind me."

Kelton slides into the bubbles and settles into the tub. He pulls me back against his erection and his chest. I am blissful and pleased. I close my eyes as he places a kiss on my back. This is one of my all-time fantasies. My ex-husband thought bathing together was a stupid idea. We never even showered together.

Kelton and I chat and wash each other. We chat and kiss. We chat and splash. We chat and moan while kissing. When the water begins to cool, Kelton suggests that we continue this in the bed. He gets out and dries himself, then offers his hand as I step out of the tub. He dries me and then guides me to the bedroom. He spends the next twenty minutes winding me up to the point of spiraling. With slow deliberate kisses that start at my feet and move up my legs. He kisses and bites my thighs. He moves to my hips, and I moan as he continues up my stomach to my breasts and nipples. First licking and sucking one nipple, then moving to the other and doing the same. I'm ready to pop prematurely. When he gets to my lips, he sucks on the bottom one as he slides a finger between my other lips and enters me. I moan even louder and attempt to reposition myself to let his finger go deeper. "Not yet," he whispers. I moan again and try to pull his body closer to me. "I want you on top." He flips over so that I straddle him as he sits with his back against the headboard. After the condom is securely in place, he pulls me on top of his shaft. I adjust as I slowly slide down, down, down to the base of his erection. "Oh, so good," I whisper and then moan. His girth fills me to the brim. Just the right thickness. I moan loudly as I close my eyes and throw back my head. Every nerve in my body has rebelled against me and is on the Kelton train of pleasure. He sucks a nipple into his mouth, and I moan. He grips my ass and assists me in creating a rhythm—our rhythm—that has me whimpering in no time. He's so good. It's so good. The apartheid has ended. A tear rolls down my cheek before the force of the orgasm grips me. I scream his name and hold on to his shoulders for dear life as my body convulses. He continues the rhythm as I try to catch my breath. He moans but isn't ready to concede yet. He rolls me onto my back without leaving me and begins to stroke. A slow deliberate stroke that goes deeper each time. Another orgasm begins to wash over me. This time it takes Kelton over with me. He growls my name as he stills inside me. We are both breathing hard and are very sated. He discards the condom in the trash and returns to bed as I start to drift off. He wraps me in his arms and pulls me close as we both fall asleep.

A few hours of rest and a repeat of exploring and stroking are our plans for the next five days. He cooks brunch every morning, and we select a restaurant within walking distance each evening. We never really get dressed during the day, and I help as much as possible with brunch. I became his sous chef in the kitchen. His specialty is stir-fry dishes.

Wearing his T-shirt to breakfast, showering together, and lying in bed, sometimes just talking, sometimes reading to each other, sometimes playing Scrabble. If we got curious, we took our time with each other. We had to remember we weren't in our twenties anymore, even though sixty is the new thirty. It took me back to the nonadult days of my early twenties, having no worries and enjoying the pleasures of sexual intimacy as many times as possible.

On the fifth day, I ask Kelton for a favor as we chill. I need a trusted expert to review the financials for Trim and Fit. The numbers are not adding up. I can't place my finger on the uncomfortable feeling I have about the investor funds. The numbers are extreme, but even more disturbing is the amount being returned to the investors. Kelton suggests that if the numbers aren't making sense, then I should drop Trim and Fit as a client. I'm not sure why he would recommend canceling the consultant contract, as they're providing a large amount of my revenue. I'd prefer to figure out the problem than give the client to another consultant.

We end the week with a quiet stroll along River Street and dinner at one of the fancy restaurants. We walk hand in hand back to the condo to pack for our flights in the morning. It turns out to be my best vacation ever.

CHAPTER 12

KELTON

My cell chirps with an incoming text. I had just gotten settled in first class and located my earbuds. I hope Pearl isn't canceling. I don't look forward to much anymore, but my woman in yellow has become very important to me. I unlock my phone and read her text. Her flight is delayed. I message her back with the address of the condo we're staying at in Savannah.

Upon securing the keys and unpacking some of my toiletry items, I explore the wine shops in the area. I requested a stocked refrigerator and selected items that Pearl and I would enjoy for the week. I choose a few bottles of wine and buy a pair of wineglasses that she can take with her to remember the week. Or maybe I'll take them. Then every time we're together, I'll bring our special wineglasses. Apparently, I'm subconsciously thinking this might happen again and again. Even though I'm still holding on to the secret of my past. I haven't decided to tell Pearl yet, but the more time I spend with her, the more I don't want secrets between us.

As I head to the condo from the wine shop, I see Pearl getting out of the Uber and making her way around the building to the entrance. I follow her. She's beautiful. Her hair is partially pinned on top of her head, and some strands hang by her ears. I long to wash her hair. I haven't told her yet, but I want to be her shampoo man any day of the week. I can massage her scalp and apply her leave-in conditioner. Each curl springing back to life. I pick up the pace, as I've already checked us in through the app and don't want her trying to call me.

I approach and tell her how beautiful she looks. She turns and gives me the smile that lights up my day. I hand the wine bottles and glasses to her while I take her shoulder bag and suitcase. She follows me to our place for the next seven days.

She's pleased with the condo and especially with the bathtub. I plan to grant her fantasy of getting us into a tub of bubbles. Whenever I'm able to get close to her without any clothes is a good thing. She checks out the refrigerator and bounces on the couch. She approves. I refuse to take any money for the accommodations, which makes this my special getaway. I assure her that if I need extra money, I'll ask. It's unusual for me to have a woman offer to pay for something. The gold diggers I'm typically with never do and always want to know how much money I have in my portfolios. Pearl has never asked me once about my income or level of wealth.

I've never been a fool with my money. Even when I take the women from the cruise out for a shopping spree in exchange for time together. When I was married, I still made sure I placed 25 percent of everything I brought home into a private account for emergencies. Chanel was always having some type of crisis that wasn't a real emergency. Needing to buy a new pair of $1,000 shoes was never an emergency in my world. Sometimes I felt guilty saving the money and not telling Chanel or having her name on the account, which was set up as a trust. Only I and my two children are listed on it. Unless someone knows of the trust, there's no way to get access to it.

The time in prison made me thankful that I had put the money away and given the papers to an attorney friend of mine. I wanted the money to be used to purchase homes for my children, grandchildren, and great-grandchildren. I never thought I'd need the funds to sustain my existence. Every penny that was placed into my trust account was earned. The amount was enough for me to purchase the stateroom on the cruise ship and to pay any bills I might have for the next sixty years. I'm sixty-two years old, and I'm sure I won't live until I'm 122. My children aren't speaking to me, so I likely will never meet my grandchildren. Someone should use the money, and that someone is me and now my Pearl.

Pearl overindulges with the wine at dinner. I think she's nervous about the week with me. I thought I would spend the evening hearing her scream my name, but she's in no shape for that or anything else right now. She slips into her peach negligee and models it before collapsing on the bed. I pull her close to me and fall asleep. I remember to place her bonnet over her hair before climbing in behind her. I didn't want her to worry about breakage or tangles in the morning. She usually alternates between a silk scarf and a bonnet. I haven't figured out why one and then the other, but the peach bonnet matches her negligee, so it must be a bonnet tonight. I just want to make sure she's happy, and I get the benefits of making her smile. And, of course, moan.

I might really be falling for this woman. I've never had such a desire to make someone happy. I attempted to make Chanel happy, but it seemed like whatever I gave her, it was never enough. The more expensive, the better. I found a seashell on a beach in Santorini that I thought Pearl would like for her collection. I mailed it to her when I returned to the States. She liked it so much that she didn't put it in her collection; instead, she set it on the windowsill in her kitchen. She said every time she's at the sink, she looks at it and thinks of me. I want her to always think of me.

The following morning, I make sure she gets water and two aspirin. Then I prepare breakfast for my woman in yellow. Lunch is a bubble bath, with us first relaxing and exploring while we wash each other. When the water cools, I recommend continuing in the bed. I'm excited to have an opportunity to run my hands over Pearl's body, with my lips following everywhere my hands touched. Giving her full control of the situation, I suggest that she start on top, directing and controlling the pleasure and outcome of our sexual encounter. I had no idea that she would enjoy giving and taking such pleasure. Her moans and whimpers are a result of each movement and touch of my hands or lips. She is definitely a loud lover, and I enjoy every single sound she makes. Predinner consists of me getting to know in what positions I can stroke her to orgasm. I get two out of her before she pulls me into ecstasy. We rest over snacks and a little sleep.

I'm not thirty anymore, even though I've heard sixty is some type of new thirty. Who knows why people say such things.

Pearl asks me to review the financials for one of her clients. She's worried about investor funds being placed into the company. After looking over the documents, I have several concerns. I tell Pearl to terminate the client, but my suggestion appears to upset her. I don't think the financials are telling the entire picture. In fact, I think the numbers Pearl has are bogus. There's no way to know for sure unless a forensic accountant reviews the books and connects all the dots. The client might be maintaining two sets of books.

The Savannah week is perfection.

CHAPTER 13

PEARL

I'm floating in the ocean on an inner tube, and Kelton touches my hand from his own tube. I look at him and smile. He's so handsome. His skin is sun-kissed. A rope connects the inner tubes so that we don't drift apart. I close my eyes and feel the sun's rays bathing my face. I hear a splash. Kelton's inner tube is empty. He's swimming toward the shore. He didn't say a word about heading back. I call out his name. He turns to look at me. He doesn't wave or yell or anything. He resumes swimming. I'm still floating in the inner tube, with his empty one tied to mine. I can no longer see him because I've drifted farther away into the ocean.

I review my schedule for the day once I arrive at the office. I'm here early because once again I awoke from a nightmare. I was afraid it might continue if I tried to go to sleep again. Jaynea has left a few notes on my desk regarding Fred from Trim and Fit. I also have a cryptic message that reads "Follow your instincts. Never second-guess your gut." Jaynea didn't indicate the person who had left it, just the time of the call: 12:14 p.m. I flip the message to view the back for additional information, but there's nothing more.

This afternoon I'm visiting the third Country Crafts store. Betty is wound tight when I arrive due to an altercation with a customer who allegedly forgot to purchase jewelry-making supplies before trying to leave the store. The officers have the older white woman in the back of the police car. She might be younger than she looks, but I can't tell age once a white person gets those crow's feet. Betty is giving a report to one officer while the other speaks with the employee who saw her drop the items into her purse. I don't want to disturb the process, so I slide into the store and act as if I'm shopping, all while listening from a distance. Betty is very professional, even though the middle-aged white woman is upset. I believe Betty personally knows the woman based on some of the comments. I move closer to where the employee is speaking to the officer. The employee gives the facts and answers all the officer's questions without hesitation. It sounds like the employee saw the incident and immediately reported it to Betty. Betty approached the woman when she left the cash register after purchasing a few cheaper items. The white woman became belligerent and began screaming about suing the store, the employees, and the management. An employee called the police because she thought the woman might get violent. The officer found the items that were allegedly stolen in a bag, and they would be part of the report. After further eavesdropping, Betty admitted that she wasn't going to involve the police and asked the woman to simply give her the items that were in her purse. "I didn't want anyone to go to jail over something so trivial. This is going to affect her livelihood, since she's a paralegal," Betty tells the police officer. The officer is understanding but continues to complete the report.

I slip out after buying a small basket. Today is not the day to address the inventory loss. I plan to mention my observation of the situation when I return to meet with Betty and the employees a few days from now, as they handled everything so professionally.

Back at my office, I ask Jaynea to reschedule my meeting with Betty.

Lunch is always planned the prior day or at the very latest the morning of the day I'm having lunch. Because my self-imposed dietary restrictions bar me from simply going to any restaurant, I need to know the menu ahead of time. This food issue has always been a part of me. I've tried to change and adapt like most adults, but I couldn't shake it as a child and now that I'm good and grown, it's not going to happen.

I decide to swing by a favorite place that has the best barbecue chicken in Essex County. Dina's Barbecue is on Market Street in Newark. It's out of the way, but it's always worth it. I hate trying to find a parking space, and the lots are always so complicated unless there's a parking attendant.

After circling the restaurant for twenty minutes, I find a parking space on the street. I was feeling nostalgic this morning and thought about my cousins. The family was close until my grandmother passed and everyone went their separate ways. I've always been family oriented, but it seems like I'm the only one. After ordering, I sit on the bench in the take-out area to wait for my number to be called. I glance at a few patrons entering the dining room and realize that one is my cousin Karyn. I haven't seen her in more than twenty-five years. She still looks the same, so much like her mother, my mother's third sister. My cousin had six children before our aunt persuaded her to get her tubes tied. Her boyfriend at the time wanted to have twelve children. I thought it was very presumptuous of him, since he didn't have to carry or birth any of them. I wave at her. She nods, but I don't think she recognizes me. I'll wait until she's seated. I don't recognize the two people she follows to the table. They might be her children or grown grandchildren.

I remember running around bases at my grandmother's home playing kickball. We were all very competitive, and once teams were selected, the instigating started. I was the youngest granddaughter and looked most like my grandmother. She had eleven grandchildren and fostered two additional children after Granddad passed away. She always smelled good and gave great hugs. She would hold on to me and give just the right amount of pressure during the hug to make it stay with me all day. Because my parents lived next door to my grandmother, I got those hugs every morning before going to school and anytime I stopped by to see her. My visits were frequent.

"Pearl, is that you?" I hear a very familiar voice ask, shaking me out of my memories of my grandmother.

I stand and spread my arms for an embrace. "Karyn. I didn't think you recognized me."

"I'm here with my two youngest children. They decided to take me out for an early dinner."

"Well, you know this is the best barbecue around since Hot Sauce closed their doors."

"That was a shame. All those years and no family member took over the business."

I study her as she sits next to me. "You look good."

"Yeah. The years have flown by."

"How are your children?"

She smiles, but it doesn't look genuine. "They're all great."

"How are you doing? I thought about you one day being in the medical field."

"No. I work as an assistant."

"I remember you told me that you loved being pregnant. I thought you'd become a doula or a midwife."

Surprise appears on her face. "Really?"

"Yeah. I believe everyone should work in a field they enjoy, and you loved the babies."

She chuckles, and a genuine smile spreads across her face that lights up her eyes. "I never thought about doing that for a living."

"I found it upsetting that the family fell apart after Grandma passed. We all had so much potential and could have all selected fields to build a network of professionals." I reach for her hand and pat it a few times.

"Wow, you're still seeing the big picture." She accepts my hand and holds it for a few minutes. We've been transported back in time in our minds. Doing our girly things and giggling over nothing. Where did the years go? We're now fast approaching the age our grandma had been when she died, worried about thinning hair, monitoring our weight, eating healthy as often as possible, passing wisdom to the younger folks, and preparing for the day we take our last breath. "Tomorrow is not promised to any of us."

"Don't we know it." I reach over and give her a warm, firm embrace, as if it was coming from our grandma. "I see your children waving. Your food must be at the table." I pull a business card out of my bag. "I hope you call me and not let more time pass."

She stands. "Or before one of us gets straight."

I laugh, since we're the group of younger grandchildren. "We'll probably see the older ones get straight before we do." I wave at her children as she returns to the table, then collect my take-out order.

The following morning, I participate in a networking event that allows me to interact with other small businesses in the community. All small business owners experience crises, but many aren't aware that outside assistance is available unless it's a legal or financial matter. My expertise and skills allow small business owners to use me as a sounding board without getting the actual board or investors involved until it's necessary. Two members participating in the event are interested in my services. I schedule appointments to meet with each of them individually at their offices next week.

After lunch at my office with Jaynea, we talk about her upcoming vacation to the Grand Caymans. She's going with two friends from college. I never had the opportunity to develop college friendships, since I was never a traditional college student. My friends were work friends and always temporary. I think about Seleste. I'll call her this evening.

I open the folder for Dollar Now, a store owned by Mia Lakes with three locations in Essex and Union Counties. She's interested in creating franchises that could be bought by a single mother wanting to be her own boss. She started from humble beginnings. She was raised by a single mother after a police officer shot and killed her father in a case of mistaken identity, according to the newspapers. The police officer was never charged, and Mia grew up with her mother struggling to make ends meet through no fault of her own. It's shameful to think of someone's life being taken by a police officer, who is required to protect and serve. That single incident took a loving husband and father away from his family. The officer returned home to his family and probably never thought again about killing Mia's father and how that act affected a child. Society wants to make it a Black and white thing, but it's simply a humanity thing. Police and their haphazard shooting never see individuals as human. Leaving children without fathers and wives without husbands. I would have crumbled and faltered if my husband was killed, making me the sole parent of a child while we were both dealing with the trauma of loss. That trauma likely stays with people for their entire lives.

I close the folder and gather my materials to meet with Mia Lakes. She has a small office near the largest Dollar Now store, which is located in an older building. Nothing fancy and posh for everyone to see. The style is simple and clean. I sit at the conference table across from Mia, and we assess and discuss the process of franchising Dollar Now. Her hair is in locs knotted on the top of her head, with a few tendrils flowing down her back. Her dangling earrings are beautiful onyx, and her makeup is light. She wears a skirt suit with an African print jacket. The skirt is straight and perfectly matches the blue in the jacket. Her shoes are pumps with a sensible heel height, also in blue. I admire her style and flair.

"I'd like to get this process finalized within the next twenty-four months. I completed all of the forms, and I also have the manual you requested." Mia slides the items across the table.

"Thanks." I place the materials in my bag. "My next step is to review the manual for duplication. Do you have any other questions or concerns?"

Mia moves a paper in front of her. "I want to make sure I completely understand the franchise concept."

"Sure." I remove my checklist from my folder so that I don't forget a step, then explain the process. "As the owner of Dollar Now, you'll grant a license to any party for the purpose of conducting business as Dollar Now using the same trademarks, trade names, trade dress, and other identifying aspects of Dollar Now. Each franchise will use the name Dollar Now as a DBA, also known as doing business as. The interested parties or franchisees will purchase the rights from you as a franchisor for a cost as well as a monthly royalty fee."

"It sounds like I'd need to hire someone to handle the franchise component for Dollar Now." Mia taps the nail of her index finger on the conference table.

"That might be best." I watch Mia as her finger taps, taps, taps. I think this process might be more than she expected. "Your focus to provide opportunities to single mothers is fantastic." I seek to remind her of the original reason she wanted to franchise her Dollar Now stores.

"Yes, I know. I'll start interviewing for an assistant within the next few weeks."

I place the folder and my other items in my bag. "Let's meet in two weeks."

"Same time and day would be great."

"I'll send you a calendar invite." I follow Mia to the front office door, and we hug as I leave. After I follow up with Jaynea via my cell, I head home, stopping for General Tso's chicken and ribs on the way.

I stretch out on the couch as I wait to hear from Seleste, who is returning my call. I've changed into my comfortable yoga pants and a T-shirt that reads No Whining. I've Had a Day! I twirl my hair on top of my head before flopping my foot on the back of the couch. I pour a little more wine into my glass. I miss Kelton and rubbing against his body.

A knock at the door surprises me. It's probably a package delivery. I look through the glass pane and then fling the front door open and start screaming. Seleste and I throw our arms around each other. It's been almost a year since we were last together. She kept saying she'd visit but then couldn't make it to New Jersey. I don't realize Weston is with Seleste until he rolls the suitcases and other bags into the foyer. I hug him too.

"This is wonderful!"

"Is it all right that we're here?"

"I hope so, since I let the Uber guy leave." Weston makes a silly face.

I punch him in the arm. "Yes, it's great you're here. Drop the bags, Weston, and get yourself a plate or raid the refrigerator. Whatever you want."

"I thought it would be best to visit you, since Weston is meeting with a producer in New York City next week." Seleste flops on the couch. She reaches for my Chinese food containers and pulls out a rib. "I'm hungry, and this looks good." Seleste licks her fingers as she eats.

"Wait! Let me get you a plate." I jog to the kitchen, but Weston has already found the dinnerware.

We sit and talk and eat for the next three hours, attempting to catch up on our lives. Weston falls asleep on the couch. I assure Seleste that they can stay as long as they want. Sometimes I get lonely in the house.

Over the next few weeks, we explore all the tourist attractions in New York City and enjoy a play on Broadway and one off Broadway. I find a fantastic restaurant in Hell's Kitchen that will become our go-to place when they visit again. We also visit many of the South Orange restaurants, the Turtle Back Zoo, and a steak place in Livingston at Weston's request. We only needed Kelton to complete the gang.

I didn't realize the importance of having the guest room on the opposite side of the house away from my primary bedroom until I went to the kitchen at 1:00 a.m. for something to drink and heard Seleste screaming Weston's name as the bed squeaked. I remind myself to oil the bed or tighten the platform base when they leave. Or I could just tell Weston where the tools are and let him solve the problem. Nothing is worse than being in the throes of passion and the bed is making more noise than the two people.

I remember having the bed frame collapse in my younger years with a lover. But we didn't stop; we simply repositioned ourselves on the floor and continued. I can laugh about it now. Apparently, the screws had worked themselves loose, and right at the moment when we were about to hit the peak of ecstasy. Wham. Bam. Boom. I was on top, and we both slid down the mattress onto the floor. Now, when a bed begins to squeak, it needs to be addressed.

I head back to my bedroom after hearing my houseguests. I pull out the Magician and think about Kelton.

<h1>CHAPTER 14</h1>

KELTON

I'm enjoying a cup of coffee on my balcony overlooking the swimming pool. I've liked living on the cruise ship for the past few years, but something feels as if it's missing. Even the women in bikinis and those who sunbathe topless don't intrigue me anymore. I spent the night with Lyndsey again. I'm going through the motions.

My cell vibrates against the table. I lean over to see who's calling. I'm hoping it's Pearl. I've had her on my mind, especially last night in the dark with Lyndsey. I wanted to hear Pearl's moans. I wanted to hear her call my name until it intensified into a scream. I wanted to tuck her into my arms as we fell asleep, exhausted. Unknown Caller flashes across the screen of my cell. I answer.

"Kelton, it's Matt Marek."

I don't say anything. Do I hang up and block the number? Do I want to confront Matt? I haven't seen him since the day the FBI raided my company. He appeared in my office that morning and quietly told me that he was sorry. I didn't understand what he was saying. Why would he be sorry? Then the FBI arrived, flashing badges and handing me a legal document.

"Hello, Kelton? Are you there?"

"I'm here." What could he possibly want? If he apologizes, I'll cuss him out until I'm breathless. How can an apology fix what he did?

"I'm sure I'm the last person you want to hear from."

"You are absolutely correct. Why do you have my number? How did you even get it?"

"Chanel gave it to me. I ran into her last week and met her new husband."

"What do you want?"

"I know it won't change anything, but I wanted to explain." Matt clears his throat with a cough.

"Okay, explain." What could he possibly tell me? He wanted a newer, more expensive car? He wanted to take his family on a fancy vacation? He wanted to keep up with the Joneses?

"Are you around? I still live in New Haven. I'd like to meet face-to-face."

"I can meet you on Friday morning at the Coffee House on Main Street at eleven thirty." I don't know why I'm giving him the benefit of the doubt.

"Thanks, Kelton. I'll see you then." He ends the call.

I'll fly to New Haven on Thursday, meet Matt to punch his lights out, then catch the train to Newark. This will allow me to surprise Pearl with a visit. I'm not sure whether I should do that or tell her I'll be in town. We never said we were exclusive. What if someone else is cuddling her? What if someone else is sliding their hands over her thighs and butt? What if she's screaming someone else's name? I quickly unlock my cell and call Seleste.

I arrive early at what used to be the Coffee House. It's now called Sesame Seed Bakery and Coffee. After ordering coffee and a scone, I find a table in the front near the window. My intent is to hear him out, not punch him out. The door chimes and in steps a shadow of the man I once knew. He's still tall but much thicker. He's dressed in a polo and jeans. He looks nervous as he scans the tables until he meets my eyes. We nod. He heads to the counter to order, then slides into the seat across from me a few minutes later.

"Hello, Kelton."

"Hello, Matt." We would normally shake hands. He didn't offer, and I'm glad. "What is so important that we needed to do this face-to-face?"

"I know you're still upset."

"I'm more than upset. But continue."

"First, I didn't mean to get you involved. I thought for sure that I would be the only person affected. I didn't expect the company to be sold and the employees to get laid off."

"Really?" I tap my fingers on my coffee cup to release some energy. "You devastated the lives of the employees who relied on those jobs to support their families, and you devastated me, my family, and my life." I realize I've raised my voice louder than the discussion warrants. I start again, more quietly this time. "You covered up the theft for seven years with lies."

"When I started, I needed only a little extra money until the baby came."

"You had twin sons with Maggie. There was no baby." I think for a moment. "Was Maggie expecting?"

"Maggie and I are divorced. My sons are sixteen years old."

"What baby then?" I remember Maggie saying she didn't want more children. It was a big discussion at a Christmas party.

"The baby daughter I had with Anasis." He unlocks his cell and shows me a beautiful little girl. Her hair is pulled into two large puffballs, and her smile matches Matt's.

I open and close my mouth, but I don't know what to say. I'm still angry with Matt, regardless of the beautiful little girl. Then I remember the name Anasis from the office. "Anasis the project manager?"

Matt nods. "We became close while working together. She's my soulmate." Matt smiles and flips through a few pictures until he gets to a selfie of him, Anasis, and the toddler. "Our relationship is so different from what I had with my first wife."

I let out a slow breath and stop tapping my fingers. "Why did you need to steal the money from the company?"

"I had to maintain my marriage to Maggie, and Anasis was having health issues while pregnant with Shai."

"You should have divorced Maggie and told me about Anasis."

"I didn't want to upset Tim and Tony with a divorce. I also didn't expect Anasis to get pregnant. She told me that she tried in the past but that she was infertile."

"So stealing and going to prison didn't upset your twin boys, Tim and Tony?"

"Well, yes, it did. I was totally blindsided when Anasis told me she was pregnant and was having the baby by herself. She wanted to end what we had."

"So you stole for her?"

"Of course not. She was making good money and owned a townhouse." He let out a breath. "Shai was born with a heart defect that the doctors thought wouldn't need to be addressed. But after three months, Shai needed surgery. Anasis couldn't work because she was caring for Shai. At first, I reallocated only enough to cover small bills. Then I needed more, but hiding larger amounts became a problem."

"Why didn't you tell me?" I'm not giving Matt any sympathy. My compassion goes to Anasis and Shai.

"I thought if I told you, then you wouldn't have plausible deniability."

"I went to prison for three years with plausible deniability. I would have preferred that you told me about the money and the baby." My voice is getting louder again.

"I know that now."

Matt takes a sip of his coffee. When he puts the cup back on the table, I slam my fist into his nose as hard as I can. Everything seems like it's going in slow motion. The force of the punch pushes his chair back into the wall. Matt's hands fly up, and he kicks the table leg, but I had already stood and grabbed both coffee cups so as not to break anything. An older female employee runs toward me.

"Sir, you will not fight in here."

I felt like a little kid being chastised by my teacher. "We're okay." I put the cups back on the table and take my seat.

"What about him?" The employee gestures toward Matt, who is holding his nose. A little blood is seeping through his fingers. The woman hands some napkins to Matt and points to the restroom.

I settle into my chair and wait for Matt to return, at which point I expected him to leave. Instead, he slides into the seat across from me again.

"You feel better?" Matt asks.

"I would have preferred not to have gone to prison than punch you."

"I'm glad you punched me. I feel so badly about everything."

"I would have preferred that you had asked me for the money."

"I started a carpet cleaning business that's doing really well."

"Why did you need to see me?" I rub the knuckles on my right hand.

"I need a favor," he whispers.

"You need a favor?" I'm incredulous. "I'm thinking about punching you again."

"None of that!" The female employee says while pointing her finger at me.

I put my hands up as if surrendering. "I won't punch anyone again." I look at Matt. "What's the favor?"

"Maggie divorced me after I went to prison. I didn't want to tell my boys about their sister, but Maggie did. I haven't seen or heard from them in quite some time."

"And you want me to do what? You want to get back together with Maggie?"

"No. I'm blissfully happy. I married Anasis, we have two girls. Shai is ten, Elly is eight, and Anasis is pregnant with our last child. I want you to be their godfather."

I shake my head. "Why would you want that?"

"Because you were my best friend before everything fell apart, and I value your friendship." Matt looks apologetic and sincere.

"I should probably think about it, since I'll likely want to punch you every time I see you."

"You'll get over it." Matt chuckles.

"You think?" I miss having someone who truly knows me. I don't have to worry around Matt because he caused the secret that I keep from others.

"Can I introduce you to my family? They're at the park across the street."

"Are you serious?"

"Yes. They're waiting there."

The train ride is faster than I expected. Two hours go quickly when you're listening to a book. I might have fallen asleep before arriving in Newark via the express train. I'm headed to South Orange and will grab an Uber when I arrive at the station.

Seleste was helpful when I called her. She and Weston had visited Pearl a month ago. I was glad to hear Pearl wasn't dating anyone. She and I need to discuss our next steps. All I know is that I won't be happy on the cruise ship anymore unless Pearl decides to join me. I didn't think I would want to settle down with one person again. However, I haven't told Pearl the truth about my past, and I'm concerned about her reaction. How do I tell her that I'm a felon and that I spent three years of my life in prison? I don't want to lose her, but I don't want to keep any secrets from her.

It's 5:20 p.m. when I arrive at her door and ring the bell. I press it again when there's no answer. She must be at the office working late. I put my duffel on the porch bench and take a seat. After a few minutes, I pick up my bag and walk around the side of the house under the carport. I hear 1970s dance music.

I unlatch the gate and head around the back. The music gets louder as I approach. Pearl is dancing around the sunroom singing "Last Dance" by Donna Summer. An orange scarf is tied around her head, creating a large Afro puff with her hair. It reminds me that I haven't had the opportunity to wash her hair yet. She's wearing blue panties with the word *sweetness* running across her cheeks and an oversize blue tank top. Her arms and hands are flying all over the place as she twirls and kicks her legs in the air.

She is the epitome of dancing like no one is watching. She's stunning, and I've missed this show tune–listening picky eater who lights a fire in my heart every time I'm around her.

I put my duffel on the outside chair and lean against the screen door, watching my woman in yellow, my Pearl. Every twirl, leg kick, and gyration makes me smile and happy I'm here. The song ends, and she leans against the kitchen island, breathing hard.

"I'm getting too old to dance like this."

"You'll never be too old."

My voice startles her, and she screams. When she realizes it's me, she runs to the door, where she struggles to unlock it before jumping into my arms. I kiss her like a starving man who's been deprived of food for years. I back her into the sunroom and push the door closed with my foot, all while never breaking our kiss. When we finally stop to take a breath, we're both winded.

"I hope you don't mind me stopping by unannounced," I say after kissing her forehead.

She looks puzzled at first, then says, "How are you going to feel when my guy friend wakes up? He's in my bed."

Seleste told me she wasn't dating anyone. Now I'm here with my Pearl, and she has someone in her bed. I can become very alpha male and mark my territory, or I can leave and tell her we can meet for dinner later this evening. We never talked about being monogamous, and I haven't been. I've been with only two or three women since Pearl, but my heart wasn't in it. There is only one thing I can say. I let out a slow calming breath. "How are you going to feel when I put him out of your house?" I wait for a reaction to cross Pearl's face.

"We never said—"

I put my finger over her lips to stop her. "I know, I know. We need to see each other more often, and we need to be monogamous." I continue to search for Pearl's reaction. "Where's your bedroom? I need to wake him and get him out of here." I walk around Pearl while she tries to hold my arm. I leave the sunroom and step into the kitchen. I ask again, "Where's your bedroom?"

Pearl stops me by putting her hand on my chest. "Are you going to put him out now?"

"Yes. I'm not sharing you. When I grab your sweetness, I don't expect anyone else's hand already there." I'm getting upset every minute I think about this guy pleasing Pearl.

"Are you serious?"

"Very much so. Where is your bedroom?" I attempt to step around her again before she blocks my path.

"No one else is here. I just wanted to know how you would handle another guy in my bed."

I let out a slow breath. I punched Matt earlier, and I'm willing to punch another guy. I can't remember the last time I was jealous. "Can I see your bedroom?"

"You don't believe me?"

I smirk. "Where is your bedroom?" I repeat.

"Second door on the left." Pearl points down the hallway. She's watching me.

I pick her up and toss her over my shoulder, like a fireman. She screams. I pat her bum. "I got something for you." I toss her on the bed. She pushes herself up as she watches me pull my shirt over my head and unbutton my pants. I crawl onto the bed as she strips off her tank and throws it on the floor.

"Your panties say *sweetness*. I want to taste your sweetness." I continue to climb up the bed and pull her panties down her legs. "I can smell your sweetness."

I didn't realize how much I needed to be with Pearl. I spend the next hour kissing, licking, and stroking her senseless. Then I pull her into a cuddle, and we nod off to sleep.

CHAPTER 15

PEARL

Kelton's surprise visit is the perfect gift. I don't usually enjoy surprises, but I'll take one from him any day of the week and twice on Sunday. Kelton brought enough clothes for the weekend. I invite him to stay for a week before flying back to where the ship is docked. He woke me this morning by planting sensuous kisses from my back to my butt. After rolling over, he kissed me and slowly entered me with two fingers while rubbing my sensitive bud. Foreplay didn't last long when I begged him to stroke me until I screamed his name. He was happy to oblige.

I skip visiting the office after Kelton put me back to sleep this morning. I'm glad I set my alarm before nuzzling into my pillow and having him spoon himself around me. I have a meeting scheduled for this afternoon.

I talk with the manager of the fourth Country Crafts store, then follow up with Betty at the third location. The manager at the fourth store seems preoccupied and not very concerned. Good employees are hard to find. His records are fine, and he knows about the inventory loss. Something doesn't feel right with this manager, but I can't put my finger on it. I make a note to thoroughly check the records for this store.

When I arrive to speak with Betty, she's ready to show me around and thanks me for not interrupting the day of the alleged shoplifting incident. She recognizes me from the picture Hazel had sent all the managers. Betty is thorough and very precise with her numbers and her processes. Her store has the lowest inventory loss, though she can't explain why. She just monitors and participates in the inventory stocking process. I thank her for her time and go to the office, where Jaynea is exhausted from being Fred's therapist once again.

When I arrive home that evening, Kelton has cooked, and he looks irresistible. The meal is very appetizing too. I can get comfortable with him living with me. I can get comfortable with him taking care of me and keeping me safe. The following morning, I don't let Kelton gift me with his lovemaking. I have an early day and tell him I'll be home in the afternoon for anything I miss this morning. I leave him in bed after prying my lips off his.

I meet with Fred once again to address his finances. The investors are pushing a lot of money at him for advertising, promotions, and gym upgrades. I want to get a handle on the current finances before additional funds are used carelessly. I remind Fred that if he plans to get a return on his investment, he doesn't need to offer services that don't interest those with memberships. The focus is on the quality, not quantity, of the services offered.

Fred continues to assure me that the money is being used to increase membership and to create two more state-of-the-art facilities that will rival any big-name gym. Of course, with additional members, an increase in profit will also exist for the investors. One of the promotions includes cooking classes and walking classes for the seniors in the community. Many of the classes are offered free of charge through a sponsor. A few of Fred's investors want to give back to the community by sponsoring programs for seniors, youths, single mothers, and athletes who can't afford a membership. Fred has hired six additional back-office workers to monitor and assist with the advertising, promotions, and sponsorships.

The increase in the digital marketing budget seems particularly excessive. The firm selected by Trim and Fit's advisory board never mentioned the amount allocated. I also ask about another line item for cleaning that appears to be extremely large. This is a result of the board's concerns for their health and the health of their family and friends after the COVID-19 pandemic. The company conducts two daily cleanings. One light cleaning midday and a second thorough cleaning after the gym closes, which includes the equipment as well as the floors, walls, and vents, and, if necessary, the ceiling. I document my concerns in a report and present it to Fred.

Now that it's been a few weeks since I submitted my report to Tamie at Happy Home Care, I contact her for any follow-up that will be needed regarding her concerns with the aides. She isn't able to speak with me at the time of my call due to scheduled meetings and won't be available until later. I assume that there were listening ears around and that she couldn't talk in private.

I connect with Tamie a few days after my call and learn that she has found the persons who were involved in the blackmailing scheme and that the matter has been addressed. I'm curious. The identity of the perpetrators is not relevant to my services, but a part of me wants to know. I ask Tamie if she needs anything else from me, but she does not. I'll have Jaynea submit my invoice with net thirty terms. I always follow up after payment with a gift of some type to remind the client that I'm available in the future. It still surprises me that Tamie didn't have Samyl address the issue, unless he was part of the problem.

My evenings at home have been perfect with Kelton's presence. We've been alternating between eating in with him doing the cooking and dining out at one of the many restaurants in walking distance from my home. He holds my hand, opens doors, and pulls me close just because when we're in public. I could enjoy this for the rest of my life.

We've discussed marriage, children, ex-spouses, our goals, future trips together, and him visiting anytime he desires. We have plans to text and FaceTime so that we can determine how we can make this work long term. We've also talked about his potential three godchildren. He didn't tell me why he hadn't seen Matt in such a long time. I believe it's due to a disagreement. That happens. I also have a few people whom I no long speak with or call friends.

I schedule Thursday to help Stephen at the tax office. I ask Kelton to join me to assist with the packing and moving. Kelton welcomes the idea. He makes breakfast for us before we leave.

I think it's only right for me to help after the good working relationship I've established with Stephen and his sister. Mari was a grade ahead of me in school. She was full of dreams and energy. We became friends during band camp. Marching band was very important to me, and I lived for it every Friday night. Mari played the clarinet, and I played the flute. Stephen made sure I always had a ride home when he picked up his sister after the game. We weren't as close after she graduated from high school. We would see each other in the community, as we both remained in the area after college. I didn't have children, and she had one daughter. I never really knew her ex-husband, but according to Stephen, he was nothing to write home about. Love is truly blind, and you cannot help who you give your heart to.

I remember the day Stephen called to tell me about Mari. He attempted to stay calm as he informed me of the situation, but I could hear the sadness in his voice. When he told me Mari was dead, a loud ringing in my ears followed that I couldn't explain. I remember feeling a panic attack starting as I walked to my car. I immediately ended the call with Stephen. I didn't say goodbye or that I'd talk to him later or ask how he was doing. I simply ended the call. Tears flowed. She was here one day and gone the next.

Mari and I had reconnected once they started the tax office and needed small business consulting to make it successful. They wanted to leave the company to their children. Her goal was to create generational wealth. I remember Mari reminding me to strategically plan to leave something for my children. I was married, but I didn't have children at the time. Unfortunately, I never would, and it was always hard to be happy for women who were blessed with them. It was a wound that would open unexpectedly on many occasions.

I greet the Santorini and Hall children and introduce Kelton to them when we arrive at the office. I had told Kelton about the next generation, the children who would inherit the tax office when Stephen passed away, which I hoped was far in the future. I wave at Stephen, who is speaking to the landlord, and introduce myself and Kelton to the other volunteers in the office. We tape up a few boxes and begin packing with everyone else. It's a bittersweet moment but an inevitable one, since Stephen still wants to pass the tax office to the next generation. I thought it would be a sad day, but music and laughter keep everyone energized.

The new office space is perfect. It's half the size of the previous one but has ample room for Stephen to continue doing what he loves until the children decide that working for themselves will be much more lucrative than being an employee. I finish the day exhausted but filled with happiness. Kelton enjoyed himself and says he hasn't worked in an office setting since he sold his tool company many years ago. Stephen and Kelton delighted in discussing tax code and crazy clients, since both had worked as CPAs. I believe Kelton had more fun than he expected when he decided to join me today.

The following day, Jaynea and I work to prepare the Dollar Now franchise manual and next steps. Mia had inquired about speeding up the process. She had presented to a group of future business owners, and they were interested in receiving more information about Dollar Now franchises. Many of the young women had already obtained funding from a special program through Essex County and the Small Business Administration. The twenty-four-month process had become an urgent matter.

Later that evening at a speed networking event for small businesses, I am introduced to a few people who might be perfect candidates for the Dollar Now franchise. I also meet a young woman who is expecting to be a small business owner for Dollar Now very soon. She tells me that she met with Mia Lakes and had placed a $5,000 deposit on one of the first franchises. I don't completely believe her because Dollar Now is not a franchise yet; there are still several things that need to be approved before that can happen. I make a mental note to speak with Mia about not taking money for a franchise until everything is approved through all levels of the process.

The speed networking concept is networking on steroids. There are finger foods and an open bar available before the event begins. Small tables are placed throughout the room to accommodate two people sitting across from each other. Upon arriving, everyone is given an odd or an even number. This evening, the event planner had decided that even numbers would move and that odd numbers would be permanent at the table. I'm number seventeen, so I'll stay at the table.

I don't know which is best, the moving or the permanent placement. Moving means you're sitting for roughly five minutes in a seat that someone else's body has warmed and sometimes didn't smell very fresh. They leave empty food plates or glasses behind as if they have a maid. The permanent person has to deal with the dirty dishes and glasses and the lingering odors. When the bell chimes, the odd-numbered person has two minutes to share their product or service elevator pitch to see if the person needs it or knows someone who might. When the bell chimes again, the even-numbered person does the exact same thing. At the end of the night, people are simply throwing their business cards at you as if the person with the most cards from all the participants will win a large unforgettable prize. But, in essence, most of the cards are useless and are tossed in the trash upon leaving.

The following morning, I present the services of my company at the Rotary Club. Afterward, I meet another person who tells me that her daughter has placed a $10,000 deposit with Dollar Now to purchase a franchise. The woman, who is a bank manager, doesn't remember the owner's name at Dollar Now, but she stopped by the bank to pick up the check and speak with her and her daughter about the franchise opportunity. I am very reluctant to talk about Dollar Now, my relationship with the business, or the fact that it is not a franchise at the present time.

After lunch at the Rotary Club, I call Mia to schedule a time to speak with her, but she is out of town until Wednesday. I make an appointment to meet with Mia upon her return, then head to the office to continue the Dollar Now franchise process.

When I arrive, I'm not surprised to find the front door locked. We keep it that way unless we're expecting a visitor, and because I meet clients in their own environment or office for assessment purposes, no one ever visits. Once inside, I flip through the mail in my inbox and set the little Foxy Brown miniature in the center of Jaynea's desk. This is my way of alerting her that I'm in the office.

I hear Jaynea in the break room. I peer around the doorway to see her dancing to a tune playing from her cell phone. It makes me smile to see her happy at work. So many employers want to quash joy. I've never liked that environment and swore I wouldn't impose the uptightness of most companies on my employees. The microwave dings, and Jaynea stops dancing to get her cup before dropping a tea bag into the hot water. I head to my office and set my things in the chair in front of my desk. I slip out of my sandals, flex my toes, and slide into my chair. I'm exhausted and probably need another vacation. Kelton returned to his cruise ship a few weeks ago, and the visit from Seleste and Weston was a few months ago. I close my eyes and lay my head back. I was immediately lonely the day Kelton left to return to the cruise ship. My home didn't have the same vibe when I would return from work and Kelton was there.

"Good afternoon, boss lady." Jaynea stands in my doorway with her cup in hand, dipping her tea bag up and down, up and down. She told me she likes to dip the bag at least ten to twelve times. I wonder if she's counting as she greets me.

"Hey yourself. What's the tune?" I ask as I start counting the dips.

"It's the new one by Janelle Monáe." She stops dipping the bag. "You look tired, or is that frustration I see in your eyes?" She moves to the empty chair in front of my desk.

I let out a long sigh. "It's frustration. I'm having an ethical dilemma with Mia Lakes from Dollar Now."

"Well, I know you, boss lady. You don't deal with unethical people. If you need anything, call me. I have a one o'clock therapy appointment with Fred from Trim and Fit."

"Thanks. I just might get a cup of your tea. It smells great, and I need to relax before dealing with this issue." I stand and stretch.

"It's in the red tea tin," she calls as she moves down the hallway to her desk.

I take another sip of my tea as I review the list of intellectual property that will be included in the Dollar Now franchises. Because all the intellectual property is currently trademarked and registered, there is no need to worry about those items. It's good that Dollar Now has been around for a while and has expanded to three stores. I finish my tea and close my eyes, knowing I need to address the deposits people are making to Mia to purchase a franchise. I refocus on the file on my desk. I need to complete the franchise disclosure document and draft a financial agreement.

The office line rings. Jaynea is out front, so I don't answer. She buzzes to tell me that Mia Lakes is on line one. It's time to confront Mia. I clear my throat and pick up the phone.

"Hello, Mia. Thanks for calling." I tap my pen on the desk.

"Diana told me you originally scheduled a time to meet at my office when I returned, but then you requested that I call you regarding the franchise process. Is there a problem?"

"Yes. I've encountered a concern that I want to talk to you about." I broach the topic without sounding accusatory. "I'm worried that many of the presentations are giving potential franchisees the belief that you're ready to start selling franchises now. Many aren't aware that the financial disclosure document must be filed and registered with the state before we begin the process."

"Oh, I'm not getting that impression at all when I present." Mia clears her throat, and I hear someone in the background speaking to her quietly. "Sorry, I'm back. Many of the individuals are simply excited."

"I just want to make sure you know that until everything is filed and registered, you cannot accept any funds from anyone or promise them a franchise."

"Of course I know that. It would be wrong of me to accept money without a contract."

She blatantly denies accepting money. Either the people I've spoken with are lying or Mia is. "Okay. I'm currently working on the franchise disclosure document and the franchise agreement. When you return next week, we can meet and review them. I'll have them sent to the office by the end of the week. That will give you time to look them over before our appointment."

"That would be good. If you don't have any other questions or concerns, I need to continue with my previous meeting."

"No, that's it. Have a good day." She ends the call without saying anything else. I want Mia Lakes's business when she begins to franchise because I'll also have an opportunity to be a consultant for each of the franchisees. I could possibly have a guaranteed number of sessions as part of the franchise contract to get new franchisees goal oriented and focused. I'll offer my services for long-term franchisees, and every year new franchisees will begin. It would be perfect, and I'd have the option to travel and interact with the franchisees in their cities, where I could learn their neighborhoods, communities, and competitors. I'll need to call my lawyer friend tomorrow and invite her to lunch. I'm afraid this franchise thing might blow up in my face, and I need to know the legal ramifications of selling franchises before filing and registering.

A knock sounds at my closed office door. "Come in." I expect it to be Jaynea, as we're the only two people here. But much to my surprise it's Kelton, with a bouquet of fresh daisies and a large grin on his face.

"I thought you might need a dinner companion and a fitness guru in bed tonight." His grin has now turned to a smirk on one side.

I stand and almost leap into his arms. He wraps them around me, cocooning me in the safe blanket of his warmth. He kisses me on the head. I smell his woodsy scent and him. I always know everything will be okay when he's around. I try to say something, but because my face is smashed into his chest, it comes out muffled. He unwraps his arms and pulls my head up so that our lips meet. His are soft yet firm as they dominate my mouth, my heart, my mind, and, oh, the warmth forming between my thighs. "I hope you don't mind me visiting unannounced again."

"You're welcome anytime." I place my head on his chest once more. It's been one of those days, and I just got a reprieve from the craziness. "What do you have in mind for dinner?"

"I'm thinking my woman in yellow being naked." He smiles and winks.

"I don't think I can be naked at a restaurant." I pull away long enough to look at him.

"Maybe take-out and we eat at your place?"

"Okay"

"And you being naked?"

From the doorway, Jaynea says, "TMI regarding my boss lady."

I raise my head, and Kelton smiles as he looks at Jaynea. "I came for the flowers. I found a vase and will cut the stems for you. You both get out of here and do your naked thang." Jaynea reaches for the daises that are still in Kelton's hand and motions for us to leave. As I step past her, she whispers, "Is this a booty call? You probably need it."

"I heard that," Kelton says as he takes my bag and my hand and leads me to the door. I'm all smiles. I'm happy he's here with me, even if it's just for one night. I'll find out how long his visit will be after we raise our heart rate, then get a little dinner. Or get dinner, then raise our heart rate.

CHAPTER 16

KELTON

I unpack my duffel while thinking about my surprise visit to Pearl. I didn't plan anything except getting on this cruise ship and traveling after the loss of my freedom and three years of my life. I was so angry with everyone, including myself. I felt abandoned all over again, just like when my mom died and no one was there to love me. Chanel and my children simply moved on without a second thought. Matt was in another part of the prison, and my friends from Tool Depot were angry and bitter because they believed I had something to do with the embezzlement.

I open the balcony door and sit in the chair overlooking the pool. I never thought someone would capture my heart again. Pearl has slowly been pulling me into her life since the very first time I met her at the ice cream truck. There are so many questions to be asked and plans that need to take shape. But there is only one difficult discussion I need to have with Pearl. I'm frightened that I might lose her if I have this conversation with her. I've made amends with Matt and even had dinner with his wife and my potential godchildren. The third and final child will be arriving in approximately two months. It's another girl. I want Pearl to meet Matt and his family, but first I must tell her about my past and that I'll be a felon for the rest of my life.

A knock interrupts my thoughts. I check the peephole and see Richard. I open the door. "Good morning, Richard."

"Hello, mighty traveler. You've been missed around the ship." Richard steps into the stateroom with two cups of coffee. "I brought you some caffeine."

I take a mug and proceed to the balcony. Richard follows and sits.

"What's going on?" I ask.

"Poker night was great. I won the final hand and largest pot of the evening."

"And I missed it." I prefer Pearl to poker night with the guys any day of the week.

"The women were looking for you. We also have some new beauties who arrived a few days ago."

"I'm off the market. You need to find a new wingman."

"Really?" Richard looks puzzled—or constipated. I can't tell.

"Why do you sound so surprised?"

"Why would you give up your bachelorhood? Why would you want someone permanent around to drive you crazy? You've been married before. You know how that can be."

"Yes, I do remember how marriage can be, and I loved it. My wife wanted the divorce, not me. I love the idea of sharing my life with someone who understands me."

"You can date and still have many understand you."

"No, I'm a one-woman type of man. Yeah, I've been with a few lookers on board, but I enjoy having a special one."

"Better you than me. I'll have many any day. So is this special woman going to join you on board, or are you going to join her on land?"

"I'm going to give up the cruise life. It's served its purpose."

"Is this you talking or her?" Richard looks puzzled again.

"I didn't realize it until I got here this morning. I haven't even spoken with her about living in New Jersey."

"New Jersey? Of all places."

"She owns and operates a B2B consulting firm."

"Don't you have enough money so that she doesn't need to work?"

"She works because that's what makes her happy."

"If I decide to settle down again, my woman can't work. I'm too old to deal with that, even if it makes her happy."

"I've enjoyed helping her and networking. She has a nice office in an excellent location, and her assistant is great."

"If you say so. Will I see you at casino night? This discussion is depressing me."

"I'll see you later." I lock the door after Richard leaves.

CHAPTER 17

PEARL

I'm swimming but cannot see the shore. I don't know if I'm going the right way. My legs are starting to cramp, and my arms are getting heavy. I stop to tread water while searching for signs of life. I don't see any birds. There is no one else around. No boats. No nothing. Just me and the ocean. The waves are making me feel like a buoy, and I try to elevate myself every time they move me higher before dropping me. I'm in the middle of the ocean with no one to help me. I'm not going to make it. This is how I'm going to die. Alone and helpless. My head goes underwater, and I try to reach the surface. My limbs are giving out, and I can't swim anymore. What am I fighting for? No one will miss me. No one will mourn my death. I go underwater again, and this time I continue to sink. I scream as I descend farther and farther.

I open my eyes and scream as I begin to hyperventilate. A few minutes later, Seleste runs into my room with a baseball bat in her hands. I woke her with my scream. She's visiting me for a few weeks since Weston is vacationing with his children and other family members in England. She sits on my bed in an attempt to calm me. My pajama shirt is soaked, and sweat is running down my face. Seleste wipes my cheeks with the sheet. I hear her tell me that everything is okay. I'm okay. I don't understanding why she's saying I'm okay when I'm drowning. I can't find my way to safety. Now I'm crying. Seleste pulls me toward her and envelops me in a large bear hug. She rocks me just like the waves were rocking me when I was in the ocean. I eventually stop crying and fall back asleep.

The Country Crafts issue is about to be solved. I tried to rush the process, but sometimes it must be played out in real time. I've kept Hazel abreast as I peeled back each layer of the onion. Inventory tracking was never the problem. Each store maintained and confirmed the inventory that was being ordered. The problem arose from the inventory that was being sold compared to the inventory that was present when manual inventory checks took place. I've used Jaynea as my mystery sleuth in the past when I need additional eyes and ears in a client's case. This one is special and has to be solved quickly and thoroughly. Jaynea can handle this situation. She's like everyone's sister or cousin. It's her superpower and gift.

Jaynea is hired through human resources as a floater to assist with inventory. On her first day, she saw a parent meet with a longtime employee, Buster, in the parking lot. The following day, eight reams of colored paper disappeared from inventory. The parent even paid through the Cash App and listed the items in the note area. Apparently, when Buster stocked items, he never put them all on the shelves. Because the boxes weren't flattened until they were returned to the dock area, Buster would keep one to three of the items in the box, put them in a red plastic bag, and toss them in the dumpster behind the store. Later that evening or in the middle of the night, he would reclaim the bags before the trash was picked up. Because Buster quickly learned the stocking protocols for Country Crafts, the managers rotated him to all the stores. Many items were purchased by a few dishonest parents who didn't understand that buying stolen merchandise was a felony. Buster even used eBay and Amazon to list and sell the stolen products.

Hazel is ecstatic to have the problem solved, but when the police are interviewed by the press, her investors learn about the level of inventory loss. One decides to pull their share, which leaves a financial need for the company. Hazel is grateful that she doesn't have to file for bankruptcy, but losing the investor might force her to close one of the four stores to remain profitable.

The following day I'm working to complete the franchise process when I receive a call from a colleague I'd met at a networking function three years ago. We occasionally have lunch or sit together at continuing education events.

"Good morning, Ashea. How are you doing?"

"Hello, Pearl," she replies, followed by silence.

"Ashea, are you there?" Now I'm concerned. She's not the type of friend I would help to bury a body or show up to check her back in a situation. But she's still a sister, and I won't allow someone to blatantly try to harm her. "Ashea?"

"I'm here. I'm having a problem asking this question without attacking you or your integrity."

"Go ahead and ask. We'll clean it up after." Why would she think I'm doing anything that might be inappropriate or illegal? I'm not dating anyone except Kelton, and I haven't had lunch or dinner with anyone who is not a client. So it can't be a wife angry with me for having a business lunch or dinner with her husband or boyfriend. Or could it? This has happened in the past, so now I intentionally invite wives or girlfriends to join us.

Just last year a wife thought an inappropriate relationship was taking place. She showed up at the restaurant where we were meeting before a networking event. We were having dinner when she approached the table and stood there for a few moments. I didn't know her. The guy stopped eating, and I could tell he was surprised. Apparently, he had been tipping, and she'd been spying on him. I invited her to join us and flagged a waiter for a menu. We had a lovely conversation after her anger subsided. When her husband excused himself, I told her that she's so much more valuable than spying on her husband. If she didn't trust him, then she needed to ask for a divorce. That was after I told her that I was a divorcée who had also experienced infidelity in my marriage. I would never do it to another person and definitely not to another woman. She stayed for dinner and joined us at the networking event. With my help, she started a small business that was once a hobby. The skill of navigating the Medicare process and estate planning is a priceless talent. One wrong checkmark or statement can harm the future assets of the heirs. She had a few business cards and thought the networking process was great. Her husband watched our interaction from a distance. I assisted her in understanding the elevator pitch and critiqued hers before the network event started. I wonder if she's still married.

"I was told you're taking money from people who want to buy Dollar Now franchises. Is that true?"

I'm startled by the question. Have Mia's actions caught up to her? "Why do you think I'm collecting money for Dollar Now?" I haven't received any funds other than the fee for my consulting work.

"My niece heard a presentation about purchasing a franchise. To get on the list, she had to pay two thousand in cash. She did that a few days later, and she hasn't heard anything from anyone."

"Who did she—"

"Don't interrupt me! She paid the money to that Mia woman, and she said that this was the process you created and that the money was being given to you so that she can get on the list."

She stopped speaking. I can tell she's upset and needs answers. "I have nothing to do with receiving money. I am not the owner or an employee of Dollar Now." I pause so that my words sink in. I hear her breathing through the telephone. "Can we meet in person to address this? I have so many questions."

"You know nothing about this?" She sounds confused and irritated.

"I know the CEO is creating a franchise model, but it hasn't been registered with the state yet, and no one should be submitting money to anyone at this time."

"My niece took the last two thousand dollars from her grandmother. She thought she was helping her get on her feet." A muffled sob escapes her. "The money was for her real estate taxes that are due in a few weeks."

"Did she get a receipt? Who told her to pay in cash?" I'm asking these important questions, but Ashea isn't listening. I think the money was for a lot more than just real estate taxes. "Can I speak with your niece? Can she call me?"

"She's in the hospital. She tried to commit suicide when she realized she wasn't going to be able to open her store this month or the next." I hear another muffled sob. "My mother found her this morning. She left a note saying she was sorry."

"Will she be okay?"

"I'm praying. Mom is so upset. You know she raised her after my sister died in the car accident." She sobs again. "I've got to go."

"I need to see any paperwork that you may have for Dollar Now and the franchise she was buying." I know this is not the best time, but I can't stop this rolling boulder unless I know where it's headed. "There might be others who are getting scammed." I didn't want to use that word, but it's appropriate. There is no Dollar Now franchise regardless of how many times Mia Lakes states there is. The franchise does not exist at the present time. I don't like dealing with unethical people and especially unethical business owners. She's exploiting money from those who don't have it so that they can obtain a slot for a nonexistent franchise.

"I'll see what papers I can find and put them in my home mailbox for you to pick up. I'll do that before I leave for the hospital. Mom is there now." She pauses to blow her nose. "Thank you for talking to me. I don't want anyone else to go through something like this."

"I'll call you tomorrow with an update."

"Thanks." We end the call without saying good night or goodbye. Nothing is good about this situation, regardless of the ending. I immediately close my computer and shove it in my bag with a few folders and my wallet. I can't confront Mia without documentation. Why would she pay in cash? Why not leave a digital paper trail that's easy to follow? Why would she think that she'd immediately open a store without a location, merchandise, and training? As part of the training manual, each franchisee must work in one of the main store locations for two weeks or ten days for a total of sixty hours before finalizing the purchase of a franchise. This will allow the person to be exposed to the processes of ordering, inventory maintenance, stocking, sales, staffing, payroll, and several other business aspects that are necessary for a store to exist and become profitable. Many of these new owners would be experiencing these processes for the first time, so it could become overwhelming.

Jaynea is on the telephone with Fred as I leave. She waves to me, and I nod. I'll call her later if I don't return to the office.

As I sit in the Chinese food restaurant waiting area, Fred enters and smiles when he sees me. I'm not ready for him to complain about something that's not going right at Trim and Fit. Especially because he likely just finished talking to Jaynea about the problem. I need to address this Dollar Now situation. I can't believe Ashea's niece did something so drastic.

"How are you doing?" Fred asks as he approaches and shakes my hand.

"I'm doing good." I know it's a lie, but in some situations, it's best to fib rather than tell the truth.

"The gym is doing well. I'm so glad you came on as a consultant. And I must tell you that Jaynea is unbelievable with her advice." He takes the seat next to me.

"I'm glad to hear that. I also believe that she's priceless."

"Do you think if I paid her enough, she might leave you and come to work at Trim and Fit?"

He smiles and winks at me this time. I am not in the mood. "Are you saying you want to hire her away from me?"

"Yeah. Good employees are hard to find."

"I know, but that's not very professional of you." I stand.

"Oh, I was just joking." He chuckles. "Come on, sit down."

I wish my order was ready. I don't want to speak with Fred anymore. He's rubbing me the wrong way today.

"I'm headed to Main Street. I probably need to hire someone to assist with dropping off towels at that location." He rubs his temple. "I might be growing too fast, like you said a while ago."

I don't respond. I had told him that was exactly the case. His investors were adamant that growth is necessary with the new funds. Fred ignored my advice and believed that what the investors said was gospel.

"Would you be going toward Main Street, by chance? I could really use an extra hand today."

I need to get rid of him. "Are you going to order?" I ask, hoping to sidetrack him.

"I am as soon as you volunteer to drop off my towels." He bumps his shoulder into mine. "The bag is in my car."

"Okay, since I'm headed that way." Just then, my order number is called. Fred waits for me and then opens the front door. I walk to my car, and he grabs two large laundry bags from his own, then flings them into my back seat. "Can you call someone to come outside to get the bags so that I don't have to park?"

"Yes, I'll do that right now." I watch as he describes my car during the telephone call. He also stresses that there are two bags and that they're heavy. "Thanks. I owe you one."

As I leave the parking lot, I see Fred get into his own car. He's on his cell. I guess he'll get his Chinese food later.

When I arrive home, I immediately strip and shower. I need the water to purify me and wash all that I encountered today off my body and down the drain. Afterward, I pull on my yoga pants and a sports top with a built-in bra. I head downstairs for food and return with a plate of orange chicken, iced tea, and the papers from Ashea's mailbox, along with my folder for Dollar Now. Why is Mia violating the franchise process? Does she need the funds, and this is her way of getting operating cash? Or is she simply attempting to cheat people out of their money? It wouldn't be the first time I encountered a minority who has embraced the white man's curse of greed. The ability to exploit and legally steal from those in need, those trying to get ahead in life. The white man's curse is strong. America was built on the white man's curse of greed. It started with manipulating and stealing from the Indigenous Americans and then progressed to exploit the Africans. When dealing with nonminorities, this is the first thing to assess. Not everyone white has the curse, but it's prevalent among most. If there are signs of the white man's curse, those people cannot be trusted, regardless of their profession or industry. It's always shameful to encounter minorities who live by this curse. The white man's curse of greed also involves thinking that their needs and their families are more important than any other person.

CHAPTER 18

PEARL

I watch the carousel from the top of the London Eye. I've visited London at least eight times, and I've had the opportunity to ride the London Eye each time. It's one of my favorite places. I've learned how to navigate through the tourists and get in line by purchasing a ticket prior to arriving in London.

I listen to the oohs and aahs from the first-time tourists in the bubble with me. I felt the same way the first time I viewed the city from the height of the London Eye. I was in London for a graduate school class. I wanted to study aboard, and the experience was wonderful, even though it was for only a short time. Now I watch the double-decker buses drive across the Westminster Bridge and over the River Thames. I'll grab the Jubilee Tube to London Bridge and walk back to my hotel. I'm excited and ready for authentic fish and chips tonight. They're always the best in London pubs.

Kelton is meeting me at the hotel. He had a business appointment today. He didn't tell me what it regarded since he retired a few years ago. Our plan is to go to Paris. When Kelton told me that he was in London, I thought it was a perfect opportunity to visit my favorite places, then we could catch the Eurostar to Paris.

I didn't want to leave the mess that I was dealing with in New Jersey, but I didn't want to miss the opportunity to escape from the craziness for a little while. It would be exactly ten days. Ten days of smiling and laughing with Kelton. Every storm cloud disappears when I'm with him. He brings the sun, and the sun makes me smile. I also need his professional eye to review the financials of three of my clients. I've removed the names from the documents for confidentiality. His expertise in accounting is an asset to me in determining whether something shady is going on. In the past, I've never encountered so much theft and money mismanagement with small businesses. It's become the norm, and I don't like it.

"Hello, lovey." Kelton's voice comes from behind me, then I feel a soft kiss on my right temple. I close my eyes and let his voice soak into my psyche. I don't want to admit it to myself or to anyone else, but I miss Kelton when he's not around. A smile spreads across my face as I turn around.

"Hello, sweetheart. I've missed you." I place my arms around his neck and push to my tippy-toes as he leans down and our lips meet. A soft and needed kiss that caresses my lips and my heart. I want more, but I remember that we're in the hotel lobby.

"I've missed you too," he whispers into my ear as he pulls me close.

I push back from Kelton to admire his cool and comfortable outfit. "You look dapper today." Kelton smiles. He's dressed in blue pants and a yellow short-sleeve polo shirt. He doesn't like sandals, but a version of boat shoes is always on his feet. I'm wearing yellow capris and a yellow striped button-down blouse. My hair is pulled up off my neck with a clamp. I love washing my hair every morning and applying leave-in conditioner while styling. Then I twist the length and add a decorative clamp. This allows a few curls to fall around my face. It usually dries within four to five hours in hot weather, but the clamp keeps it in place. Kelton rolls a few of the curls around his finger, then lets them spring back near my cheek.

"I love your hair."

"You love washing my hair."

"Yes, I do. I plan to do just that tomorrow morning in the shower." He smiles deviously.

"Is that all you're going to do in the shower with me tomorrow morning?"

"No. I have other plans, but we will get to washing your hair."

"I also see you're in sunshine yellow today."

"I wanted to match you. My woman in yellow is always beautiful." I smile and squeeze him around the waist. "What's the game plan for the next few days?"

"Why would you think I have a game plan?"

He reaches for my hand and leads me to the restaurant across the street from the hotel. I follow without question. "You always have a game plan. That's why I love you." He kisses me on the cheek as we walk.

I'm speechless because he's just said he loves me. I'm sure it was a slip. I'm also sure he's not been monogamous, but we've never talked about it because we aren't together on a regular basis. The topic keeps popping into my mind, but I'm not ready to address it yet. A few other reasons are the fact he has all those bikini-clad women on the cruise ship who want to get with him and then into his bed. There is a constant rotation of beautiful women on the ship every seven days. I'm sure he sees buying dinner and gifts for the women as a trade-off for sex or as just part of being with someone. Men have attempted to buy my time and justify it. I've never been able to use men in that way. Why would I need a man to buy me clothes, jewelry, or other items in exchange for sex? It's very unfortunate that some women feel this way is much easier than generating their own money by working for it or investing it.

"You already know we're headed to Paris tomorrow afternoon via the Eurostar." Kelton motions to a booth after we enter the restaurant. I place my backpack on the seat and scoot toward the wall. Kelton slides in next to me. He likes to sit next to me instead of across from me. "I have tickets to the Louvre the day you have meetings. Other than that, we'll be eating good food and enjoying each other's companionship to its fullest."

"I agree, and we start tonight by enjoying each other." He winks at me as the waitress arrives.

After ordering traditional fish and chips, Kelton slides his hand into mine and interlaces our fingers. I always feel so wanted when he does that. I'm sure he doesn't know what it does to me. It's always the beginning of foreplay. Every simple touch, caress, and kiss warms my soul. I didn't think another man could capture my heart after my ex-husband ripped it out of my chest and stomped on it; it's been on life support for so many years. I didn't like my I-hate-men years, but I couldn't trust them during that time. But the pain slowly subsided, and my heart healed enough to be removed from life support. "Oh, I also wanted to ask if you could look at some accounting reports. I see the problem, but I can't determine what might be triggering it."

He laughs. "You think I'll be able to identify the cause?"

Our food and drink arrive. I bless our meal and begin eating.

"Yes, once a CPA, always a CPA. I'm sure you can identify things in numbers that most of us can't." I pat his hand.

"We'll see," he says with a smile. "A new client?"

"No, it's a client I've been working with for a while, but now he's expanding faster than necessary. He has new investors who are demanding growth."

"There's nothing wrong with growth as long as you don't do it too quickly. Rapid growth doesn't allow for control of all business aspects. Something always falls through the cracks."

"Yeah, I agree, but I can't get him or his investors to slow the process. I can't do anything about that, but you'll tell me about the numbers."

"No problem. You might have mentioned this client before."

We continue chatting about where he has traveled on the cruise ship. I mention that Seleste and Weston are living together in Aruba and remind him that we probably need to visit them there soon. Afterward, we walk around the neighborhood holding hands and laughing. Even the silence is comfortable with Kelton. We eventually make it back to the hotel, where we hear live jazz on the hotel patio, but the wall surrounding the patio doesn't allow us to see anything. We decide to get a nightcap after we drop off my backpack in the room.

When we return to the patio, the band is playing a jazz song that encircles my heart and squeezes. I can't remember the artist, but I remember the song. It must do the same thing to Kelton because instead of getting a table and sitting as we had planned, he pulls me onto the dance floor. I love to dance, and it's always hard to determine whether a guy likes to as well when you meet him for the first time. I would never end a relationship with a guy because he doesn't dance. My ex-husband was charming but would not dance. Many times we listened to jazz together, and I had the overwhelming desire to dance and be held, but instead we just sat at the table, and I tapped my foot to the beat.

Kelton starts with hand dancing and twirling me as if I'm a queen in a fairy tale. He never lets go of my hand and alternates between them. I smile as we dance. I can't stop smiling. Kelton makes me feel so wanted. Then he changes things up and pulls me to him for a slow waltz. I knew because I took dancing classes with my ex-husband. I purchased a Groupon thinking he might like dancing if he had professional training. He complained at each of the first three classes, then refused to attend the fourth. I showed up by myself and danced the waltz alone. He accused me of trying to change him into the man I really wanted. My dancing has been very limited since that day. I group dance with my girlfriends or cousins when the opportunity is available, such as at birthdays or weddings, but nothing until meeting Kelton.

Kelton finishes the dance by pulling me into a tender embrace. He kisses the top of my head, and I melt into his chest. This is perfection at its best. I think about how many other women he has probably embraced like this, but I force that thought out of my mind and sigh into him again. This is pre-foreplay. We eventually get our nightcap and take it with us to our room. Foreplay ensues, followed by heavenly touches and orgasms throughout the night.

The following morning, we grab a cab and head to Saint Pancras International railway station. I like the idea of last-minute shopping in the mall that's attached to the station—or I should say the railway is attached to an indoor mall. Kelton gets us a few snacks, even though we purchased seats with a meal. Because I'm such a picky eater, I usually have many questions about sauces and gravies that can never be answered when the items are prepackaged. I buy a few pairs of earrings and a summer dress. Kelton finds seats outside the store, then gets coffee and scones for us. We finish our snack and enter the Eurostar station at the appropriate time. The monitor indicates that our train is delayed. An announcement identifies an electrical problem as the cause.

We had selected the 12:25 p.m. departure time because we're in no rush to get to Paris. Worst case, we'll stay another night in London. As long as I can press myself against Kelton when I sleep, I'm good. Cuddling and spooning are my current addictions. I can't get enough of him.

We board the train two hours later and have a pleasant trip. Kelton eats our meals, and we share the wine. I eat another scone that he bought for me. We chat and laugh before we fall asleep holding hands. Kelton repositions me to lean against him as we sleep. We arrive in Paris and take a cab to our hotel.

The meal at the fancy restaurant at the end of Avenue Raymond Poincaré is delicious. We can see the Eiffel Tower as we dine, and our hotel is walking distance between it and the Louvre. That evening I pull out my client paperwork to share with Kelton. I tell him that I've removed the name of the company due to confidentiality but that I need a professional eye to look at the numbers. Kelton had bought two bottles of wine from the restaurant. He opens one and pours me some in our traveling wineglasses that he purchased in Savannah. We move to the balcony as the sun sets. Kelton puts on his glasses and looks over the financials. Every once in a while, he makes a low moaning sound, then flips to the next page. I close my eyes and enjoy the feeling of being in Paris with Kelton. I can definitely get used to this. I've been traveling for quite a few years alone, but it's so much better to be with someone. Someone with whom I can enjoy conversation and laughter. Someone who ignites a spark when he touches my hand, brushes a kiss on my neck or my cheek, wraps his arm around my waist to pull me closer when he feels I'm too far away, and slowly undresses me during a dance. You never know what you're missing until you experience something you can't live without. I believe I'm at the point of acknowledging that I don't want to live without Kelton in my life.

I'm not sure what that looks like or if it's even something he wants. I watch as he reviews the documents, calculating something every once in a while. He looks so sexy in his glasses, I'm getting flushed thinking about rubbing myself against him.

"My original assessment is that money is being posted, but it cannot be from sales because the membership numbers aren't growing. Where is the increase in sales coming from? The investors' money is coming into the business, but it's also being paid out as profit to the same investors." Kelton removes his glasses and looks at me. "How much do you trust this guy?"

"He's just a client. I don't really know him."

"Hmm. You're going to need to ask about the increase in sales."

"Do you think it might be a typo? Maybe a transposed number?"

"Really? What does your gut say?" Kelton asks with force.

"I'm not naive. Clients contact me for help, and I assist them."

Kelton places his glasses on the table along with the financials. He takes a sip of his wine, then scoots his chair closer to me. "I didn't call you naive."

"You insinuated." I don't look at him when I speak.

He scoots a little closer and moves my chin with his finger so that our eyes meet. "I've learned that people will sacrifice anyone's livelihood to protect a lie. I don't want you involved in something that might blow up in your face."

"I know people lie." I shrug.

Kelton pushes my chair back, then turns it toward him before pulling me onto his lap. "If the client can't explain the increase in sales revenue without an increase in membership, I would end the consulting job."

I wrap my arms around his neck. He's providing me with safety and protection as he explains his decision. This is the first time the silence between us has felt intense. He doesn't want to push me to do anything other than ask more questions, but if the answers don't sound logical, then I should terminate my contract with the client. "Okay. I hear you loud and clear."

He smiles and kisses me.

The remainder of the week moves like lighting. We eat, we pleasure each other, and we relax. We lay entwined in the sheets every evening and every morning. We enjoy nonadult days that remove all responsibilities other than to eat what we want, when we want. Sometimes healthy and sometimes not so healthy choices. We relax in the hot tub, and I sunbathe naked on our balcony. We relax on the penthouse patio with others as we watch the sun go down in the evening. We relax with good wine as we cuddle. Each day the sun wakes us, bringing with it a new beginning.

It might be time to decide if we want to go to the next step. The idea keeps popping into my mind, even though I refuse to mention it to Kelton. Would he be interested in leaving the cruise ship and joining me on land? We can continue to travel. I would even do my consulting remotely and limit the number of clients I accept each quarter. I can reposition a few of my finances to ensure there's enough money to continue traveling. Kelton and I never talk about money, and I'm not sure if he needs to adjust any of his finances. He must be well off to live on the cruise ship and never mention needing to work.

Kelton enters the room holding a bottle of wine and some chocolates for me. I love chocolate with red wine. I'm packing my suitcase. I can never understand why my items don't fit into the suitcase in the same way they did at the start of my vacation. I can't be the only person who has this problem. I did buy a few new items but not enough to make me pull out the emergency duffel I carry with me.

Kelton hands me a glass of wine. I accept and clink his glass to celebrate the end of our mini vacation in Paris.

"Can we talk about our relationship?" I'm nervous because I'm not sure how to tell him I want to spend more time with him. If we're monogamous, we can eliminate the condoms. I can't get pregnant, but I don't want to get an STD, since I assume he's sleeping with other women.

Kelton takes a seat and crosses his legs. "Sure. Is there a problem with our relationship?" he asks with curiosity.

"No." I hesitate and then sit on the end of the bed. I look at my toes, then at Kelton. "I want to know if . . ." I pause. I'm asking for something I thought I would never want again. How will this work? Will he move into my home? I panic and quickly change my mind, asking him instead, "When do you connect with your cruise ship?"

"What does that have to do with our relationship?" Kelton looks puzzled.

To redirect his question, I hand him a small gift that I purchased for him. "Don't open it until you get back home. Or to your stateroom." I kiss him on the cheek. "This was a fantastic getaway. It amazes me how just being with you is enough excitement for me."

Kelton takes the gift and smiles. He pulls me onto his lap and nuzzles my neck and my ear, giving me a reason to push my suitcase off the bed.

CHAPTER 19

KELTON

I've been looking forward to the week in Paris with Pearl. I need to complete some banking in London, so we start there. The banking goes very smoothly, and I return to the hotel for dinner with Pearl. We complete the evening with dancing and drinks. The dancing moves to our hotel room, which is our foreplay into much more throughout the night.

The following morning, we head to the train to travel to Paris. Unfortunately, it's delayed due to electrical problems somewhere on the line. After two hours of waiting in the station, we board and travel from London through the English countryside, under the English Channel, and into the French countryside before arriving in Paris. After a light meal and some wine, I pull Pearl into my chest, and we nod off for an hour. It's one of the nicest short trips.

Pearl insists that we stay in the art district but close to the Eiffel Tower. I select an independent hotel that allows us to see the tower from our balcony. Pearl would have been happy with any French balcony, but I think she deserves one where she can watch the lights shining from the Eiffel Tower. I would love to bring her back for the New Year's Eve celebration. It's spectacular.

For dinner, we opt for a restaurant where we can sit with the locals and some tourists in the shadow of the tower. Pearl has been to Paris before, and like so many, she enjoys the magic of the area and the people. Her French is horrible, but mine is much better. After mixing up words a few times when ordering, she decides to use only one or two words to get her point across instead of speaking in complete sentences. When she orders snacks, she holds up the number of fingers and points to what she wants, then says thank you in French. She is beautiful to watch. So independent, determined, and curious about everything.

The day I conducted my banking task, she ventured to the Louvre, where I met her a few hours later. After much back and forth, she agrees to use the translation app on her cell phone if she needs to speak French. I'm more concerned how the French will treat her if she mispronounces a word or mixes one up with something else. The negotiations result in me agreeing to a bubble bath and that we'll have a nonadult day while overlooking the Eiffel Tower doing very adult things the next day.

That evening we walk along the Seine River and hold hands, with the intent of getting a late dinner before returning to our hotel. Cyclists whiz past us in the bike lane, and walkers power by us slow-moving American tourists. I stop to lean against the rail and pull Pearl into my chest. I couldn't be happier at this moment. In the past when things became so content, I would expect a tsunami to occur in my life.

During my marriage, I thought I was happy with my life as a husband and father of two great children until it blew up in my face. I'm not sure if I should be happy that Matt forced me to move out of an uncomfortable relationship with my wife. Like I said, I thought I was happy. I thought she was happy. I tried to provide everything my family needed and some of what they wanted. Chanel and I were planning to be empty nesters in about five years. Instead, I went to prison, the family dynamics shifted, and I was dismissed from my family's life.

"What are you thinking about?" Pearl asks curiously.

"Having you close to me." I kiss the top of her head.

"It looked like you zoned out. If you ever want to talk about anything, I'm always here."

"I know you are, my lovey. I guess we should stop at the restaurant at the traffic light for dinner." I point to the place across the street.

"Sounds good to me. Are you going to let me order in French?"

"You're going to tell me what you have a taste for, and I'll make sure you get a meal without any gravies, sauces, cheeses, or condiments."

"You're so good to me."

We continue walking arm in arm toward the restaurant. Afterward, we return to the hotel. It amazes me that at my age, my libido seems to be in overdrive when I'm near Pearl. I've been previously concerned about needing medication for my sexual activities— Richard even shared with me the name of the doctor who writes him a prescription and where he gets his supply—but not with Pearl.

The week progresses with astonishing speed. On our last day, Pearl asks to discuss our relationship. I also want to talk about things between us becoming more permanent. We text, chat, or FaceTime at least once a day if we're not in the same city. I want to take this to a more permanent place, but I'm so frightened she'll leave after learning about my prison stint. Pearl changes her mind when I repeat the *relationship* word. Instead, she pulls out a small box from her suitcase and gives it to me. She asks that I wait to open it until I return to the ship.

We kiss goodbye at the airport. I'm headed to Fort Lauderdale, with a layover in Charlotte. Pearl is traveling to Newark on a nonstop flight. Our relationship will go online once again until the next time our paths physically cross.

When I arrive back on the ship, I see Richard holding court near the upper swimming pool. The women are jockeying for position next to him as he judges who has the softest, smoothest legs. I watch him and wonder why he doesn't feel a need to settle down with one woman. We all have our reasons, and many times the hurt we've encountered forces us to hide from real intimacy.

CHAPTER 20

I roll over in bed and check my watch to see my sleep score. Last night I earned a perfect 100. I'm glad to be in my own bed, but I wish Kelton was here with me. We left Paris yesterday. I returned to New Jersey, and Kelton headed to Fort Lauderdale.

I stretch, then touch my bonnet before pulling it off my head and stuffing it in my pillowcase. I'm ready to start the morning. I jump into the shower, and before I know it, I'm in my office drinking coffee at my desk. Jaynea has not arrived yet. I'm early so that I can get a head start on the activities that need my attention. I've already spoken with Mia and have spent the last three weeks documenting everything in her file. I've also included some notes about others who have issued money to purchase a franchise for Dollar Now even though there is no official franchise at the present time. I need to schedule a meeting with Mia regarding the operations manual. I reviewed the manual last week, and it looks great. She's captured the different processes to make the franchisee steps flawless. I made a few notes regarding clarifying some of the terminology. This franchise contract with Dollar Now should be very lucrative for my bottom line. I could possibly have Dollar Now as my only client, along with the franchisees. This will allow me to travel with Kelton or settle in Aruba with Seleste and Weston.

"Hello!" Jaynea has arrived.

I stand and head to her desk. "Good morning," I say with a smile.

"You look radiant. There must have been some good lovin' going on in Paris." Jaynea wiggles her eyebrows.

"A woman never kisses and tells." A smile is still on my face, and I can't help it. The muscles just won't relax.

Jaynea picks up the decorative box on her desk. "What's this?" she asks and does a shimmy.

"A little something to say thank you for holding down the fort while I ran away with Kelton." I sit down next to her desk.

Jaynea slides into her chair and slowly lifts the top of the two-inch by two-inch box. "Oh my goodness." She holds up the earrings. "They're beautiful!"

"They spoke to me as I walked by them in the store. I'm glad you like them. I also assumed you'd have something to match the color."

"Yes. Yes, I do!" She gets up, and I stand to give her a hug. "Why are you here so early?"

"I wanted to review the mail and write a few summaries before I meet with clients this week." I walk to the hallway. "I'll let you get situated. We should have a staff meeting after you get your coffee."

"Sure. Give me ten minutes."

"Okay."

"Pearl, I also wanted to tell you that I believe someone has been watching the office."

I turn around. "Someone is watching the office? Did you recognize the person?" It wouldn't be an ex-boyfriend because my ex-boyfriends are slim and none. And I'm positive it wouldn't be my ex-husband. Unless he realized what he gave up when he traded me in for a thinner, firmer, perkier woman.

"No. I thought maybe it was an ex-boyfriend of yours," Jaynea says.

"Ha, I doubt that. I'm thinking you're the big-time dater. Are you sure it's not one of your ex-boyfriends who wants you back?" I ask.

"No. My ex-boyfriends know better."

"Keep the front door locked and watch your back when you leave the office. Also make sure no one is following you when you go home, and I'll do the same."

"What is this world coming to? We can't even work and be safe." Jaynea heads back to her desk to get a legal tablet. "I'll be in your office in a few minutes."

The meeting is very productive. Once this Dollar Now franchise is active, I might assign Jaynea permanently to it and hire someone else for the office tasks. As I reorganize my folders in my briefcase, my cell alerts me to an incoming text from Mr. Paris.

Kelton: Hello, lovey. I'm missing you. I should have asked you to join me in Fort Lauderdale. We're headed to Saint Thomas, one of your favorite ports.

Pearl: I'm missing you too. I should have asked if I could join you, then I would be headed to Saint Thomas.

Kelton: Would you mind if I visited you in a few weeks?

Pearl: I would absolutely love to have you visit!

Kelton: Have an amazing day. Love you!

Pearl: You're using love.

Kelton: I said it the other day.

Pearl: I believe I'm falling in love with you too.

Kelton: I'm glad, because I would hate to tell any other guy that you're not available.

Pearl: Would you do that?

Kelton: Yes, I would, because you're already spoken for. By me. Love you!

Pearl: Love you too!

Jaynea leaves for lunch and to swing by Trim and Fit to drop off mail that was delivered to Pearl Consultants by accident. I think about Jaynea describing the guy as creepy looking, standing between the cars in the parking lot and taking pictures of the office. I'm also torn between calling the police or confronting the guy myself. I'm not a fan of the police because they always appear irritated and annoyed when interacting with the minority community. I'm working in my office when I hear her return.

"Pearl!" Jaynea calls.

I stop what I'm doing and run up the hallway. "What's wrong?"

"We might want to contact the cops."

My eyes follow where Jaynea is pointing out the front window. "Is that the same guy from the other day you mentioned?"

"No, it's a different one, but when I left, there was another guy standing near the cars by that bush over there. Now there's a new one taking pictures with his cell."

"Get away from the windows." I move to Jaynea's desk and pick up the receiver to dial 911. Before I can complete the call, a loud pounding on the front door startles us. "I'll see who it is. You move to the coffee area. If something happens to me, call 911 on your cell and hide."

Jaynea nods and runs down the hallway, peeking around the corner.

I go to the front door to find officers in black gear standing on the other side. Now I'm scared.

"Open the door. We have a warrant," the large man calls through the glass. I'm frozen in fear. My hand is shaking as I unlock the door. A few officers rush in and push me against the wall, asking as they go where the other employee is. Jaynea hears the ruckus and steps into the hallway with her hands in the air.

Jaynea babbles something, but everything is incoherent to me right now. I finally hear Jaynea admitting to purchasing bootleg movies from a guy last week at the gas station. I don't think ten officers would show up for bootleg movies. I'm being handcuffed. I'm numb and don't understand what's going on. Jaynea screams as they handcuff her too. I believe she also says she's been buying and reselling knockoff designer clothes and bags online. I still don't think the officers are here because of these activities, unless she's trying to pass off the merchandise as genuine.

An officer is talking to me and waving a piece of paper in my face. I don't understand what he's saying. I can't reach for the paper because my hands are cuffed behind my back. I'm so confused, and now I've got to pee. My heart is beating, and my head is beginning to hurt. I wonder what's going on as I'm escorted to a police car.

A few hours later, I'm led toward the booking desk. A gentleman in a suit is standing on the other side of the glass, staring at me. I don't know who he is. I told the officers I wanted an attorney. I wasn't going to tell them anything. I've seen enough shows that reinforce the buttoning of my lips.

I was a faithful follower of *Homicide: Life on the Street* with Andre Braugher. He would break people in the box. They would lie, deny, and cry, but he would have them wound up. Before you knew it, the person would be admitting to the crime and explaining how they did it. I was also a fan of *Law & Order*. Dun-dun. I learned to never say anything. Simply lawyer up.

"Pearl Jermaine?" the well-dressed man asks as I step through the door with the officer.

"Yes." I know I look horrible. I'm sure I have tear stains on my face. I tripped and fell as I entered the station because I was confused about which officer to follow. With my hands cuffed behind my back, my balance was off. And, while in the cell, I tried to pee quickly without sitting on the seat and peed on my ankle. I tried to wipe it away, but once the smell is on you, you need to thoroughly wash. There was no privacy either, and I was embarrassed.

"I've been hired as your attorney."

"Who called you? Who hired you?"

He extends his hand. I'm sure mine has traces of urine on it. There was no soap to wash my hands after my accident. I wipe my hand on my thigh, and we shake.

"I've filed the necessary paperwork to get you released. I'll drop you off at home. You're not permitted to leave the state."

I want to cry. I'm a very grown woman, and I just want to cry. I know it won't make anything better, but I need to cry. "Everything is back at my office. Including my purse and my house keys."

The gentleman leads me by the elbow toward the front door of the police station. "My name is Jester Jackson. I'm a friend of Jaynea's."

"Is she all right? Did you get her out?"

"Yes, she's fine. A little shaken, which is to be expected."

We walk toward a black BMW. I smell like pee, and he hasn't said anything. I haven't even talked about paying him. "I took the liberty of stopping by your office to collect your purse and lock up. There was an officer waiting for someone to arrive before leaving your office unattended."

"Can we go back so that I can confirm everything is in order?" I slide into the car as he holds the door. I don't want him to feel that I don't trust him, but I have confidential papers that must be secure.

He gets into the driver's seat. "You're worried about confidential files?"

I hold my purse strap as if it's a lifeline. "Yes."

"I'm sure they took the documents you're probably speaking about, but we can still stop."

A few minutes later, we pull into the parking lot. I prepare to leave the car after locating my keys in my purse. Jester pats my hand, and I look up at him.

"For tonight, it's best to confirm only that the front door is locked. Tomorrow when we meet, you can deal with the office inside."

Jester doesn't move. I'm baffled by his request. "Why can't I go inside? What did they do?" He doesn't answer. "Okay," I say quietly.

He slides out of the car, walks to the door, and pulls on it. It's locked. I should be relieved, but I'm not. I'm so confused and embarrassed. He drops me off at my home with a bag of Chinese food. I'm still a little shaky. Jester will be at my office at eleven tomorrow morning. During the drive home, Jester said I can still consult, but he suggested I might want to wrap up my current clients and not accept any new ones until this blows over. I think this is all an error. Maybe a case of mistaken identity. I saw a movie about a woman who was mistaken for someone else and had to deal with legal trauma because of it.

The following morning, I arrive at the office at ten thirty. I'm horrified to see that my two desktop computers and my laptop are gone. My file cabinets are open, and files have been removed. They even took or drank all of the K-Cups and most of the snacks that were in the coffee cabinet. Were my coffee and snacks going to be used as evidence against me? My desk drawers are open and have been rifled through. Some of my pictures are askew on the wall. I guess they thought I was hiding a safe behind them.

Jaynea arrives, and her shocked expression quickly turns to anger.

"I've never experienced anything like this. I've seen it on television, and last year they raided a friend's barbershop, then realized the alleged 'bomb chemical'"—she makes air quotes with her fingers—"was actually a balm for natural hair. It was shameful how they went through everything and destroyed his shop. He sued for seventy-five thousand in damages to the walls, chairs, equipment, and supplies."

"Good morning, ladies," Jester says as he enters the office. "I thought this place might look like a battleground." He glances at the file cabinets and desks.

"Will they give me my files back? I have a few pending clients along with active ones who are not Dollar Now or Trim and Fit." I sit in a chair near Jaynea's desk. I'm trying to hold back tears by blinking. When I read the warrant and the charges against me yesterday evening after my very long shower and while sitting on my bed with a bottle of wine, I realized that these two clients' practices have blown up in my face.

"I don't want to go to jail," Jaynea says angrily.

"Can we sit in the conference room and discuss the charges?" Jester asks.

I lock the front door and attempt to straighten the small waiting area near Jaynea's desk.

"I need coffee," Jaynea says.

"What I really need is a strong drink, but caffeine will do for now."

In the conference room, I find a few boxes on the table, along with some supplies. Printer manuals and HR policies have been pushed to one side of the large table. On the other side are crumbs, as if people ate here and failed to clean up behind themselves. I quickly straighten the papers and place everything in the empty box. I'll sort the items later. I clean the table with a Clorox wipe and push the chairs under it.

"I've never encountered anything like this before." I sit next to Jester. "Jaynea will be in shortly." Just then, Jaynea enters with a carafe of coffee, mugs, and creamer. "I'm glad you keep a hidden stash of K-cups."

The three-hour conversation is intense. Jester leaves to speak with someone about getting the charges dropped against Jaynea and will be in touch. I didn't realize she had been delivering packages that were sent to our office for Trim and Fit. She thought she was being nice by bringing the deliveries to Fred at the gym. Apparently, Fred would call Jaynea when the boxes were to arrive. The packages contained money. I also didn't know that the few boxes I dropped off at the gym were full of money. I've told Jester that I will take full responsibility and don't want Jaynea involved in any of this craziness.

I'm charged with participating in money laundering for Trim and Fit with the delivery of the bags that Fred claimed were clean towels. I'm also charged with embezzlement from Dollar Now. Mia Lakes told the officers that I instructed her to accept money prior to creating the franchise. She also stated I've accepted $50,000 from people to get on the franchise list. Jester will follow the paper trail, which should lead to the money.

I'm overwhelmed by the entire situation. I would never participate in a money laundering scheme or take any money I didn't earn. Jaynea has a headache after the meeting. I tell her to go home and take a sick day.

I stay and clean up the mess that was created by the officers. I don't even know which officers. Everyone was dressed in black and carrying guns. I definitely wouldn't be good trying to identify someone in a lineup. After a few hours, I have the office organized, but I don't have the heart to call anyone or do anything else. Where do I start?

CHAPTER 21

KELTON

I look at the moonlight cascading over the large chair and across the Persian rug. Sleep is gaining, and my eyelids are getting heavy. It's been a good day, and I don't have a worry in the world. The sheets smell like magnolia blossoms. A sound from downstairs wakes me. I roll over and look at the ceiling while straining to hear the noise again. There it is, like muffled talking. Then a large bang, as if someone has rammed into the front door with a car. I jump to my feet and put on my house shoes. The voices are coming up the main staircase. I slide down the hallway and hide in the shadows as I head to the back stairwell. The objective is to get out the back door and run like my life depends on it. I should have never agreed to help Pearl determine what was going on with the health club. I swore I would never get into another situation where I did not have full control. I spent three years in prison because my COO decided to embezzle company funds. I was totally blindsided. I still remember the day the CFO found an error in our finances and initiated a deeper dive into some of the expenses with his team of accountants. I thought it was probably just a bookkeeping error or a number entered incorrectly into our accounting software. Technology has improved the process of locating and correcting typographical mistakes. After a few weeks and many records of proof, the CFO reported that the COO and two other accountants had embezzled $2.7 million over the past six years. I was shocked and dumbfounded. Eventually it was discovered the CFO and the COO, Matt my former friend, were pocketing money for personal use. How could I have missed such a large gap in the company's finances?

I slip down the back stairwell to the door. I open it slowly in the hope that no one hears me. It surprises me that the alarm didn't go off when the officers entered the house. I always set the security alarm before going to bed every night. What if the alarm chimes when I open the back door? It will alert everyone that someone is leaving. I twist the knob and gently pull the door while praying no chime will sound. Nothing happens, and I sprint as fast as I can across the backyard and to the fence. My legs are getting heavy and tired, and my breathing is ragged. I pump my arms as if I'm in the last leg of a marathon and the finish line is the fence.

I wake in a cold sweat. It was only a dream. I move my legs to the side of the bed and place my head in my hands. I'm in my stateroom, my suite. I'm breathing hard, as if I was actually running toward the fence. It was so real.

It feels like a repeat of the day I was arrested for the embezzlement charges. The task force broke down my house door, yelling and putting handcuffs on everyone, including my children who were asleep in their beds until the noise startled them, and they ran to the hallway. The officers threw them to the floor and handcuffed them. My daughter was crying and screaming for help. I can still hear her screeches of terror as if we were in a horror film, and the monster had found us. My son wrestled with the officers in fear of his life. My wife put her hands up, and she went to her knees not knowing what was going on. How could a law-abiding person get caught in such a situation through no fault of their own? *It's the company you keep*, my lawyer said. But how do you know the history of people you interact with? Our only saving grace was the fact that we are of European descent or what they classify in America as white. People only identify me as a person of color when I spend time in the sun and my light skin becomes a beautiful brown like my mother's complexion. At least being white would guarantee that I would not be shot because the officers are fearful of their own shadow or that my wife and daughter would not be stripped of their clothing and made to stand naked for hours. A tactic slavers used to control slaves in the US. A tactic uncivilized police departments use to humiliate minority populations.

I remember when Pearl told me she became fearful and horrified when she learned about officers breaking down the door of Breonna Taylor's apartment where she lived with her boyfriend. The officers justified the blatant killing because her boyfriend had attempted to protect them. In America white police and white judges believe in terrorist tactics used by slave patrols in which killing and humiliation are acceptable. Society and police unions confirm the practice is not biased or racist.

The inhumane actions and justifications first came from the person who requested the no-knock warrant with false information, then from the judge who agreed with the false information, and finally from the officers who shot at everything that moved. Then the cowardly officer who killed her. Breonna was penalized for not being of European descent and for having a boyfriend who attempted to protect her and himself. It's the company you keep. Why should she suffer for her ex-boyfriend's actions of sometimes getting mail delivered to her apartment? The officers took her life and never batted an eye at the offense. It was a cowardly approach from all parties. We can only hope that each person's cowardly actions will one day allow them to experience the same. Making their family relive the anguish and never find peace.

I was once told the pain will ease in time. But it's not true. It's a total lie. The pain never eases. Unfortunately, we learn to live with the pain. We learn to adapt. We learn that God does put more on a person than they can handle. But sometimes those people never recover from the brokenness that occurred.

I pick up my cell and stare at it for a moment. I've been avoiding Pearl's calls for the past week. The last time I spoke with her, she told me about the embezzlement and money laundering charges. She was scared. I couldn't tell her that I was also afraid for her because I had been set up before. I lost everything I valued. The company I built and the family my wife and I created. My children were my pride and joy, and I wanted them to excel beyond what I was able to accomplish in life. Now my daughter and son won't even accept my calls. They were upset about not being able to go to the college of their choice. They had to attend state colleges and use financial assistance. My ex-wife filed for divorce when the house and all our assets were frozen. It was nice of her to visit me in prison to tell me that I was an incompetent and useless husband and father. I swore I would never get caught in another situation like that again in this lifetime. I remember my ex-wife's words: "I've never known anyone so stupid to get charged with embezzlement and not actually embezzle a penny." I press the button on my cell, and it begins to ring.

"Hello," Pearl answers.

"Hello. How are you?"

"I didn't know what happened to you. I've left a few messages," Pearl says with concern in her voice.

"It might have been bad cell access." That was the best lie I could come up with. "How are you doing?"

"I can't sleep, and I can't figure out what happened. I keep looking over the numbers and trying to piece everything together. I can't afford to hire a forensic accountant. It's a puzzle that's missing a lot of pieces," she blurts out in a rush.

I say nothing while I listen to her speak in confusion and fear. I take a deep breath and let it out slowly. "I know you're upset, and I'm sorry I couldn't help you," I squeak out.

"I thought you had ghosted me because you haven't answered any of my calls."

I can hear the panic in her voice. I'm sure she's been crying. I really want to be there to wipe away her tears. "I'm sorry I haven't been available, but I've met someone."

Pearl's voice sounds garbled. She repeats my words slowly. "You met someone."

"Yes, someone special to share my life." This is like a Band-Aid. I just need to rip it off and move on.

"Oh." She's silent. I can feel the hurt in that single word. I can feel her disappointment. I just want to wrap her in my arms and never let her go. The silence is unbearable. She clears her throat. I'm sure she's wiping tears from her eyes. "I wish you the very best with your new friend. Your special someone." She ends the call.

I had to sever our relationship. I've completely fallen in love with Pearl, but I also thought my ex-wife totally loved me until she filed for divorce. I don't want the courts to know I've seen any of the financials. I never want my name plastered across the paper again. I don't want to give anyone a reason to pull me back into something that I did not create and cannot control. Nor do I want to sit by until Pearl is placed in jail. I promised when I left prison that I would never go back for anyone. I'm not even sure whether I, as a felon, can visit her in jail. A knock sounds on my stateroom door. I raise my head and plaster a smile on my face. Richard opens the door and pokes his head inside.

"I know you've been down in the dumps, but I found us a few women who are eager to mambo the night away with us."

"Sounds great." I keep the smile on my face as I approach Richard.

"I guess you finally broke up with Pearl?" he asks as we walk to the elevator.

"Yes, I did."

Richard presses the down button. "I know you liked her, but only an idiot would get caught in an embezzlement web." Richard looks at me, then punches me lightly on my upper arm. "And you never know. She might have actually taken the money. She could have been misleading you, simply trying to get you to take the fall."

"Yeah, I'm sure you're right." I have completely betrayed Pearl.

We step off the elevator, and Richard waves at the two women at the bar. "You definitely don't want your woman sitting in jail for the next few years. It would be so embarrassing to tell people your girlfriend is in prison." Richard laughs and points. "Yours is the one in fringes. I think she might be too thin to get them moving like Tina Turner, but tell me if she can. Then I'll spend time with her tomorrow night." Richard laughs again as we approach the two women.

I say nothing as Richard laughs about the situation with Pearl. That is why I never tell anyone about my stint in prison. I can still hear Matt, my COO, say that I got only three years in prison. That's supposed to be my silver lining moment, having only three years of my life stripped away from me. I guess he forgot I lost my respect, my company, my wife, and my children along with all my assets, except for a few that I had in a retirement vehicle no one knew anything about. Thank goodness for trusts. I would trade my entire hidden retirement trust for a loving wife and to have my children in my life.

The women are excited to dance, dine, and drink. I still feel badly about lying to Pearl when all I want is to have her in my life. The woman with fringes rubs circles on my thigh under the table throughout the meal. After dinner, her fingers walk up my leg and closer to my groin. I look at her with a fake smile. She doesn't notice it's phony, and she probably doesn't care. She finally asks if we can leave and go to her room. I don't decline her offer in the hope that the distraction will stop the pain in my heart.

I'm sitting on my balcony enjoying a cup of coffee. I'm glad I didn't bring the fringes woman back to my suite. When a woman's thighs are so thin with a gap, she's not going to be good in bed. I guess it's like a man's ability to dance or the size of his hands or feet.

She tried to make the fringes move when she was on the dance floor yesterday evening. The dress was red and spandex. It would have hugged her in all the right places, except I believe she forgot to put the right places inside the dress. As we danced to an upbeat song, she looked like a praying mantis. Her legs would go from pigeon-toed to slue-footed. At one time I thought she was having a medical episode. Her legs were planted, but she was shaking and gyrating her hips and shoulders as if she was going to regurgitate her dinner. I knew I was probably wasting my time before I agreed to leave for her stateroom that she was sharing with her friend. The attempted lap dance was more of a bony dance. The entire experience was definitely an effort for her and for me to watch. A woman needs a little extra padding on her body in the right places. My mind wandered.

Of course, she asked about my net worth while seductively removing her dress. This is the reason I got that vasectomy a few weeks before I met Pearl in London. It amazed me that the entire procedure only took thirty minutes, and I'll never worry about creating an unplanned child again. I won't be surprised if she contacts me in a few months about being pregnant. She insisted on using her own condoms. There are two things I refuse to tell anyone, especially women. First is my net worth and where I have my money, and second is that I had a vasectomy. I will go to my grave with that information.

CHAPTER 22

PEARL

The words keep ringing in my ears. "I've met someone." I didn't think I'd heard him correctly. I wanted to ask him to repeat it, but I knew that his statement had registered in my head. "I've met someone." I thought the situation with the embezzlement charges and the money laundering was overwhelming enough to break me, but I knew I had Kelton's support and that he would be my brick wall in this mess. I thought I wasn't alone until last night. Until I heard those words. More tears roll down my face. I can't stop them. I curl into a ball on my bed and pull the covers over me. My head hurts, and it feels like my bonnet is squeezing it even tighter.

"You'll never make it without me," my ex-husband had told me. We'd been married eight years, and I thought it was perfect. I admit, it took a little time for me to get into a routine of married life because it's different from dating life. When you're dating, you don't take into consideration doctor appointments, dental appointments, laundry, cleaning, car repairs and breakdowns, mammograms, Pap smears, annual physicals, eye appointments, caring for your parents, caring for his parents, family illnesses and deaths, and how everything affects you mentally and physically. And then there are the finances.

Even if you go through marriage counseling prior to the wedding, it doesn't prepare you for real life. It's like when an elderly family member is diagnosed with an illness—you know in your heart that they'll never be the same. The doctors can prolong the inevitable, but that person is going to die. Everyone knows it. Even the person knows their time on this earth is coming to an end, but does anyone acknowledge that fact? You prepare for them to get better. They go through radiation or chemo, and everyone expects a good outcome. Some may even be told that their cancer is in remission. But when the person finally dies, which can be in three months or less or three years or more, everyone is so shocked that they didn't live longer. In many cases, the person wants to go. They want to end the pain as well as the poking and prodding that goes along with medical treatments. It's like marriage. You attempt to transition from dating life to married life by juggling and merging the day-to-day stuff into a marriage that will result in happily ever after. I waited until I was thirty years old to get married. I thought getting through the party/adventurous twenties would ensure a happy future.

I became my grandmother's caregiver when I was nineteen because my mom didn't have the flexibility at her job to take time off. My grandmother was always there for me throughout my childhood. When I needed advice, she was the first person I called, not my mother. When my grandmother needed me, I dropped out of college to care for her. I will never regret a day of taking her to doctor visits, cooking her meals, cleaning her house, scheduling her appointments, and bathing her each and every day. I had the opportunity to be washed in her wisdom. The wisdom that comes only from someone who has survived a lot. I was grateful when she passed and that she was no longer suffering from Alzheimer's disease. It was heartbreaking. So many give up and simply put their family member into a facility to save themselves from seeing the daily decline. My grandmother's home was the facility, and I was her home health aide and sometimes her nurse and doctor. She passed away a few weeks after my twenty-first birthday. Happy birthday to me.

I made sure I had enough money to enroll in the next semester to complete my college education. My grandmother stated in a letter she had written to me before Alzheimer's took her mind that I had sacrificed enough and that she left me some money to cover a semester. I didn't tell my mom that I was taking a few classes each of the two years I cared for my grams. I enrolled part-time and thought I would stay in Gram's home until I finished my associate's degree in management. I always saw myself running a small boutique. I would become a small business owner. My dad thought I would be a big-time CEO one day. I'm sorry that he died from a heart attack when I was fifteen and never saw me run my own business.

I finished my associate's degree and then started on the next step to complete my bachelor's degree in business administration. Unfortunately, I learned from the county that Gram's house was going to be auctioned due to unpaid taxes. When I asked my mom about it, she wasn't surprised. She said she had tried her best with Gram's life insurance, but there wasn't enough to continue covering the expenses, and I needed to find another place. At the time, her new boyfriend was not interested in anyone sleeping on her couch, since he was paying her rent.

Luckily, Mom was able to sell Gram's home to a real estate investor who paid cash. However, most of the proceeds were used to clear the house title and to cover a few hospital bills. I believe Mom received $10,000 afterward. There were outstanding liens for repairs, a home equity loan that I don't think Gram even knew about, medical bill liens, and of course the tax liens. Gram told me in a letter given to me by her attorney that she made sure to leave my mom and me something to build on. The house that she and Grandpa paid off was to be our legacy of homeownership, and she wanted us to build on that legacy. I never shared with my mom what Gram told me about the house. I don't think Mom really cared. She gave me $1,000 and told me it was from Gram. I packed everything I owned in my car and put a few pieces of furniture that I wanted in a friend's basement for a few weeks until I could find something affordable. It took me a few years to get on my feet, but I scraped and sacrificed until I was able to return to my goal of earning a bachelor's degree.

I was eligible for grants and obtained a scholarship to complete my studies until my heart fell in love and my mind followed. I saw Andrew in the supermarket. My heart skipped a beat. I couldn't explain it. We spoke as we waited in the checkout line. He asked for my telephone number, and I gave it to him. He was an electrician. I was twenty-eight, and he was thirty-three. We spoke every night and never left each other's side on the weekends. When he popped the question, I immediately jumped at the opportunity to build a life with him.

You never see heartbreak coming until it hits you like a Mack truck going 110 mph. "I've met someone," my husband had said. We had been married for eight years. How do you meet someone when you're already married? Why are you looking? What happened to your commitment to me?

During our marriage, I dropped out of college once again because he would be unemployed during the winter months since he liked working on new home builds. You can't wire a new home when they don't build them in the winter. I lost my grants and scholarships because he made too much money for me to qualify, even though his money was not being used to pay for my college tuition. The college didn't care. I was back to paying for every credit out of pocket. I didn't know I would lose those state grants and scholarships if I married. It was already sad enough that I had given up my dream of becoming a small business owner for him. I just wanted my bachelor's degree so that I could head directly into corporate America. I lost my way and my identity because of loving him, then that Mack truck hit me and left me battered and bruised.

I shut down. Nothing made sense. I started doing temporary work after I moved out of our apartment. That was at his request because I couldn't afford the rent on my salary. I didn't argue or cry. I was just numb. I sacrificed so much during our marriage, and he sacrificed nothing. While moving the last box into my car, I asked him why he felt he needed to find someone else. He told me that I refused to give him a child until I finished college. He didn't need a college-educated wife because it was a waste of money. He also said my ambitions were the reason I couldn't carry a child full-term. "Wives are just going to quit their jobs and stay home after they have their first child. Why waste the money on educating women?"

At that moment I realized that he did not want me to be independent. His words of support while we were dating ended after I said *I do*. He knew that if I had a college education and a skill, I could not be controlled. I would not be controlled if I was able to make money to care for myself and any children I may have in the future. How barbaric to keep a woman uneducated, unskilled, and pregnant. He needed me to be financially dependent on him and him alone. Without him, I would not be able to afford adequate housing and everything that goes along with basic human dignity. I realized that he was never committed to our marriage. Marriage counseling did not help prepare us for the future. He lied about our dreams merging and becoming one. I would never be enough, because when he got tired, he would move on and never look back. The magic spell that had captured my heart had dissipated.

I promised I would never fall for anyone else the way I fell for Andrew, yet here I am lying in bed wishing I'd never met Kelton Anderson. He too has moved on to a perfect woman who is not me.

I drag myself out of bed. I haven't showered or changed into fresh clothes in five days. I can't even remember if I've eaten anything. I found a piece of peppermint candy in my nightstand when I was looking for the photo of my wedding day. I keep it hidden there to remind me that I'm a survivor. But what am I a survivor of? I gave up on my marriage because I wanted to have an education and the ability to be independent if I chose. Was I wrong all those years? Should I have accepted my ex-husband's terms and quit college and had children? Tears stream down my face. "I've met someone." I flop my butt on the bed and place my head in my hands. Is this my punishment for not giving up my education and having a child? Should I have accepted the role of being dependent on a man to bring home the money? I sob louder. I'm all alone, and everything I have will be snatched away from me. How am I going to maintain a home from a jail cell? How will I pay my bills? How will I afford an attorney for the trials, the appeals, and whatever else is part of this web of lies?

I've changed my mind about eating, showering, and dressing. I pull myself farther up on the bed and yank the sheet over me as I curl into a ball once again. Maybe tomorrow will be better.

"Wake up, sleepyhead."

I hear a familiar and calming voice. I roll over on my back.

"You'll sleep the day away. I just had some fresh fish delivered, and I want to prepare it for dinner tonight."

Fresh fish? I don't eat fish. I've always been worried that I might get a bone stuck in my throat and that it will pierce something. My idea of fish is a fillet from the frozen food aisle in the supermarket. I would never call it fresh. I haven't heard anyone say anything about fresh fish since my grandmother. Mr. Cross was my granddad's best friend in the neighborhood, and they owned a small boat together. When my granddad died, Grams told Mr. Cross the boat was now his. Every time Mr. Cross went fishing, he always split the catch with my grandma. I guess he was thinking about my granddad and wanted to make sure his family was taken care of.

I remember Grams telling me stories about the Depression. That the family always ate well. My granddad and Mr. Cross would go hunting a few times a week for deer, raccoon, or rabbit. When they weren't hunting, they went fishing. Since Coloreds, as Grams said, were not being hired anywhere, they knew they could live off the land because of their blessing of the knowledge of survival from hunting and gardening. They never missed a meal, Grams said about the Depression. They heard about many hungry people standing in bread lines in the cities. That didn't happen around here. Roughly thirty families lived in the colored neighborhood, and everyone ate well before, during, and after the Depression. They never told the whites in town. They gave the appearance that they needed food. It was the right thing to do to prevent being burned out or shot like so many other colored communities such as Tulsa and Rosewood.

I stretch and pull the covers from over my face. I see Grams standing in front of the dresser, pulling her hair up and pinning it. I look at my arms and hands and realize I'm six years old again. This is my wonderful grams, who I would stay with after Granddad died. I slept with her in the big bed. However, she made sure I had my own covers because she said I just toss and turn while pulling the blankets off her.

"Get up, sleepyhead. I'm going to start your breakfast."

I jump up and fold my blanket, placing it on the end of the bed. I head to the bathroom with my clothes for the day. Before I know it, I'm in the kitchen eating a breakfast of pancakes and scrambled eggs and chatting with Grams about my dreams.

I wince every time she chops the head off a fish, then slices it open to remove the guts. Gram will have those fish smelling good by dinnertime. She always removed all the bones and gave me the fish in a loose fillet. Being a picky eater, she went out of her way to make my food very bland but tasty.

I remember the time she saved me from eating scaly potatoes. Everyone in the family was excited to eat these scaly potatoes. Why would potatoes have scales? I buttoned my lips and refused to eat them. At dinner, I just pushed them around my plate. My mom yelled for me to put some in my mouth. But I just couldn't. The following day for breakfast, my mom reheated them and made the same request. She refused to make more than one dinner for picky me. I held out by drinking water. Gram came by to see me after two days. I was crying at the kitchen table because my mom said she was going to force-feed me the scaly potatoes. Gram told my mom that sometimes children are picky eaters, even when all the other family members aren't. My mom gave in and threw the scaly potatoes in the trash. She never offered them to me again when everyone else ate them. I got plain egg noodles without the gravy, which was perfect. Thank you, Gram! I later learned that the scaly potatoes were not scaly; they were scalloped potatoes. I still never ate them. Too much going on in that casserole. I like my food plain, recognizable, and not touching.

I can hear Gram's words: "Child, you can become anything you can dream. Don't let anyone ever stop you from achieving your dreams and doing the right thing. I didn't have that opportunity, but you—oh, you can do anything."

I open my eyes after six days of wallowing and decide my life is not over yet. It's time to make a plan of action, even if I'm going to jail for something I didn't do. I jump out of bed and head to the shower.

CHAPTER 23

KELTON

*E*ver since I told Pearl that I found someone, I've been moping. My woman in yellow is all I need to make everything okay. I did the same thing to her that my ex-wife did to me. I tossed Pearl to the side and abandoned her in her time of need. I vividly remember sitting in my cell, waiting for my name to be called for the visit. Chanel had said she was coming, and I needed to see a friendly face. When my name was finally called, I conducted myself according to the visiting policy and listened to the guards' instructions. While I waited for Chanel in the visiting area, I attempted to straighten my loud orange jumpsuit. The commissary prisoners were able to wear beige pants and matching polos as their uniform. My goal was to work in the commissary area.

When Chanel finally arrived, our meeting was very brief. She informed me that she was filing for divorce. She was not there for an embrace, a kiss, or to hold my hand across the table as a sign that I was still important in her life and that the family missed me. She told me that all the assets were frozen and that the children never wanted to hear from me again. This was the result of the damn visit. The friendly face that I'd long anticipated to see in the visiting room destroyed the remaining fragments of my life. And now I've done the same thing to Pearl.

I sip my coffee and boot up my laptop. I subscribed to a few of the local newspapers in the Newark area in the hope of gaining insight into Pearl's case. I also reviewed the court schedule to see when she would appear next in court. I needed to know everything.

In the meantime, I've been double-dating with Richard. He says he's helping me get back in the field. The women he picks are all the same. Most are widows who married a much older man in the hope that he would die soon after the wedding. Now they're living off their dead husband's life insurance policy payout—also known as life insurance widows—a pension if he had one, and his social security. None of them have any interest in getting married again because if they do, they'll no longer be eligible for their late husband's money. Because they can't marry and kill off the new husband, they opt to stay single and go shopping in exchange for a roll in the hay. Some have invested much in a plastic surgeon. When a woman's breasts are standing at attention as if they're eighteen years old but the woman is actually knocking on the door of seventy, there's a problem. Perky breasts are nice to look at, but there's something so beautiful about breasts that have matured with an arch that sits in the palm of your hands. Most have marks from facelifts, tummy tucks, and butt tucks to eliminate saggy cheeks in the face and backside, hanging guts, and fat pockets on the back. Thin is definitely in when the woman eats like a bird, just a few sunflower seeds and some water. There is nothing good if a woman stands sideways and there is no noticeable difference between her butt area and her gut area. If they're both flat like a pancake, they fail to understand the beauty in maturing. The thigh gap is also a problem. Who told women their thighs are not required to touch?

My name being called pulls me back from my deep thoughts.

"Hey, Kelton," Richard says as he enters my stateroom.

"Good morning. You're running late. I unlocked the door thirty minutes ago."

"Someone gave me a reason to stay in bed this morning."

"Oh."

Richard takes a seat on the balcony, where I'm sitting with my cup of coffee. "Your friend needs what type of favor?"

"They've been set up to take the fall for someone who has been stealing money from a company. I have another friend conducting a forensic accounting, but he needs to access unknown bank accounts that might exist in countries outside the US. You once told me you had someone who does computer geek stuff."

Richard rubs his stubble. "I haven't spoken with him in years. I guess I can try his old number. Is this about that woman?"

I don't say anything.

"You don't owe her anything."

"I know."

"No one else I've introduced you to has gotten that woman out of your mind?"

"Her name is Pearl. And to answer your question, no. She's really special." A smile graces my face.

Richard pulls an orange juice from my refrigerator and returns to sit with me. "I remember when I fell in love with Desiree. She was my heart and soul. There was nothing I wouldn't do for her."

"Richard, you actually fell in love?"

"Haven't we all? Sometimes the pieces can't just be put back together to make it whole."

"What happened to Desiree?" I'm interested in Richard's truth about love.

"She disappeared in the middle of the night. I was supposed to meet her at her apartment, but she never arrived."

"Did you report her missing?"

"I did after forty-eight hours, which was the required timeline then. In the meantime, I searched for her. Her clothes and things were in her apartment. Only a few personal effects were gone."

"What did the police say?"

"After the investigation, which consisted of speaking with a few neighbors, they concluded that she ran off with someone else in the middle of the night."

Richard looks defeated. He'd fallen in love with Desiree, and she disappeared.

"How did the police determine she ran off?"

"Because of the personal items that were missing. I was worried that she might have been kidnapped. They didn't hop to that conclusion. I searched for years. I even tracked down her mother in Vietnam. Via a translator, she told me she had not seen Desiree in more than ten years."

"Desiree had no contact with her mother?"

"The mother lied. I know Desiree sent her money and spoke to her at least once every few months. Her mother lived in a remote village that did not have access to telephones."

"Did you tell the police?"

"They didn't want to hear anything about a missing American Vietnamese woman. Let me emphasize *Vietnamese* woman."

"Have you tried looking for her now, in the age of technology and social media?"

"She was in my past." He downs the rest of the orange juice. His eyes look lost as he talks about Desiree. Richard's current actions are the result of him falling for Desiree and not being able to live that life of love.

"Love never dies." I think about Pearl.

"I'll tell my geek friend to reach out to you. I hope he can help you." Richard heads to the door. "I'll see you at dinner. We have two hotties tonight."

"Thanks," I say, though I'm talking about the geek help, not the two hotties. I also believe Richard did use technology to try to locate Desiree. He's afraid, and it's easier to be afraid and not do anything than to do something and learn the truth. Ignorance is bliss.

CHAPTER 24

PEARL

I'm numb. I don't feel anything. I'm not sleeping or eating much, just enough food so that I don't faint. I keep waiting to wake up from this nightmare. I try to spend as much time as possible in the local park, feeling the sun on my face, the wind blowing my curls, and listening to the sounds of life. The birds chirp overhead. They're sitting on a limb. Just two of them singing. I wonder if one is serenading the other. Or maybe they're simply chatting about something going on in the bird world.

Today I decided to walk to the park and conquer the two-mile path. Prior to my world crumbling to pieces, I would ride my bike and speed by everyone moving slower than me. When I would opt to leave my bike at home, I'd usually power walk to the turnaround spot, then slowly stroll back, expressing gratitude for the blessings I've received. When Kelton entered my life, it seemed that I didn't have much time to cycle or walk unless it was holding his hand on the beach. Now I don't have either focus in my life, my beloved consulting company or Kelton. My work has come to a standstill. Pearl Consultants is no longer consulting. I loved solving business problems and watching companies grow to their full potential. It's like having a child and watching them progress through all the stages: infant, toddler, young child, preteen, teen, and then adult. Not all businesses complete each stage, and some die before experiencing any growth. I guess I loved doing what I did.

I'm wearing my sunshine yellow dress. I need to remember that the sun rises every day regardless of the circumstances, even when it's overcast. It's the same dress I wore that night Kelton saw me in Aruba. He's moved out of my life and found someone better. Maybe someone who isn't such a picky eater, someone who doesn't have the extra pounds, someone who looks good in a bikini, someone who doesn't have all of my issues. Tears cloud my vision as one escapes. I'm wearing sunglasses, so no one will see my eyes. I swipe at my cheek.

It seems like the men I think I can grow old with always find someone better. Will I ever trust again? Should I ever trust again? I now realize why so many women are single by choice. Your heart can only take so much hurt before it turns cold and unfeeling. I've met bitter women and have wondered what could cause them to be that way. I believe I now know. The bitterness slowly creeps into your life, shielding any emotions that might make the heart feel. Then you become critical of everything because your ability to discern is broken.

I buy ice cream today. It's my nemesis. Just one lick goes to my hips and prevents me from getting into my pants. I'd sworn off ice cream for the past eighteen months. I love it with a passion, but it doesn't love me back. But because I'm in the worst place in my life and in my career, I think that warrants the best dessert in the world. I get two scoops of pralines and cream on a waffle cone. My mouth is in heaven along with my tummy. I think I can feel my butt cheeks growing with every lick.

I've been standing in this same place for the past twenty minutes. I can't seem to decide which direction to go at the fork in the road. I've been worried that my increased anxiety over my situation might trigger a panic attack. I haven't had one since Gram died and I was living out of my car for a few months. I was always afraid someone would break into my car while I was asleep.

I look toward the tree where the two birds were sitting. They've flown off into the day. I need to move. I don't want to have a breakdown while in the park eating ice cream. I decide to take the path back to my home. As I walk, I realize I haven't made the difference in life that I'd wanted to. Nor did I ever think I would be in trouble with the law.

This morning is moving day. I decided not to renew my office lease for Pearl Consultants. I wanted to, but if I can't afford the rent because of lack of clients, it will be detrimental to my funds. I moved my telephone line to my home. I've donated most of the items from the office to the youth center. The others are being placed into my home office. I wanted to keep everything, but I don't know if Pearl Consultants will survive. I'm not sure that *I'm* going to survive or where I might end up after this fiasco.

I've spent the last few days boxing up the office. Jaynea is stopping by to collect her things. I've included a gift of thanks and a generous bonus inside her box. I hear a knock at the front door and turn to see Jaynea waving at me.

"Good morning," I say as I let her in.

"Yeah, good morning." Jaynea moves toward her former desk. She's wearing a blue geometric-patterned long T-shirt dress with navy leggings and beige tennis shoes. Her hair is died blackish-brown, and her fingernail polish is a tawny color. I've never seen her toned down. She doesn't look like the same Jaynea who lives life in full bold and sometimes neon color.

"Did you get that position with Marlowe Consultants?" I watch as Jaynea avoids making eye contact with me.

"Yeah. I got it." When she finally looks at me, there's anger in her eyes. "I don't appreciate you taking on clients who caused the cops to arrest me as if I were a criminal," Jaynea says hotly, her hands on her hips.

I'm taken aback that she's blaming me. I'm also angry that I was taken into custody and am now looking at jail time. "I didn't know the clients were going to cause this type of problem." I try to console her and not go on the attack.

Jaynea continues to give me the evil eye. Is she trying to read my mind? "Well, Mr. Marlowe said you've always been unprofessional and that's why you're being charged with money laundering and embezzlement."

I'm surprised by her comment. I sent her to Marlowe Consultants because she needed a job and she's good at what she does. I've never been a fan of Elvin Marlowe. He's always been threatened by me. He even tried to badmouth me at one of the networking events. I had to pull him to the side of the room and put him in his place very professionally. I was best friends with his sister in high school. Catherene died after graduation in a horrific car accident. I never asked Elvin if he blamed me for letting her get into the car with her boyfriend, who was driving that night. Of course, the boyfriend lived, but all four of the passengers died, including Catherene.

I decide to avoid a pissing contest with Jaynea. I'm also rethinking her bonus check, but I pick up her box and give it to her. The sooner she leaves, the better off we'll both be. "These are your personal items. Is there anything else you wanted from the office?"

"No."

"I wish you the very best." I step toward the front door. I can see the movers backing the truck near the entrance. I'm glad they're on time. The sooner this is finished, the better.

Jaynea leaves with the file box. I watch her walk across the parking lot, the famed Black Panther pack that she loves on her back. The Black Panther looks ready to pounce on any evil that might be lurking to harm the innocent. I need the Black Panther to help me fight the evil that has taken over my life.

I open the door for the movers and greet them as I refocus on the task at hand. While they work, I bring my personal things to my car. The movers are heading to my home first and then to the youth center.

After everything is delivered, I return to the office, sweep the floors, and clean the fingerprints from the kitchen nook cabinets and light switches. I then say goodbye to the place that was formerly Pearl Consultants. I don't believe an action that wasn't mine has destroyed my hard work and the future of my business.

I remember the first day I saw the office space. I had looked at six different locations. I needed that warm feeling, that feeling of belonging, and this was the place. I started with a single desk and two file cabinets. It's been a good journey. I'll complete the remaining consulting cases and close the company for good. Tears well up in my eyes. I've lost my small business and the guy I thought would be with me into old age. I'm alone once again as I try to figure this out. It reminds me of the day my father died. Mom said we would be okay. Neither of us were ever okay again. Or when I buried Gram, I realized I didn't have anyone to love me or a home to call my own.

The following week Seleste and Weston visit me in South Orange. Seleste has been calling a few times a week to check on my mental state. I'm glad they're here. She wanted me to visit them in Aruba, but I'm not permitted to travel outside New Jersey. When Seleste learned that Weston had some business in New York City, she was excited to join him. Weston stays a few days and then returns to Aruba for some previously scheduled music concerts. Seleste remains for another week.

The following morning, Seleste makes a list of all the things we can do to have fun. This is conducted over a beautiful breakfast spread. Prior to our meal, we showered and dressed in our most comfortable everyday attire. That was the beginning of the plan. Seleste thought I would have a better attitude if I wore something colorful and had a hearty breakfast. I'm wearing orange yoga pants with wide legs and a T-shirt with the message Highly Educated, Beautiful, and Proud. Seleste enters the kitchen in pink yoga pants that hug every part of her body and a T-shirt that reads I'm Perfect and I Know It! We both look at each other's shirts and laugh.

Because my breakfast skills are limited, I assign myself to slicing and dicing for Seleste. I mix the mimosas and set the table. Seleste prepares the eggs, bacon, and hash browns. We laugh and talk about the desires we had as teens, then in midlife, old age, and our golden years. That's the age when we won't feel like doing anything other than sitting in a comfortable recliner with our legs up so that our ankles don't swell. We both agree that we're now in our old age and won't be in our golden years for another decade or so.

Our potential list of fun activities over the course of the week consists of the following:
1. A show on Broadway
2. Butterfly forest
3. Skydiving
4. Rom-com binge-a-thon
5. Atlantic City casinos

We'll play it by ear after we complete our list. If we see a Broadway show, I'll need to leave New Jersey for New York. If I leave for New York, maybe I could fly to Aruba. Would someone really be looking for me over a weekend? The court didn't ask for my passport. I think about it as I sip my mimosa. No, I don't want to give anyone a reason to lock me in a jail cell before it's time. I'll visit New York for the show and return to New Jersey.

After a full week of activities, laughs, and sometimes tears, I wave goodbye to Seleste as she rides away in an Uber. We completed everything on the list as well as a few other spur-of-the-moment adventures. It amazes me that we get along so well. I know people from high school, college, or professionally who I'm not as close to as I am with Seleste. They're the ones with whom I thought I would share my old-age experiences. Now I guess my old age will consist of going to jail. Seleste has not judged me or disowned me due to this crisis in my life.

Mia Lakes from Dollar Now has denied accepting any money. I've been told not to have any contact with Mia or have anything to do with her business. She's hired a big-time attorney to make sure she doesn't go to jail. I read in the newspaper that Fred Armstrong tried to skip town, and now he's in jail awaiting his trial. The article claimed I was involved through my business, Pearl Consultants. Three potential new clients cancel their appointments with me after the article is published.

If you're innocent until proven guilty, why does the media publish articles without all the facts? How can a person remain innocent when all the fingers are being pointed at them as if they are guilty? How does the average person pay their bills if they cannot find work? I've tapped into my emergency savings, but not everyone is as fortunate.

I pour myself more coffee. I've been officially charged, but there's no way for me to investigate the allegations unless I'm able to speak with Mia Lakes or Fred Armstrong. I thought about hiring a private investigator, but I don't want to waste the money. Jester Jackson told me I'll probably get jail time for the franchise incident because people were financially harmed. He's estimating ninety days. What worries me is the money laundering charge because I did deliver the laundry bags and the packages. I didn't know what was in any of the bags or boxes that I dropped off at the gym. I thought I was doing Fred a favor. Jester believes I might get five years or possibly more if the prosecutor can find additional evidence that I actively and knowingly participated.

If I'm sentenced to anything more than one year, I'll probably need to sell my house. I've been trying to calculate how many months I can pay all my bills and keep my home. I fought long and hard to purchase, renovate, and pay off my house. I could afford only a foreclosed property because I didn't want to finance a turnkey home. I have a duplex bungalow that is completely paid for. I rent out the other one-bedroom, one-bath unit with a side entrance. My tenant has been renting from me for ten years. I should have received my gram's home, but my mom made sure that was not my reality.

Do I rent my home while in jail? Do I sell it? Do I just lock it and let it sit? What do normal criminals do? Is there such a thing as a normal criminal?

After I review my financials and pay some bills the following morning, I schedule an appointment with my therapist. I haven't seen her since my mom died, when I needed to release my anger toward my mother. I didn't want it to eat away at me in my old age, so I found a professional to talk to. I schedule a Thursday appointment, which follows a meeting with Jester.

He's received some information about a plea deal. I want to know the particulars, but he prefers to speak with me in person.

Another woman sits opposite me in the therapist's reception area. The office has five very busy therapists who all are melanated. When I was referred to Sindra Ojo, I was told she was a unicorn. I wasn't sure what that meant until I learned that minority therapists are a rarity, so when you find one, you don't let them go.

When my mom died from that disease that strips people of their dignity, I needed someone to help me put things in perspective. We really never got along, but she was still my mom. Her boyfriend disappeared as soon as she was diagnosed. He took anything of value, then dropped her off at my home. I found a nursing facility close by and visited every evening until she passed. I asked myself the same questions other family members likely do. Did my mom want to be here in that condition? Was there anything I could do about it other than take one day at a time and pray for mercy?

The meeting with Jester did nothing to calm my fears. The plea bargain was to plead guilty to two of the four charges and accept thirty months in jail. It would mean acknowledging that I was guilty and automatically becoming a felon for the rest of my life. Throughout the entire meeting, I kept telling myself that I did nothing wrong. Why am I going to jail when I did nothing wrong?

"Ms. Jermaine? Ms. Ojo is ready for you."

Lost in my thoughts, I don't hear the receptionist, and she has to tap me on the shoulder to get my attention. She walks me to the door and opens it. Sindra is seated behind her desk. I sit on the couch, and she moves to a chair across from me.

"Good morning, Pearl," she welcomes me warmly.

"Good morning."

"How are you doing?" She shows no worry or weight from listening to people's problems. I expect her to have aged a little, but her beautiful coloring shows no sign of that. Because I've always felt comfortable with Sindra, there are no need for formalities. "I'm not doing well. I've been told that I might end up in jail for thirty months. It could be less or it could be more."

"How are you handling that?"

"I'm not. I'm not eating or sleeping."

"Do you think not eating or sleeping is healthy?"

"No, I know it's not healthy," I snap before taking a breath and continuing more calmly. "But I have no appetite, and I just stare at the ceiling in my bed."

"What electronic devices are on during bedtime?"

"None."

"None? Not even your cell?"

"No one calls me anymore. If I turn off my cell, I still won't sleep."

Sindra repositions herself in the chair. "You sound upset. Can you explain why?"

I let out a long breath and close my eyes. "I'm being accused of something I didn't do. I'm afraid I'm going to end up in jail for a crime I didn't commit." I take in another deep breath and let it out.

"Let's talk about eating."

"I'm not hungry, so I don't eat."

"But you know you can't survive without eating."

"Yes, I know, but I have no appetite."

"You don't need an appetite to eat." Sindra makes a few notes, then looks at me.

"I guess you're going to tell me to eat at least three small meals a day even if I don't feel hungry."

"Is that what you want me to tell you?"

"I don't know. I guess."

"It sounds like you just created a plan."

"Okay. What about sleeping?"

"Do you believe the body must rest?"

"Yes, of course."

"What is your plan to make sure your body gets at least six hours of rest?"

"I'll set aside the time and stare at the ceiling."

"Maybe close your eyes during that time."

"I'm on a sinking ship and can't seem to find a way off to survive."

"If you saw someone in a boat bailing water to keep it afloat, what would you say?"

I think for a few seconds. I make the assumption that it's someone I don't want to die. "I'd tell them to abandon the sinking ship and save themselves."

"What does that look like?"

As I drive home, I reinforce the idea that I need to abandon my sinking ship. And I need to envision abandoning it. Because I don't want anyone going down with me or feeling guilty, I also need my friends to abandon my sinking ship.

CHAPTER 25

KELTON

*g*lance into the cooler of fresh cut flowers. I want to get something as beautiful as Pearl to say I'm sorry for crushing her spirits and ending our relationship. She was overwhelmed by the charges of embezzlement and money laundering. I heard the fear in her voice, but I wanted only to protect myself from the hurt and shame of going through another scandal. I know Pearl doesn't like fresh cut flowers. She says it all the time. She prefers flowers that aren't going to die within the next week or so. I can hear her say, "If someone thought enough of me to send flowers, I don't want them to die." I drag my hand through my hair that needs a trim. I've been so preoccupied with Pearl that I missed my scheduled barber visit on the cruise ship.

"Sir, can I help you select something?" the petite saleswoman asks with a smile.

Her voice brings me back to reality. I clear my throat. "I'm looking for something really nice to send to someone special." Even though I know she'd prefer something else. Why am I here? Because I feel guilty, and Richard thought a bouquet of flowers would be just the thing to say *I'm sorry for being a selfish asshole.*

"Let's look in my book, and maybe you'll see something. Then we can select a particular flower or color." She motions for me to follow as she walks away from the cooler and toward the front counter. Forty minutes and multiple recommendations later, I continue to flip through a book of flower bouquets. I can't find the perfect thing that says *I was a total idiot, and you've been the best thing in my life in a very long time.* And let's not forget that I was afraid she might automatically discard me if she knew my secret. I close the book a little too hard, startling a customer at the checkout. The shop assistant glares at me, but that could be for wasting her time trying to choose something that I know would not be the best gift.

"I can't decide. Let me think about it," I say to her. As I walk past the front desk, I don't make eye contact with the customer, but I do nod to the helpful employee. I feel them both watching me as I push the front door open and exit the shop. My telephone rings as I head toward my rental car. I pull it out of my pants pocket and see Seleste's name on the screen. "Hello, my Aruban friend."

"Hello yourself. Where are you?"

"I'm in Saint Thomas for the week."

"I spoke with Pearl today. She's seriously stressing."

"I've been following the case, and she's not going to get probation. The state wants to use her as an example." I run my hand through my hair again. I'm getting stressed trying to figure out what to do.

"Really? How would you know? They might look at her stellar track record of no criminal history and reconsider." Seleste pauses to take a deep breath, as if she really believes the prosecutor is going to give Pearl a slap on the wrist and tell her not to do it again.

I don't want to tell Seleste how I know this. I don't want to share with her the horrific nightmare that reshaped my life. I don't want to think about the time I thought I would wake from the nightmare but never did. I don't want to relive any part of the night before I went to trial. Or the day I was found guilty for something I didn't do. I don't want to think about how this uninitiated action on my part ended my marriage and my record as a loving, caring family man. I don't, but I say it anyway. "Unfortunately, I know firsthand what it means to be charged and sentenced for a crime you didn't commit." It's quiet on the other end of the phone. Did we get disconnected and she didn't hear my confession?

"I thought I recognized you, but I couldn't put my finger on it," Seleste replies slowly and quietly. "The newspaper said your employee was the embezzler, but the prosecutor charged him and you as well." Her tone is so reserved. No excitement or shock. I'm waiting for her to end the call. I'm waiting for her to react along the same lines as Richard when he heard about our shipmate who was selling guns to unsavory people. I remember how he ridiculed the guy without any shame. How he judged as if he's never done anything wrong.

"Kelton? Kelton, are you still there?" Seleste asks.

"Yeah, I'm still here. I thought you would hang up or tell me how horrible I am." I take a deep breath and wait for her judgment to wash over me.

"I followed most of the case because I was surprised that could happen. I could have been in the same position when my husband stole from his job and the items were discovered at our home. I'm sorry you were found guilty and had to go to jail."

"Me too, and it was prison."

"So what can we do to help Pearl?"

"You're not going to judge me?" I ask curiously.

"Of course not. I have no right or authority to judge anyone. You might want to judge me, and I don't want that either."

"I don't know. I simply don't know how to help Pearl." I clear my throat as if phlegm is building in it. "What I do know is that prison is not a place where they expect you to remain human given the inhumane treatment that exists behind bars." I'm surprised that I survived. There were many days and nights when I thought suicide would have been better. I had nothing else to live for.

"Did Pearl tell you what she's doing tomorrow?" I should be the one staying in contact with Pearl, but I relinquished my love for her in her dire time of need. Now I rely on Seleste to tell me everything.

"She'll be at her attorney's office all afternoon to prepare for the trial."

I nod as if Seleste can see me. "Thanks. We'll talk soon."

A few days later, I arrive at the Essex County prosecutor's office with my attorney in tow. I'm dressed for comfort in a lightweight beige windbreaker, khakis, and a blue short-sleeve polo shirt. Everything this morning has been so surreal. I left my emotions in the hotel room as I slid my feet into my deck shoes before departing. I took an Uber to the storage unit, then to my attorney's office. I want to be comfortable as I share information with the prosecutor to protect Pearl from the charges of embezzlement and money laundering. My lawyer is completely against this visit. I know what's at risk. I promised myself when I got out of jail that I would never put myself in that situation again.

I know Pearl's clients are blatantly lying to save themselves from being locked up. They're using Pearl as a scapegoat, and the prosecutor doesn't care as long as someone is held responsible and the media gets a front-page story. The prosecutor wants to get his name in the paper and have a press conference to propel his career toward a better and higher position. Maybe even governor one day. My attorney says something as we get out of his car at the Essex County Veterans Courthouse parking lot. I don't hear him. I only see his lips moving. I finally process his question and tell him that I did not bring my cell phone. He nods, and we proceed to the building. This should all be over rather quickly.

When I called Seleste a few days ago, she insisted there was another way to handle this. She even put Weston on the telephone in the hope of changing my mind. But their pleas fell on deaf ears.

CHAPTER 26

PEARL

A tear falls down my cheek. I don't wipe it away. I let it roll toward my jaw and drip onto my chest. That simple tear has friends that follow. Both eyes fill now, and they are flowing. I grip the steering wheel tighter as my chest gets wetter and wetter. The tears continue to be pulled by gravity and slide down my chest, over my breasts, and into my bra. Some take the shortcut and run between my breasts. I thought my divorce was the hardest thing I would ever do. At the time, I couldn't believe that someone who had committed to me would wake up one day and stop loving me.

Now I'm totally confused by how I could be forced to endure the lie that I embezzled money from a client and participated in money laundering. I scream at the top of my lungs to let it all out. I scream as loudly as I can and for as long as I can, thinking it will exhaust my body. It's also an attempt to relieve some of the stress that has taken up residence in my neck and back. I have a headache. When I pull into my circle driveway, I don't recognize my house. Someone has been here. It must be a mistake. A prank to draw me even deeper into this embezzlement and money laundering scheme. I stop to take it all in. I put the car in park and get out.

Much to my dismay and the ugly horrible day I've had to go along with the preceding days, someone has planted yellow marigolds in my previously empty flower beds. The shade of yellow varies, wrapping around the bushes and toward the front steps. On both sides of my steps sit large beautiful pots of geraniums in bright reds and pinks. What a lovely mistake someone made today. Some landscapers must have planted these flowers at the wrong house. They'll be royally pissed tomorrow when they learn of their error. I'm sure someone will return and rip them out of the ground tomorrow. Leaving my flower beds empty, wanting, and lonely. I absorb the beauty of the flowers and how they make my house look so welcoming. "I planted a few flowers the first year, but this is spectacular," I say out loud to myself. I walk back to my MINI Cooper and pull the car into the garage, then go back to view the flowers again. If someone doesn't return to remove them, I'll need to water them daily. They're just what I needed to take my mind off the craziness. As I head back to the garage, I see a card taped to the front door.

Dear Lovey,

I'm sorry for everything, and I miss you dearly. I wanted you to have flowers. A lot of beautiful flowers for you to enjoy. If you never speak to me again in this lifetime, I will understand.

Love always, Kelton

I read the card a second time and then a third. Why would Kelton do this? I'm sure his special someone wouldn't be happy to know he's sending flowers to his ex-girlfriend. The flowers are from Kelton; they're not a mistake. A landscaper didn't plant them at the wrong house. Kelton sent me flowers to purge his conscience.

The next morning I wake and glance at my nightstand, looking for my cell. It isn't on the charger. I remember attempting to call Kelton a few times throughout the night. It's not like him to not answer. Yes, I might have drunk a little too much wine, but I wanted to give Kelton a piece of my mind. He doesn't get the opportunity to clear his conscience after dropping me like a hot potato.

I pat the sheets to locate my phone. I attempt to contact Kelton once again, but it rolls to voicemail. I leave a message this time and thank him for the flowers. I'm not one to leave nasty messages. My gram taught me better. I also spoke with Seleste yesterday evening. Since I couldn't get in touch with Kelton, I wanted to tell someone about the beautiful flowers. I miss Seleste, but I don't want her to see me cry during this court process. Our friendship has grown to a real sisterhood, and I don't want her to take pity on me. I remember the discussion with my therapist about abandoning my sinking ship. I need Seleste to abandon my sinking ship even though we speak regularly. She even mentioned that I could stay with her in Aruba if I decide to disappear before the court case. I thought about leaving the States and hiding in that Caribbean island for the rest of my life. But my passport would eventually need to be renewed, and then I'd get caught. That's if the Aruban government didn't find me because I outstayed my visit.

Once this incident blew up, Seleste knew it wouldn't be possible for me to visit Aruba, so she stopped inviting me. She's still going strong with Weston. However, she doesn't want marriage, and because he already has two children, there's no need for more. It seems like a perfect match. It also sounds like she gets along great with his kids, especially as she and her son are estranged.

I stretch as I walk to the kitchen to start the coffee. I let all of my remaining tasks scroll through my mind. I see a shadow cross the lawn. I've been worried someone will try to trash my house, and now that I know the flowers are actually mine, I don't want anyone to remove them. I run to the front window and see someone watering the flowers. I pull the curtains back and knock on the window. The young woman with the hose smiles and returns my greeting. I've been miserable, and my inevitable fate of jail isn't going to disappear because someone sent me flowers, but they sure are making me feel good.

I return to the kitchen after showering and pulling my hair on top of my head into a large puff. Since my current attorney, Jester Jackson, is a criminal attorney, I hired an estates planning attorney to act on my behalf if I get jail time, and I've rented a large storage unit. By paying for the first month, I received two months free. The unit is large enough to store all of my household items. I'll sell the house if I end up in jail. My attorney will have access to my main bank account containing $200,000. This will cover my storage unit until I am released and any outstanding utilities once I sell the house. My vehicles will be kept in the parking lot at the storage facility. Once I sell my house, my life will consist of two cars and some furniture. My only debt is a student loan I took out while earning my master's degree, and I set up a direct payment for it. Jester said the prosecution is requesting a sixty-month sentence.

I drum my fingers on the kitchen counter, where I'm writing and drinking my coffee. I try to enjoy a little something every day that I take for granted. The sun on my face, a walk in the park, reading a book in my hammock on the sunporch, and eating ice cream, which is my all-time favorite food, even if it goes directly to my butt. It doesn't stop anywhere else; its only destination is my butt. However, I'm sure I'll lose weight in jail because I'm not going to get my desired way of cooking. My attorney is requesting probation. I refuse to plead guilty because I'm not guilty. I'd like to have all of this vanish into thin air. I'd like for my clients to admit their guilt.

My telephone rings, startling me out of my thoughts. It's Jester. As my mother would say, speak of the devil.

"Good morning, Pearl. Do you have a few minutes to speak?" Jester is always pleasant and gracious, even when dealing with the legal system. I always thought it was glamorous to see lawyers on television. I realize now that there's nothing glamorous about that work. When he first took my case, he admitted that he was not a trial attorney. But he came highly recommended and is a friend of Jaynea's. I've also come to understand that he's a negotiator.

"Yes, I'm available to speak now. Do I need to come back to the office again today?" I drum my fingers on the counter in anticipation of the purpose of his call. Did another client come forth and accuse me of something I didn't do?

"The prosecutor has dropped all charges."

My mouth flies open, and tears well in my eyes. The clients admitted to the truth. I no longer need to worry about spending time in jail or selling my house. I can breathe again and enjoy my flowers. I need to find Kelton. Maybe he's no longer with his special someone.

"Pearl, did you hear me? The prosecutor has dropped all charges."

This time when I open my mouth, actual words come out. "Thank you. Thank you." I let out a long heavy sigh. "Did the owners finally admit to embezzling and money laundering and that I was simply trying to get them to do what was right?"

"Unfortunately no, they did not admit their wrongdoings. I believe an employee is taking the fall. I didn't get all the details, but someone admitted to orchestrating everything."

"Really? So an employee is going to be prosecuted instead of the owners?"

"No, the owners will still be prosecuted, but this employee knew a lot of the details and admitted to participating in the schemes. It all made sense. I have a few more things to do to confirm that they cannot try to prosecute you again. I'll be in touch."

"Thank you again. Before you go, can I know the name of the employee who came forward?"

"Sure. His name is Kelton Anderson."

"Did you say Kelton Anderson?"

"Yes. He turned himself in to the prosecutor's office yesterday. He had an attorney and knew a lot about how the organizations operated. He's now sitting in a jail cell instead of you." He clears his throat. "Do you know him?"

"I've got to go. Call me with any other details. And thanks for everything." I quickly end the call. Kelton is taking the fall for me. Why? I didn't want to go to jail for something I didn't do, but I definitely don't want someone else to go to jail in my place.

CHAPTER 27

PEARL

I'm relieved that I'm not going to be convicted, but I can't believe Kelton would admit to participating in these schemes to exonerate me. This is a man who worked as a CEO for a medium-size tool manufacturer. He grew the business after many years as a CPA in other companies. He's led a stellar life. He doesn't say much about his ex-wife or his children, but I know his children don't speak to him. They're probably estranged like Seleste and her son.

I call Seleste. I'm not sure of my next steps, but Kelton cannot do jail time for me.

"Hello?" a groggy voice answers.

"Oh, did I wake you?" I hear Weston in the background asking if it's an emergency, then Seleste telling him to go back to sleep.

"Pearl, is everything okay?"

"I'm sorry. I didn't mean to wake you. I'll call back later."

"Don't you dare hang up on me," Seleste threatens. "Give me a minute." A short time later, I hear a door close. "Pearl, are you still there?"

"Yes. You were probably up late yesterday with Weston's band. We can talk later."

"Are you calling about Kelton?"

"You know." My mouth goes dry. "Why didn't anyone tell me? Why is he taking the fall for my mess?"

"Because he loves you."

I sit frozen at my kitchen island. "He's with someone else," I finally squeak out.

"If you hear noise, I'm making coffee. Kelton called a few days ago and told me that he was going to admit to the charges and take the fall."

"Seleste, none of this is making sense. Could you please explain?"

"I need to share some information with you in person. I'll be there in a few days. Weston's band had a gig last night, but I also spoke with an attorney in the States to address the quandary that Kelton has created. All in the name of love."

"I don't understanding anything you're saying."

We hang up after Seleste gives me the number for Ayaba Adesanya, an attorney in Hoboken. She also instructs me to not feel intimidated by her large presence. I'm not sure what that means. Apparently, she's a family friend of Weston's, and she plays to win. She's well known among the wealthy families in New Jersey, New York, and Connecticut. How will I pay for a big-time attorney?

I contact Ms. Adesanya to schedule an appointment. She was expecting my call. It surprises me that the number I dial is for her cell phone and not her office. She knows my name and says to call her office and give my contact information to her assistant. I do as she instructs and am scheduled to meet with her at 11:00 a.m. tomorrow.

Later that day, I sit in front of my house enjoying the flowers. I was upset when I thought I'd have to leave my home and live in a jail cell for a few years. I couldn't eat, sleep, or breathe. Now that won't happen, but I still can't eat, sleep, or celebrate. I've been placed on pause. Seleste is on her way to explain, and tomorrow I meet with the killer attorney. Kelton is sitting in a jail cell at the county lockup. I don't want to tell Jester about knowing Kelton because it might blow up in my face.

I go to bed that evening feeling as if I've run a marathon. My sleep is not restful.

"Kelton!" I scream from the shore. I can't see him. The sun is going down. He was in the water, but now he's gone. He simply vanished. "Kelton!"

I call again. After a few moments, I feel a hand on my arm. I turn to see Seleste. She doesn't say anything. She reaches for my hand and leads me toward a large house overlooking the shore. I try to tell her that I've lost Kelton. She still doesn't say anything as she guides me to the home's multilevel decks.

I awake in a cold sweat. I can't catch my breath. I'm having a panic attack. I close my eyes and try to focus on my breathing and a pleasant thought. My respirations begin to level out. My head hurts, but it might be from not eating much the previous day. I look at the picture on my nightstand of my gram and myself. It was taken at a family gathering before she fell ill. *I miss you, Gram. You would give me strong words of advice during this ordeal. May I one day have your wisdom.*

I head to the kitchen to get coffee and turn on the television. Much to my surprise, I see a press conference with a woman explaining a situation about embezzlement and money laundering. I wonder if this is becoming the in thing this year. Then I see her name flash under her picture. It's the killer attorney, Ayaba Adesanya, with whom I'm meeting today. I missed the beginning of her speech, but she ends by saying that her client is innocent and that it will be proven. I wonder how she's going to do that when Kelton has already pleaded guilty to the charges. I realize I've been pulled into a world I know nothing about. I dress and drive to Hoboken for my appointment.

This initial meeting with Ayaba Adesanya is intense. I brought the information that I could locate on my backup drive. The task force officers took everything else. I explain all my interactions with each of the clients. First Dollar Now and my contracted activities with Mia Lakes. Why she wanted to offer franchises. Then when the problems began and the allegations from potential franchisees. Then we shift to the second client, Fred Armstrong with Trim and Fit. How he initially contacted me about staffing issues and how the growth from his new investors was taking a toll on him and the company he created. Ayaba records everything while taking notes. She doesn't want to miss any detail that might help in the case, so recording is a must in her line of work. She'll contact me in a few days after she's devised a plan of action. She also asks permission to contact Jester Jackson. I agree and will touch base with him after our meeting to inform him of the situation.

Before I leave the conference room, I ask how Kelton is doing. I need to know. She tells me he's okay. That's all she says. I didn't know what to expect, but I feel miserable. I want to visit him, but I'm afraid he'll decline to see me, and then I'll feel even worse. I thank Ayaba before leaving her offices.

Seleste arrives a few days later. I'm waiting for her at baggage claim and am ecstatic to see a friendly face. Someone I have grown to respect and who has become my sister in life. I didn't understand our last conversation. I also didn't understand why she knew so much about something I was not aware of but should have been. We collect her luggage and head to my car.

After arriving home by way of the Ethiopian restaurant in South Orange, I put Seleste's luggage in my guest bedroom. Returning to the kitchen, I find her logging on to my Wi-Fi so that she can share information with me. I set the dining room table and move our take-out food there. Seleste follows with her laptop.

"Are you upset with me?" Seleste asks.

"About not telling me about Kelton or because you know something I don't?" I ask angrily.

"Both." We made small talk in the car about her trip and where Weston's band is playing. I even asked if Weston is going to join us. He might in a few weeks, but he's working on a project and won't be available for a while.

Without saying a word, she approaches and wraps her arms around me. The last time she hugged me so tightly was when I had that nightmare, and she sat with me until I fell back to sleep. Now she wraps me in a warm, motherly, everything-is-going-to-be-okay hug. I begin to sob. The tears are flowing, and I can't stop them. I see her wet T-shirt shoulder through my blurry eyes. Instead of pulling away to prevent her shirt from becoming drenched, she simply brings me closer and tighter. As I sob, she rocks me from side to side and rubs my back. When I finally stop, she slowly pulls away to look at my puffy eyes and tear-streaked cheeks.

"Feel better?"

"Yes."

"Go wash your face. I'll be right here waiting for you to return."

I go as ordered. I feel so much better. I needed to be able to cry in a safe place where I wasn't going to be judged. I found that in a true friend. When I return to the dining room, Seleste is prepared to talk and eat dinner.

"I don't know how much you know about Kelton's past," Seleste begins.

"Just what he told me. I know he's divorced and has two children. Please don't tell me he has more than one wife."

"No, I believe he was married only once. Did he tell you why he is divorced?"

"I never asked, and he never said." I put a forkful of food in my mouth, and it tastes heavenly. Maybe my appetite has returned.

"Kelton was the CEO of a tool manufacturing company in New Haven, Connecticut. His COO was embezzling from the company. Kelton was eventually charged because he was the CEO; his CFO was also charged." Seleste stops speaking, probably because my mouth is hanging open.

It takes me a minute before I can form words. "Oh my goodness. He was convicted of a crime he didn't commit?"

"Yep, and it was embezzlement."

"And now he's being charged again for the same crime, and again it's something he didn't do." I frown. I'm trying to not cry again.

Seleste turns her laptop toward me. "I pulled these articles for you to read. They're all in a file folder here." She points to her screen. "I followed the trial only because I encountered a situation with my ex-husband that was illegal. That's a story for another day."

I look at Seleste, then back at the computer.

"You can start with the articles in order in the folder. They'll walk you through everything. He ended up serving three years of his five-year sentence."

"Why would he admit to my charges? I would never want to go back to prison for anyone."

Seleste clears her throat. "He called me a few days before he planned to meet with the lawyer who was going to prosecute your case. He told me that he didn't want you exposed to prison life. He had already endured it once and knew what to do to survive."

The tears I was holding back reappeared, and this time they ran down my cheeks. "He didn't want me to go to jail." I wipe my eyes with my napkin.

"Yep. He remembered what you had discussed that last time you were together."

"In Paris, I asked him to look at some numbers. I had my clients' folders with me."

"He recalled your concerns and connected enough dots to convince the prosecutor that he was involved and not you."

"Why didn't you call me?" I ask with anger in my voice.

"He convinced me that this was best for you and asked that I not tell you until he was in the county jail."

"But you're my friend, my very good friend."

"I'm friends with you both. He didn't have to tell me. He just wanted me to watch over you while he was in jail."

"So I thought I was dating Mr. Good, but he's actually Mr. Bad Boy with a felony record."

"How was the sex, now that you know?"

I wipe my face again and smirk. "Now you're trying to make me laugh."

"I just want to know if the sex was good coming from Mr. Bad Boy himself."

"Oh, the sex was definitely from a bad boy, and now I know why. This is even more of a reason to find an alibi and get him released."

"I brought an alibi with me. It might be helpful for part of the case."

"Really. What is it?"

"First you need to read the articles to understand what happened to him and process why he decided to admit to something on your behalf. I have an appointment with Ayaba Adesanya on Tuesday. You can come with me."

"Okay. Thanks for being our friend and for letting me cry all over you."

"Anytime."

We spent the remainder of dinner talking and laughing about life in general and about relationships. Especially because Seleste and Weston have become a permanent item. Afterward, I forward the file folder and contents from Seleste's laptop to mine via email. She wants to FaceTime with Weston, and I don't want to stop the magic from happening. I sit on my bed and read one article after another. Kelton had insisted that he was innocent of any wrongdoing. The prosecutor said he was ultimately responsible being the CEO. Matt Marek was the COO and was responsible for the embezzling. I remember hearing that name before. Why? It finally dawns on me that Matt is the guy who wanted Kelton to be his kids' godfather. *Matt Marek wants Kelton to be their godfather*, I repeat in my head. Matt is the reason Kelton went to jail, and now he wants Kelton to watch over his daughters and give worldly advice? It sounds insane. I close my laptop and place it on my nightstand before turning out the light to end another day.

The following morning, a delicious aroma wakes me. I follow it to find Seleste in the kitchen. She loves to cook, and since moving in with Weston, his two grown children visit on a regular basis for meals.

"Good morning," I say from the doorway.

"Good morning. I hope you slept well."

"I did. What smells so good?"

"I whipped up a cinnamon coffee cake to go along with breakfast this morning."

"Oh, it smells divine. Is it ready for me to taste a piece?" I ask with a smile on my face.

"It should be ready once you're showered and dressed. No more pajamas all day. I bet you went days without showering and changing into fresh pajamas."

"I don't know what you're talking about!" I run down the hallway to my bedroom to get ready for the day.

Seleste and I devise a plan to gather more information from the two clients who had planned to destroy my life. We toss around going undercover. I can change my hair and eye color, and we can plant listening devices and gather intel. We realize we've watched entirely too many investigative shows and opt to first speak with Kelton's killer attorney before doing anything that might negatively affect his case. We spend the next few days eating all the marvelous food Seleste cooks for brunch and dine at several of the great restaurants in the South Orange and West Orange areas for dinner.

On Tuesday, we arrive early at Ayaba Adesanya's office. We sit in the conference room and listen as Kelton's attorney shares the information she's gathered and what needs to be done to get him out of jail. Ayaba understands our need to help but doesn't want us to put ourselves in harm's way. After much debate and discussion, we decide that Seleste will contact Mia Lakes to purchase a Dollar Now franchise. She'll first speak with someone who has deposited money to get on the list to purchase a franchise. This will leave me out of the introduction. I also have a list of those who were upset due to submitting money for a franchise.

Seleste and I agree not to do anything else other than meet with Mia and attempt to purchase a franchise. We'll record the meeting and submit a personal check to get on the list for documentation purposes. Then we'll get the information to Ayaba.

Ayaba and Jester are meeting to develop a strategic approach to address the money laundering. She and her investigator have already started following Fred's employees. We give our word that we will not interfere with anything regarding Trim and Fit. We leave the law office and head to an early dinner to devise a plan of attack.

CHAPTER 28

SELESTE

Three days later, I have an appointment to meet with Mia Lakes at her office. My cover is that I was referred to Mia through a contact who had attended her presentation at one of the community centers. I wear a business casual dress and sensible pumps. Nothing with fancy labels, even down to my purse. When my husband died, I exchanged most of my clothing for designer labels with the help of his life insurance policy payout. My new wardrobe has nothing but fun colors and accessories that would not qualify as business attire. Pearl and I had to go shopping for this very casual and sensible outfit. I checked Pearl's closet, but my curves are more voluptuous than hers, so shopping we went.

I don't want to appear overly professional, as my story is that I was formally a cashier at a small supermarket in town until my husband died. His life insurance policy of $50,000 will allow me to purchase a Dollar Now franchise and finance the balance through Dollar Now Corporation. I've brought along a portfolio to take notes. I received materials from Dollar Now via mail prior to the meeting. The purpose of the appointment is for Mia to answer my questions and discuss the next steps before running my own Dollar Now store. When I told the receptionist, Bay, why I want to be a franchisee, she said I was the perfect candidate for the Dollar Now future.

The real purpose of the meeting is to record everything. Because Kelton knows certain details, the prosecutor doesn't have any problem allowing him to be charged with the transactions, even though it doesn't make sense. At the meeting with Ayaba, I brought pictures and receipts showing that Kelton was visiting me and Weston in Aruba during the dates they accused him of receiving packages and dropping off boxes and laundry bags. Because the prosecutor has no video or audio evidence, it's all hearsay from Fred Armstrong. But someone is going to take the fall for this money laundering scheme, as the prosecutor is trying to make a name for himself.

Pearl and I discussed whether video or audio would be better for the meeting. We finally agreed that both would be best. My sensible purse has an outside pocket area where I can put a cell phone to record. Pearl insisted that we buy a second cell phone and not use my personal device. She doesn't want someone calling during the meeting. We don't want anything to interfere with our plans. We named it Project Get Kelton Released.

The receptionist places me in the conference room with a bottle of water. I try to stay calm as I wait for Mia to arrive. But I'm nervous, and my palms are starting to sweat. I wipe them on my dress. If I start perspiring at my temples, I'll say I'm having a hot flash.

I once had a hot flash while in a meeting with my former male boss. I felt the warmth moving up my torso. When it hit my neck, perspiration formed near my hairline. I tried to ignore it, and I hoped my boss wasn't paying attention to my flushness. Then he said, "It must be that time." This was his excuse for not promoting me. "What if you have a hot flash while meeting with a client?" He acted as if I was a serial killer. What if I killed someone during the meeting? My hot flash was not going to kill someone, but I wanted to kill him. One day I timed my hot flash. It lasted a total of seven minutes from beginning to end. Seven minutes of not having control over my body. Is that a reason to not promote a woman? Maybe when a woman gets to that beautiful time in life, they should be permitted to retire and sit on a beach while enjoying a cool breeze. That way, it won't embarrass the employer or any clients.

"Hello. You must be Seleste." Mia enters the conference room and extends her hand.

"Hello." I stand, and we shake. I'm glad I wiped my hand on my dress earlier.

"Welcome to Dollar Now." Mia settles herself at the head of the table. I purposely sit to her right. I can see the receptionist area through the floor-to-ceiling glass windows.

"Tell me a little about yourself."

"I'm forty-five years old. My husband died about a year ago."

"I'm sorry."

"Don't be. I didn't know how badly I'd had it until I met a real man. Now I'm treated wonderfully." I'm already sidetracked, talking about my relationship with Weston. I get back on topic. "I received a small insurance payout from his death and thought I should make an investment in my future. I met a woman named Kathleen at a support group for grieving women. She told me about Dollar Now. I'd like to invest my money and run my own company."

"Well, it seems like you have a plan."

"I don't want to work for someone else. I don't ever want to answer to a boss again."

"Oh, you still have a boss when running your own business."

"Who?"

"Your bosses are the customers. You try to keep your customers happy."

"Yes, of course."

"At the present time, Dollar Now is in the process of filing all the necessary paperwork to begin franchising."

"I was told about the process when I called to schedule this meeting."

"Good. There's been some confusion with other people in the past."

"I want to start as soon as possible."

"Is there a reason you want to begin so quickly?"

"I told my boss to stick my former job where the sun doesn't shine."

"Oh."

"He wouldn't promote me because I was having hot flashes. He said I would embarrass the company and make the customers feel uncomfortable. But if I could learn to control my hot flashes, he would consider giving me a promotion."

"Wait, your former boss told you to control your hot flashes?" Mia chuckles.

"Yes, he did. When he said it, he really believed it was possible."

Mia chuckles again. "I encountered something just as stupid that caused me to start Dollar Now. Let me tell you about the company."

Mia gives me the history, where the current stores are located, and why she chose those particular areas. She also says she wants to create franchises so that women can run their own businesses and control their futures without dealing with the foolishness of misinformed male bosses. I'm really impressed with Mia. I understand why Pearl respected her so much before this franchise fiasco.

"What are the next steps?" I ask.

"We need additional information, and I'd like you to visit one of the Dollar Now locations to make sure it's what you really want. I'll send Bay in to obtain the information and give you the Dollar Now store locations."

"Okay."

Mia buzzes the intercom and tells Bay to bring some forms for me to complete.

"I have another meeting outside the office. I'll leave you in my receptionist's capable hands."

Bay enters with a folder and passes each document to me one by one as I complete them. I start thinking this might be a bust. Mia Lakes is smart enough to not get caught. As I finish the last sheet, Bay says, "Now that you've completed all the necessary forms, the next step is to meet with Pearl Jermaine to discuss the specific franchise process and how you can obtain one of the first twenty-five franchises."

I can't believe that Bay says Pearl is going to explain the process of getting one of the franchises. I wonder if maybe Pearl is living in an alternate reality. A few minutes later, a woman with the same body size and hair as Pearl enters the conference room. She's also wearing contacts to match Pearl's eye color. Bay introduces her as Pearl Jermaine. This imposter explains the franchise process and how I can be guaranteed to obtain one of the first twenty-five so that I can quickly begin running my own company. I get so excited that we'll have evidence, I knock my purse to the floor. I compose myself and reposition my bag to continue recording both Bay and imposter Pearl. At the end of the presentation, imposter Pearl gives me a final paper that requests $2,500 to get on the list. I complete the form, then write out the check. Bay opens her laptop and processes the payment as an ACH. My cell pings like always when funds are withdrawn from my checking account.

"What's that chime?" Bay asks.

"Oh, it's my cell phone. Anytime I use my debit card or write a check, I receive a text." I unzip my purse, making sure I didn't mess up the recording of the second hidden cell phone. I pull out my cell and open the text app to show Bay and imposter Pearl the message indicating that $2,500 was deducted from my account.

"Wow, that's neat."

"Yes, I had a problem with identify theft in the past and promised myself I'd never deal with that again. Do I need to sign anything else?"

"No. We'll be in touch in a few days."

"Thanks." I place the Dollar Now folder and prospectus inside my portfolio before I stand and shake their hands. I can barely contain myself as I leave the office. When I get to the car, I turn off my hidden cell phone's video and audio, then tap the recording to make sure it's good. Pearl and I tested and retested the process at her home before I felt comfortable enough to pull off this charade. I quickly call Pearl after ensuring that my doors are locked. I've seen many shows where the undercover person is killed before submitting the evidence. I don't want to become a statistic.

"Hello," Pearl answers anxiously.

"We got it! We got it!"

"Where are you?"

"I'm leaving the parking lot now. I'll be at your place in thirty minutes."

"I'm waiting. I thought I'd have a heart attack before you called. Did you lock your car doors?"

"Yes. I'm locked inside my car. I also thought I was going to have a heart attack before I finished the meeting. See you soon."

Pearl has a glass of wine waiting for me. We hug, knowing we've busted the group. I show Pearl the video; she emails it to herself and puts a copy on a flash drive. We don't want the video to disappear or get corrupted. The more copies we have, the better for everyone working to free Kelton. But is Mia Lakes involved?

We decide to call Ayaba tomorrow to schedule an appointment to share the video with her. We'll both sleep well tonight. Weston calls to check on me later in the evening. He's working on a project, and I haven't seen or spoken to him in two weeks.

CHAPTER 29

JAYNEA

"Good morning, Simon," I say as he enters and swipes his membership card. I'm sanitizing the exercise equipment. He never speaks, but I always acknowledge all members. I've been working at Trim and Fit for the past three days. After each shift, I write everything down in a small notebook. I don't want to forget anything. I've been undercover for Pearl before, but this time the people involved would be willing to kill if necessary to keep their secret.

The last time I spoke with Pearl was when the office was closing and she gave me a file box of my things. I was pissed off, and I made sure she knew it. She said nothing. She showed no anger toward me. I tossed the box under my kitchen table because none of the items on my desk there would be acceptable at Marlowe Consulting. I even had to dye my hair a brownish black and remove my orange polish. Neutral colors only on the nails. That's fingers *and* toes, Mr. Marlowe clarified. He hired me because Pearl always hires the best, but he wasn't happy that Pearl allowed me to dress in my personal style. Mr. Marlowe made air quotes when he said *unprofessional*.

I needed my business card holder and remembered it was in the box under my kitchen table. When I opened it, I saw that Pearl had put a letter of recommendation on the top of my things, along with a second envelope. Inside was a $10,000 bonus in the form of a cashier's check. I began to cry. I was so mean to her, and she didn't want me to worry about money until I found my next job. I sat on the floor and collected myself before calling Jester. I wanted to help Pearl. He said that Pearl was no longer being prosecuted because a guy named Kelton Anderson had come forth and admitted to the crime. I assured Jester that Kelton could not have been involved and told him about every encounter I'd had with Kelton. Although I didn't have many interactions with him, he didn't give me the impression that he was a criminal, even after Jester said that Kelton was a felon and had served time for embezzlement before. I was shocked, but I would trust Kelton because of the caring way he treated Pearl. He'd never do anything to sacrifice his time with her. He even admitted to that one day at the office.

I watch the vehicles park in front of the gym. The laundry is being delivered this morning. The employee who normally handles the clean laundry has refused to let me assist him each morning. Is this where they're hiding the money? Pearl told me she dropped off clean laundry bags at a few of the locations when Fred had asked, but she hadn't been happy about it. The delivery guy is running late this morning, and the regular employee is working with a new member. I wave at the delivery guy, and he puts the bags behind the receptionist counter. I open them and pull out the towels, placing them on shelves in the gym. There's nothing suspicious about the bags or anything inside them. The past few days, the regular guy unpacked the towels, but nothing looked suspicious those days either.

The following day, I volunteer to deliver the used towels to the laundry facility. My boss has mentioned that I'm trying to get a raise. I'm really not. I couldn't survive on the little money I get from this part-time gig.

I scan the laundry facility while making a mental note of the staff and the laundry process. No one looks guilty. Will I know what I'm looking for when I see it? After work, I inform Jester that nothing seems out of place. Every once in a while, I see a guy show up with new equipment boxes, even though there's no room on the main floor to accommodate new equipment. The boxes are stored in the back under lock and key.

After realizing I received a $10,000 bonus, I didn't need to immediately begin work at Marlowe Consulting. I told Elvin that I had a family emergency and wouldn't be able to start for two months. I also said I'd be working part-time at Trim and Fit because I didn't want him to show up and ask what I was doing. My wish is to have Pearl Consulting reopen.

I'd return and be so very grateful to have my dream job. I've even thought about going back to college to complete my undergraduate business degree. I could become a project manager for a few clients under Pearl Consulting. You don't know what you'll miss until it's gone.

Every other day I contact Jester to give him an update. I consistently document everything and send my notes to him each evening. I'm hoping that if one night he doesn't hear from me, then he'll realize something is wrong and launch a search. I didn't have the heart to contact Pearl. I want to find something to help her and Kelton before I reach out to her. She could have easily removed the envelope from my box before giving it to me. But she didn't. She showed me to the door without arguing. That's a true friend.

I learn from Jester that Stephen Santorini completed a project for Kelton. I'm surprised when Jester asks if I know Stephen. I didn't interact much with him and it was only via the phone, but I know that Pearl has had a long-term relationship with Santorini Tax Office because of Stephen's sister, Mari. Jester wanted to know if Stephen is trustworthy. Kelton had given Stephen some information and requested a forensic accounting. Kelton told Stephen to only give the information to him, Pearl, or me. Because no one knew who could be trusted, I was pleased to know Kelton felt like he could include me.

Pearl once told me that Stephen loved what he did and could locate a toothpick in a bale of hay. I never had the pleasure of meeting Stephen in person, but he sounds like someone I would want on my side if I was in need of tracking money. Stephen located quite a few offshore accounts and determined where the money was being funneled and what questions to ask Trim and Fit's interim CEO. He reminded Jester that people like those at Trim and Fit would kill to keep the organization safe from prying eyes. I also learned from this discussion that Stephen began his career at the FBI and helped bring many criminals involved in embezzlement and money laundering to justice.

Instead of confronting the interim CEO of Trim and Fit, I volunteered to place an audio bug in his office and another at the receptionist desk.

The bugs aren't legal, and I discussed this with Ayaba's investigator. The investigator didn't tell either attorney because he wants them to have plausible deniability if the listening devices are discovered. Some days I even join the investigator at his office to listen to the hours of recordings.

CHAPTER 30

WESTON

I work for myself because I don't like the bull that comes with having a boss. I'm doing this only because I've fallen head over heels for Seleste, and when my woman isn't happy, I can't be happy. Even the sex isn't right when everyone is unhappy. I need my Seleste back in my life fully and in my bed completely. She's been worried about Pearl.

"Sir, do you need me to deliver anything else?"

"Weston, my man, you've been doing a great job. I might have some additional deliveries of gym equipment."

"Okay, Mr. Tallen."

"Don't call me Mr. Tallen. That was my dad, and I hated him. Call me Sebastian."

"Do you want me to deliver the gym equipment now or later?"

"You'll get a telephone call, then I'll need you to go to the address on the text. Are you still sleeping at the gym?"

"Yes. I was told I could stay until I save enough money to get my own place."

"It's tough being an immigrant. I remember when I moved from Ukraine to New Jersey. We had some assistance from nonprofits and churches, until we didn't. Then I had to get creative in order to find food and shelter each day. But I knew liquor and got a job off the books at a distillery. I slept in the back room there that was the size of a broom closet. I worked ninety hours a week with two other immigrants. But look at me now. I have a large home, nice cars, and expensive clothes, and I can buy any woman I want. It took the right connections and skills to become an American. The land of milk and honey."

"Yeah, I want that too."

"Go back to the gym. Keep the van tonight. You might get that call and then the text at any moment. Don't forget to take that list of gyms. I've marked the locations."

"Okay, Mr. Tal—I mean, Sebastian." I head to the main location where I and seven others rent rooms in a warehouse behind the gym.

I receive a call the following morning around seven. The texted address follows. My instructions are to pick up new equipment from a location I've never visited before. I'm to deliver the boxes to three gyms.

I drive to an old warehouse with graffiti on the outside walls. I ring the doorbell and am directed to the overhead doors in the loading dock area to collect the boxes. They're large and packed with Styrofoam peanuts on top. I pack sixteen boxes into my cargo van. A guy in designer clothes gives me a list and instructions to deliver five boxes to the first two locations and six to the last location. I have to complete the task in less than two hours. Then he pokes me in the chest. I guess he's trying to intimidate me, but it only pisses me off. He says that if any of the boxes are opened or come up missing, I might not see the light of day again. His threat causes me to remember Seleste, and I humble myself. Or rather I play the character of a scared immigrant.

"Yes, sir. I will complete the task in two hours."

"No speeding, and do not stop anywhere else."

"Yes, sir." I quickly get into the van, set the GPS on my phone, and head to the first location. I pull my personal cell from my inside pocket and take pictures every time I stop at a red light. I'm standing outside the warehouse at the last location when a man in a brown uniform approaches the guy who signed off on the delivery. The man flashes a badge, and I see a gun on his hip. I attempt to move behind the van, but he sees me and tells me to stand near the clipboard guy. He demands that I open one of the boxes. Once I cut the seal, the guy rummages through the peanuts, takes a few pictures, and leaves. I want to see what's inside the box, but the clipboard guy tells me to get in the van and wait. I watch him make a call, and he returns the peanuts to the box as he talks. I could have done that instead of sitting in the van. When he hangs up, he tells me to not speak of this to anyone and return to the main gym location.

A few days later, the warehouse is shut down, and everyone is forced to leave the rented rooms. We all complain as we pack the few items we have there. I have enough money to rent an efficiency for a few days. During that time, I'm able to call Seleste. I miss her so much. She shares about her project with Pearl with me, and I tell her I'll see her soon.

Ayaba contacts me and says they have the information I sent and are able to prove that none of the money is being laundered through the clean laundry bags. They're moving it through the equipment boxes. They pack them with money to be distributed to three different locations for counting and depositing into the gyms. The boxes are delivered every two to three days. Ayaba's investigator is the guy who took the pictures. She assures me that I was not discovered while I was sending her information. It's also been determined that only three of the twelve Trim and Fit gyms in New Jersey and Pennsylvania exist. The others are ghost gyms; they're on the books and showing a profit, but they're not real. The twelve locations are needed to distribute the vast amount of money so as not to arouse suspicion.

I pack my things and head to South Orange. I have to see Seleste. I need to do a lot more than just see her, but I'll start with that and kissing. It's 7:00 p.m. when I finally arrive and ring the doorbell. I didn't call to tell anyone I was on my way. Seleste opens the door and almost drops her wineglass when she sees me. The storm door is locked and prevents me from entering.

"Hello, my beautiful."

"Weston! Weston!" She fumbles with the lock. Realizing the wineglass is part of the problem, she puts it down and finally gets the door open. She jumps into my arms, then hugs and kisses me.

"I guess you're not mad anymore." I hold her as she cries.

"No. I just want this to work between us. I don't want any secrets. I thought you were seeing someone else."

Pearl joins us and gets in on the hug.

"I'm glad you're here. Seleste has been worried about you."

I rub both of their backs, then close and lock the doors.

"I thought you gave up on us and . . ." Seleste mumbles into my chest.

"Never. You're my light in the darkness." I kiss her. "I had to go undercover for Ayaba to implicate Trim and Fit. I didn't want you to worry about me. We need to get Kelton out of jail."

Seleste stares at me in awe as she wipes away her tears.

"You went undercover at Trim and Fit?" Pearl asks.

"Yep. Ayaba needed someone she could trust, and she couldn't send in her investigator. I volunteered, but I had to remove myself from my old life and not tell anyone what was going on." Now Pearl is crying. I didn't expect all these tears. Pearl is babbling; nothing coherent is coming from her mouth. I pull her into another embrace with Seleste. Eventually, they'll both stop crying, and then I can possibly get something to eat.

Everything came to light when Sebastian Tallen was picked up from one of the gyms. He decided to save his hide by turning state's evidence in exchange for witness protection. He implicated the other investors, all of whom had fled the US. Many just happen to have taken vacations in locations unknown. Sebastian also confirmed that Pearl never transported any money or had knowledge of any money laundering, even on the day he met with her. He also confirmed he never heard of Kelton Anderson and didn't understand why the prosecutor thought he was involved. A major money laundering ring operating in two states was brought down. The prosecutor held multiple press conferences along with his task force, and they all smiled for the camera.

I tell Ayaba I owe her big when she visits Aruba. You can't find many half sisters like her who are willing to work pro bono to discover the truth behind fraudulent charges. She'll have front row tickets to any concert I host now and for the rest of my life. She makes a significant name for herself when she presents all the information to the prosecutor. She was already known as the killer attorney for the wealthy in the tristate area. Before, she always worked behind the scenes as a fixer when possible. This case forced her into the limelight to distract the prosecutor while both her experienced and novice undercover teams gathered information.

She might have told herself that she took the case free of charge because of her little brother. She might have told herself that she became an attorney because she loved the law or because justice is blind. But justice has never been blind when people can see the color of one's skin and decide to impose their biases on minorities. Neither of us could do anything when our father was accused of killing a white man in Newark when he was with us in Atlantic City and had at least twenty witnesses. My mother's alibi was thrown out, as were those from the other family members who were with him. We saw our father slowly die a painful death from the white man's justice system. He was sentenced to life. He would never leave the confines of that prison. I recall the visits to see him. The man who was bigger than life was stripped of everything and began to wither. He died from cancer in jail. Alone. I remember when my mom got the telephone call. She screamed, then sobbed uncontrollably. She always believed he would be proven innocent. The justice system didn't work. My mother didn't leave her bed for ten days. I remember because I had to call my aunt and tell her I thought my mom was going to join my father. She showed up the next day and climbed into bed with her sister, my mother. We closed the door at my aunt's request. It was a *grown people discussion*, she said. The following day, my mother was in the kitchen making a breakfast fit for kings and queens. I know she cried from time to time about my father, but she never slipped back into that void of despair.

My sister, Ayaba swore she would never let another family be forced to endure a situation that could be prevented. After struggling to get her undergrad and law degrees, she passed the bar the first time and began working at a prestigious law firm. During that time, she gathered all the documents from our father's case and forced the court to reopen it based on new evidence that wasn't presented. His conviction was overturned, even though he died an innocent man in prison. The exoneration was too late to make a difference in my life, in her life, and in my mother's life.

CHAPTER 31

PEARL

Weston and Seleste return to Aruba a few days after Weston ended his undercover assignment for Ayaba. The trumpet player had been handling the band and engagements in Weston's absence. Weston is happy to be his own boss again. Seleste assures me that she'll call in a few days to check in.

I meet with Jester, who tells me that Jaynea was instrumental in learning the processes of Trim and Fit. She chose to go undercover as an employee. Fred Armstrong would have recognized Jaynea's name, but he was in jail awaiting trial, so it was safe for her to be there. She worked a swing shift to meet all the staff and to observe any wrongdoings that were occurring.

Jaynea became upset when she learned that Kelton chose to take the fall for the embezzlement and money laundering charges to protect me. She wanted to help us both. I only wanted her to find adequate employment with Marlowe Consulting.

When I heard what she'd done, I invited her to join me for lunch at the diner on South Orange Avenue. I'm sitting in a booth in the back when she enters. She's dressed in army fatigue capris with strappy sandals laced up her leg. Her shirt is neon orange, as are her fingernails. Her hair is in Bantu knots. When I first met her, she appeared intimating. After getting to know her, I realized she's very bold and lives life to its colorful fullest. Knowing her has been invaluable to me.

"Hello, boss lady." Jaynea drops her bag on the booth seat.

"Hello, Jaynea. I'm not your boss anymore." I get up to give her a bear hug. Our embrace reminds me of all the times we laughed and sometimes cried at the office.

"I want you to be my boss again."

"I don't think I have it in me to go through something like—" The waitress arrives to take our order. Because this is one of the many restaurants where we met to discuss strategy, we know the menu, and we order without looking at it.

"I'm afraid this situation has made me decide to discontinue Pearl Consulting." I take a sip of water.

"But you love your work."

"I know. But I would have spent time in prison and been labeled a felon for the rest of my life. I was so scared."

"I was scared when the task force raided the office, and I was placed in handcuffs. I've always watched those reality TV shows and wondered how people could be surprised." Jaynea laughs. "I was one of those surprised people."

I laugh too, and tears form in our eyes. "It's funny now, but it wasn't funny then."

"No joke," Jaynea says as she wipes her eyes with her napkin. I do the same.

The waitress returns with our meals. She asks if we're putting liquor in our lemonade. We both say no but that we'll take some if she has it. She wishes us bon appétit and disappears.

After blessing our food, I bite into my French dip. Jaynea puts ketchup on her chicken nuggets and fries.

"I'm sorry," Jaynea says. "I'm so, so sorry that I treated you badly. I was angry because I liked working for you and doing what I did. Even when clients like Fred drove me crazy. It was part of the job, and I enjoyed it."

"I know you were angry. There was nothing I could do to stop the allegations, which is why I didn't argue with you about the comments Elvin Marlow made."

"I didn't even know you gave me the bonus until I needed my business card holder. I simply pushed the box under my kitchen table and left it. I was so angry with Mia and Fred that I could have given them a piece of my mind."

"There was nothing you could do except fight the allegations." I take a bite of my sandwich. "So how long did the box sit before you cashed the check?"

"It was a few weeks, but I cashed it as soon as I found it. Thanks for the bonus."

"I wanted to make sure you got the money. The prosecutor froze all of my accounts. If I hadn't had cash stashed, I wouldn't have been able to pay my own bills."

"Do you always keep cash hidden?"

"Yes. I remember stories being passed down from my great-grandparents about the Freedman's Bureau and Freedman's Bank that managed the deposits of the ADOS. Many never got their money from the bank."

"Who are the ADOS?"

"Oh, you don't know ADOS? American descendants of slavery are those who were stripped of their country, culture, and language. We're the descendants who built the United States and who were forced to work for free for fourteen generations. Or you could say our wages were stolen by the whites in America either through the forced labor when we were enslaved or through cheated wages, since whites never compensate labor equally. To think corporations continue to pay minorities less for the same job as nonminorities."

"They're part of the problem."

"Yes, they are, and the supervisors and managers who enable companies by hiding and participating in unfair wage compensation should be ashamed."

"I'd heard of ADOS before but wasn't sure what the acronym stood for."

"It's also a shame that many ADOS are still using the European name of their last enslaver. Can you image if every white woman was raped by a visible minority male, then forced to take the name of their rapist? Or if every white male was forced to take the name of their CEO and not get paid for fourteen generations."

"If that happened, they'd have a new point of reference regarding the white privilege they say doesn't exist. We all hope and pray that one day the level of understanding and compassion will be the same for all."

Jaynea gets the waitress's attention and asks for another lemonade. "Has Kelton been released?"

"Tomorrow."

"Do you plan to see him?" She wiggles her eyebrows.

"I think he's had enough of me. He was willing to sacrifice his freedom for mine. I'm so grateful. But I'm sure I'm probably the last person he wants to see."

"I like him. He seems like an upstanding guy who cares a lot about you."

I look at Jaynea and decide how much to tell her. Should I reveal that Kelton told me he'd found someone special and that it wasn't me? Even though he sent the marigolds that are overwhelming my flower beds. I think he did it out of pity for my situation. "I think he has someone else special in his life."

"Why would you say that?"

"I just know. So you start at Marlowe Consulting soon."

"Look at me." Jaynea makes a sweeping motion over her hair and attire before flashing her neon orange fingernails.

"I thought Elvin Marlowe changed his dress code." I chuckle.

"He was so uptight about that. Another employee told me he critiques the staff's wardrobe weekly. When I interviewed, I was completely neutral, and he thought my hair wasn't straight enough. I didn't say anything to him, but he knew he was violating the CROWN Act."

"Yeah, that sounds like Elvin."

"He even made a conscious effort to look at my footwear. We were in his conference room discussing rules. Then he looked under the table at my shoes. I was wearing sandals. He told me that he prefers pumps because they're business oriented. Sandals are for the beach or a date."

"So what's your plan?"

"I thought about returning to school to finish my business administration degree at Rutgers. I applied for a scholarship that will help with books. My financial aid adviser said I'm eligible for grants to cover my tuition."

"That sounds great. If you don't get the scholarship, tell me. I have another resource for textbooks."

"Thanks. I'll also need to work part-time to pay my bills."

"I'll keep my ears open for you." I pay the lunch bill, and we exit the diner.

"I think you need to reach out to Kelton. At least to thank him for his sacrifice. I'll be in touch."

"I'll be in touch with you also." After an embrace and a smile, we depart.

The following morning around eleven, Jester Jackson calls to tell me Kelton has been released. Apparently, Jester is now collaborating with Ayaba on a few cases. This opportunity might work out for both of them and could even result in the merging of their law practices.

I've stopped having nightmares since everyone pulled together to help Kelton and me through this harrowing experience.

My cell rings again, and I lean over to see who's calling. It's Ayaba. I want to thank her for all of her assistance.

"Hello, Ms. Adesanya," I say.

"Hello, lovey."

I immediately become flushed. I didn't expect Kelton to call me. The last time we'd spoken, he stomped on my heart with steel-toe boots. After all the good times. I remember when he told me he found someone special to share his life. I thought I was his someone special. We'd experienced so much together. But he did sacrifice his freedom for me.

"Hello, Kelton," I manage. "I'm glad you're out."

"I wanted to make sure you were okay. I know you were worried about me."

"I'm much better. I do want to thank you for making the ultimate sacrifice of your freedom for me. I'll never understand why you did it, but I truly thank you for everything."

"Can I see you? I want to talk to you in person."

"You don't need to do that. I'm doing much better now that you're free. I also wanted to thank you for the flowers."

"Are you sure we can't meet somewhere?"

"I think you should get back to your special someone. I wish you the very best in life." I end the call. Tears begin to fall from my eyes. I can't believe I fell in love with Kelton. Once again, I opened my heart to someone, and they crushed it. I need to give up on love and focus on my next steps.

I received a call last week from Hazel at Country Crafts. She wanted me to know that she didn't believe I would ever do anything that was published in the newspaper. I told her that all the charges had been dropped but that I hadn't decided whether to continue consulting. She asked if I would occasionally reach out for lunch or dinner. I also heard from Stephen. He was happy that the forensic accounting he performed helped get Kelton released. He wasn't able to conduct a complete forensic audit due to lack of information, but what he did helped immensely. The silver lining is that the task requested by Kelton brought together the next generation, as Stephen, his two children, and his niece all assisted in tracking the money. This was the very first time they'd shown any interest in Santorini Tax Office.

Jaynea and I share an Uber to the Bayonne cruise dock. I had been happy locked inside my home. I just wanted to wallow, but Jaynea insisted that because she was returning to college in September, we had to chill on a cruise. She obtained a scholarship for textbooks and grants for tuition. She'll have her degree in four to five semesters. She said it was the last time she'd be able to vacation for a while. I gave in and decided to go with her on the five-day cruise.

We arrive at the dock and stand in long lines to check in. We hand off our luggage, receive our medallions, get our pictures taken, and confirm our drink package. Jaynea insists our balcony rooms were a gift and refuses to accept any money. Our cabins are next door to each other.

Even though she's flirting with every man she sees, she continues to text a guy she started dating a week ago. We're early, so we can't get into our cabins yet. We decide to enjoy the pool area on the top deck. I take a nap while Jaynea checks out the food options.

She wakes me almost two hours later, once we're able to get into our rooms. Our luggage is already inside our cabins. Jaynea had taken it in while I was sleeping. I get myself settled and step onto the balcony. Jaynea is already on hers, sipping a drink. The purple and blonde streaks in her hair glitter in the sun. All of her clothes have purple in them or match the hue. I bought a few new clothes but didn't go all-out shopping. I think about Kelton and wonder where he is. I called Seleste last week and told her I was cruising for a few days. She's never visited Bermuda. I told her it's one of the prettiest islands and has pink sand. A knock on my door brings me back to reality.

Did I forget something near the pool? I open the door, and my heart lifts to see Seleste and Weston.

"We're a few doors down and wanted to visit before we see you at dinner."

"Oh my goodness." I hug Seleste and then Weston. Jaynea has joined us in my cabin. "This is great!"

"I have plans for us this evening. We're having dinner, then going dancing in the Sausalito Club all evening. Wear something comfortable and sexy."

"Should I put the emphasis on comfortable or sexy?" I ask.

"I'm thinking sexy first," Weston says as he flops on my bed.

"I got your sexy." Seleste steps onto the balcony.

"We'll meet at the elevators in one hour for dinner, then we dance." Jaynea shimmies out the door and motions everyone to follow except me. "We have five days to live life to its fullest!" Jaynea shrieks.

I close the door and jump into the shower, then slip into a sexy yellow dress. It's lightweight with a drop bodice that flares around my thighs, stopping two inches above my knees, and has a V-neckline that allows my breasts to show. I tie the belt around my waist and twirl in front of the mirror. My shoes are flat sandals that tie up my legs. I remember to put a knot in the laces after I tie the bow. If I'm dancing all night, I don't want to stop to keep tying my laces or, even worse, trip and fall. I wrap a yellow patterned scarf around my curls to pull them up and off my face. My makeup is light, with bold red lips and smoky eyes to bring out the hazel color. *I'm ready for anything*, I tell myself as I put my medallion around my neck.

Dinner is great. I haven't had so much fun in quite some time. The last time Seleste and Weston were at my home, we were still anxious about getting Kelton out of jail. This time there are no worries, and we dance and drink until midnight. Several guys want to dance with me, and some are great on the dance floor, but I don't want to take anyone back to my cabin. I'm not ready. I believe celibacy is the best option right now.

I motion to the group that I'm stepping onto the deck area. I lean against the railing and breathe in the cool salt air.

"Could I have a dance?" says a deep but familiar voice.

I turn around and see someone in the shadows. "I'm resting now. Maybe in a few."

"You look lovely in yellow."

"Thanks."

"Could we talk?"

"About what?" Now I'm thinking this guy is a stalker, until he steps out of the shadows. "Kelton?"

"Hello, lovey."

I don't have words. How did he know I was on this cruise ship? I purposely didn't agree to any cruise in the Caribbean because I didn't want to run into him. "Is your special someone here?"

"Yes, but I need to tell her something."

I attempt to move around him and return to the club. He reaches for my hand. "You're my special someone. You always have been."

"You said—"

"I know what I said. I was scared that you would find out my secret." He drops my hand.

I can see he's aged a little more around the eyes. He's also thinner than the last time I saw him. I fold my arms across my chest. "What secret?"

"I'm a felon. I've spent three years in prison."

"Did you serve your time, or did you escape?" I watch him to ensure he's not lying.

"I served my three years and two additional years on probation." His gaze never leaves mine.

"What do you want, Mr. Anderson?"

"This is what I know. I don't have very many more years left, but I want to live them to the fullest. I would prefer to live life experiencing fireworks every day than to live a life that's lukewarm. You, Pearl Jermaine, set my heart on fire every time we're together. I wait with bated breath until the next time we meet. I don't want that feeling to ever go away. You're the only one who makes me feel that way."

Kelton's hands touch my waist as he repositions himself in front of me. I've missed his touch, his smell. I breathe him in and close my eyes as I pull him close.

"You asked what I want. I want you, Pearl Jermaine. Only you for my remaining years. Do you think you could be mine and only mine?"

A tear rolls down my cheek. Kelton gently wipes it away.

"Yes."

Kelton kisses me softly as he pulls me close. Suddenly, I hear clapping and shouting from behind us. It's our friends, Seleste, Weston, and Jaynea, who have been through the valley and over the mountain with us.

PEARL

One month later

We've decided to use my home in South Orange as our main residence. Kelton sold his stateroom to Richard when he decided to admit to the charges of embezzlement and money laundering on my behalf. He'd packed his possessions and placed them in his storage unit in Connecticut. Because he moved into my home, I told him there was no need to keep the storage unit. I wanted him to make my home his permanent residence.

We visit Connecticut as often as possible, since Kelton agreed to be Matt's children's godfather. They already have a godmother, but I've become their second godmother. We arrange our schedule to be at every birthday and a few activities such as dances, soccer games, and a swim class graduation. Kelton and Matt have reestablished their friendship. Anasis and I have become good friends. I've even included her in girls' night when Seleste visits. Sometimes mothers must remember that they're still women and need time for themselves.

Jaynea is doing well in college and is on track to graduate in two years. She was concerned about the number of credits she needed to take each semester, but everything is going well. Especially her job on campus working in the library. She met an inspiring young man who has also returned to college after two tours overseas in the army. He loves the outrageous style only she can pull off. He's protective and understanding of her and her dreams for the future. He wants to have lunch with Kelton next week. I'm not sure what that's all about.

Kelton purchased a home in Aruba, and it's there we spend most of our days. I haven't decided what to do other than enjoy the time with him, walking, talking, dancing, and cooking. Our sex life is fantastic. We've christened every possible place in my South Orange home as well as in our home in Aruba. We have dinner parties with Seleste and Weston as often as possible and when we feel we need a change of pace. Each year we choose a place on the globe and visit for a few months.

The last time we heard from Ayaba and Jester, they had merged their law practices and their lives.

1. If you spent time in jail or prison, would you tell your friends?
2. Would you sacrifice your freedom for a friend?
3. If you were Pearl, would you have fought for Kelton to free him? Why or why not?
4. Do you think the relationship between Pearl and her mother stemmed from jealousy?
5. Have you ever met someone and felt an instant connection, as what happened with Pearl and Seleste?
6. Would you want a friend like Weston? Why or why not?
7. Did you believe that Weston was having an affair, since Seleste didn't know where he was during the undercover assignment?
8. Would you have forgiven Matt and become a godparent to his children?
9. What is the most memorable moment in the book?
10. If money were no object and you could vacation for ten weeks anywhere in the world, where would you go?

www.ingramcontent.com/pod-product-compliance
Lightning Source LLC
Chambersburg PA
CBHW020720130726
47899CB00011B/583